Whacker McCracker's Café

Whacker McCracker's Café

The story of Waiheke Island's infamous eatery

HarperCollins*Publishers*

National Library of New Zealand Cataloguing-in-Publication Data

Ward, Tony, 1943 Dec. 20-
Whacker McCracker's café / by Tony Ward.
Originally published: Waiheke Island, N.Z. : James Marketing, 2002.
ISBN 1-86950-557-7
1. Restaurants—New Zealand—Waiheke Island—Fiction. I. Title.
NZ823.3—dc 22

First published 2002 and reprinted in 2003.
This edition published in 2004 by
HarperCollins*Publishers (New Zealand) Limited*
P.O. Box 1, Auckland

ISBN 1 86950 555 7

Cover design by Seven Visual Communications

Printed by Griffin Press, Australia, on 50 gsm Ensobulky News

This book is dedicated to the wonderful entrepreneurs

on Waiheke Island responsible for creating the restaurants,

bars, vineyards and cafés that give pleasure to so many.

Prologue

'You! Whacker McCracker, running a café? You can't even make toast! You'd make more money running a brothel on Great Barrier Island!' Greg Reed, my accountant, cheerfully advised me. Roaring with laughter too, I should add. 'And after five of them, you're currently wifeless.'

'You're right there. Five of the piranha-snapping, Pauanui-loving things. I'm gloriously free.'

'So running a café is going to make you gloriously happy? Sounds like a midlife crisis.'

'Mate, a little café away from all the city bullshit, on a peaceful, sun-drenched island, is the ultimate dream. The kids have gone overseas and the ad agency is a daily drama. It's not the money thing any more. I'm fifty-two. I want to do things *I* want to do. If that's a midlife crisis, great!'

'Have you ever been there? It's an arsehole of a place.'

'Twice. I went over years ago to collect wife Number Two, who was staying with friends. I don't think she liked it much. Reckoned it was a refuge for DPBs, hippies and eccentrics. She made it sound a bit like a lunatic colony. But you know what she's like.'

'I most certainly do. Bloody gorgeous, but unable to keep her shapely legs together when she met your next-door neighbour. And the second time?'

'Three years ago. A client had a brainstorming day at one

of the vineyards. Not much brainstorming was achieved — everyone got totally pissed. Coming back on the ferry, I chundered all over the managing director's shoes and we lost the account.'

'Then why in the world do you want to go back? It's not a place for someone like you. The second love of your life was right — it's for loonies. What's the real reason?'

'Simple. It's near Auckland, but has a big moat around it that'll keep Number One, Two Three, Four and Five well away from me.'

'Those ex-wives still pestering you?'

'Frequently.'

'But why a café?'

'Less stressful than running a brothel.'

My friends, colleagues, kids and the five exes all decided I'd flipped when they heard my plan, but I wouldn't be talked out of it and it took just three months to finalise the sale of my shares in the agency and get other business and personal matters sorted out.

Finally, on a pleasant winter's Tuesday morning, a middle-aged, gloriously wife-free Auckland businessman, who, in the words of his accountant, 'couldn't even make toast', migrated to Waiheke Island on Mr Fuller's ten o'clock ferry. To open a small, quiet café and live what he believed was going to be the ultimate dream lifestyle.

And this is what happened . . .

Walking down the main street of Oneroa on a Monday, my sixth day on the island, I came across *The Glorious Ocean View Café*. It was closed. There was a notice in the window saying it was for sale, phone Peg Pinney if interested. I phoned.

Peg answered. Yes, she'd closed it. Within two minutes flat I found out that her husband had acute piles and was completely incontinent, the daughter who lived with them was experiencing yet another Immaculate Conception, and Peg had arthritis and giddy spells. I could understand why she had to give up *The Glorious Ocean View Café*. We chatted a bit and I agreed to meet at the café at midday.

She arrived right on time and unlocked the door. Frilly curtains, white tableclothes, uncomfortable chairs, a horrible food display unit, dreadful signs and an all-round 1960s atmosphere. The kitchen, which was surprisingly big, was at the back, with amazing views, facing the sea. The café was in the front facing the road. Arse about face. Wow! The potential! The opportunity! The challenge! I instantly loved *The Glorious Ocean View Café*.

Peg just wanted out. She was stuck with a lease for two more years; she couldn't make money out of it — and nobody else had shown any interest.

I don't procrastinate in business. If I feel something's right, I go for it. Within minutes we had a deal that included her staying on to help me get it cranked up again.

Brad Crocker, my lawyer, shook his head when I told him of my new venture. However, after the standard lecture about how it won't work that professional people normally give to middle-aged clients who want to open a bar, café or restaurant, he sorted things out. Just one week later, it was mine. I was the proud owner of *The Glorious Ocean View Café* in Oneroa. The café where the patrons didn't get a glorious ocean view.

I had a yarn over the phone with the building owner, Grant Mitchell, about a few internal alterations I wanted to make and he was very enthusiastic. As long as I left the alterations behind when I vacated the place, it was fine with him.

To get things cracking, I needed a carpenter. A copy of the *Gulf News* was acquired and the Work Wanted column read. Four carpenters were seeking work. Russian Roulette time. I phoned the first. No answer. I phoned the second and got his wife. 'He's busy. Got heaps of work on. Doesn't need any more.'

'Then why does he advertise?'

'To get business.' A brilliant reply to a silly question.

The third call was to an answerphone advising the carpenter was away that week and would return all calls the following week. Obviously completing a new skyscraper in the Big Smoke.

I dialled my fourth dynamic, enthusiastic Waiheke Island carpenter seeking work and actually spoke to the horse's mouth. He listened to what I had to say, and then said, 'It sounds like a piece of piss, mate. How about I come up and have a bird's-eye?'

We agreed to meet at *The Glorious Ocean View Café* at four. He arrived in his ute at four-thirty. 'So you're the stupid bastard who bought Peg's old dump,' were his first words to me.

'It's got potential.'

'Potential? You sound like a Willie Woofter from Queen Street. It's a pull-down job, this one. Anyway, the name's Mal. Good to meet ya.'

'Hi Mal. All that's wrong with this place is that the view isn't being utilised. People like to sit and look at the sea. I want to move the kitchen from the back to the side. And reduce it a bit, by getting rid of the pie warmers and the glassed-in shelves for the cakes and sandwiches.'

'Piece of piss.'

'Guess I'll have to apply for a permit.'

'For this little job? Not necessary. Not structural.'

'Are you sure?'

'Positive. I haven't applied for a permit for years. Don't need 'em over here for simple jobs.'

'What jobs have you done recently? Perhaps I could go and have a look at one to see your standard of work.'

'Mate, I've done bloody heaps. All over the place, not a complaint. Tell you what — I'll get crackin' on your place. If, at the end of day one you don't reckon I'm a shit-hot carpenter, you can tell me to piss off and not pay me a cent.'

'OK. That seems fair enough.'

'When do you want me to get cracking?'

'Soon as possible. I'll have to get a few plans whipped

11

up first. Do you know anyone on the island who could do that for me?'

'Plans? My speciality, mate. Always do me own plans. If you know what you want, just tell me as we go along and I'll work it out on me pad. Works every time. Promise.'

Not only had I found a second James Fletcher but I'd also found a second Christopher Wren. I was impressed. Rather than mess around, I asked if he could start tomorrow.

'Piece of piss. Eight sharp. Just one thing mate . . . it will be a cashie? I'm twenty bucks an hour, cash in the hand. Plus, you pay for the materials — just lend me your eftpos card and tell me the pin number. I'll look after it.'

Now the cashie thing was a problem. I'd had a run-in a few years back in the third-wife era with builders, cashies and the IRD. Since then, I'd done everything pretty much by the book — especially with more expensive items.

'Ah . . . no . . . I can't do cashies. You'll have to invoice me and I'll give you a cheque. I don't mind if you add on a couple of bucks an hour to cover the tax.'

'C'mon mate, I don't want to have to write you an invoice. Haven't even got an invoice book — it's always cash over here. Why should I pay bloody tax to support all those no-hopers down in Wellington? Don't do anything for me.'

I had to agree the man had a point, so I came to a compromise. 'I'll pay you in cash — twenty-two fifty an hour to allow for GST. But you'll have to get an invoice book and bill me. Are you registered for GST?'

'No way! It's bureaucracy gone mad. I like to save the people I work for twelve and a half per cent.'

I was starting to have a soft spot for Mal. I liked his principals. Mal was starting to have a soft spot for me too.

Twenty-two fifty an hour was a lot healthier than twenty dollars an hour. And, come hell or high water, there was no way he intended passing on any of it to increase the revenue of the New Zealand Government. We agreed we'd meet again at eight in the morning. I'd go home and do a few sketches of what I had in mind, and a miraculous revamp would occur to *The Glorious Ocean View Café*.

'How about we go across the road and have a couple of beers before we call it a day,' suggested Mal, as we were locking the door.

'OK. Just a couple.'

'Whacker your real name, mate?'

'Yeah. My dad's nickname was Whacker. He liked it and when Mum and Dad had me, they decided to call me that. No middle name. It's good having an unusual name — nobody forgets it.'

'Nice name, Whacker. Nice name. Where are you living?'

'I've rented a bach near Palm Beach. It even came with a bicycle.'

We walked across the road to the bar. Five hours later we left. Great mates. And pissed as parrots.

I didn't get up to the café at eight the next morning. I got there about ten. Mal was waiting outside in his ute, reading the paper. 'Well mate, I was here at eight, so you owe me forty-five bucks. Right. Let's get into it.' Mal's cheerfulness wasn't contagious as we entered the café and cast a quick eye around. 'That dunny's going to be a problem.

We can't change that. Squillion bucks involved in changing dunnies.'

The dunny was *crème de la crème*. As long as you were a gent. The view facing out as you stood to pee was the ultimate glorious ocean view. Due to the unexpected delay in getting home the previous night, there were no sketches so I told Mal the changes I wanted.

'Make us a cup of tea Whacker and while you're doing that, I'll have a bit of a play-around on this old envelope.'

I made the tea and he got planning. In the space of a couple of minutes he sketched a plan, moving the kitchen to the side and making the glorious view glorious for the patrons. 'Hey Mal, that's not bad, not bad at all. Where'd you learn to do plans like that?'

'Jail, mate. Last time I did a drafting course. You can do some bloody good courses in jail these days ya know.'

Boring old me didn't know, but as a taxpayer it was nice to find out that if those inside no longer spend all day cracking rocks, they picked up a few useful skills. I wanted to know more but decided it wasn't the right time.

'Perfected me carpentry in jail too. Time before last. Great instructor we had, that time. Depends so much on the instructor ya know.'

I fully agreed.

'Going as straight as a politician on election night now. Haven't been inside for over two years. A reformed man. Plus, I haven't been caught.' He laughed. 'Right now we're going to need a few things. I'll have to pop down to Placemakers. Just lend us your eftpos card, give us your pin number and we're in business.'

The thing is, do you give an ex-jailbird you've known for less than twenty-four hours your eftpos card and pin

14

number to buy building supplies? Will he also buy a television set, a stereo and god knows what else? Well, it's Waiheke, so of course you do.

'One other thing, Whacker. I'll need a helper. You'd be no bloody good — we'd never get it done. You Willie Woofters from Queen Street should stick to being Willie Woofters *in* Queen Street. Buggered if I know how you're going to run this joint. Anyway, I'll pick up a young bloke on the way back who's worked with me before. Wally. Great guy — honest as they come, and ten bucks an hour. You'll have to pay him cash in hand because he's on the dole. Better give me a key to this place too, so I can come and go.'

Mal was taking over. He had the confidence and assurance I assumed came from his time spent under Her Majesty's lock and key, in which case I knew a few people in Willie Woofterland who'd benefit from a month or two inside. I had a couple of spare keys to the café so I gave him one. He drove off in the direction of Placemakers, with my eftpos card and pin number, while I went back to the bach to sort out a few things.

When I came back, Mal was sitting at one of the tables, yarning to an extremely large gentleman. He introduced me to Wally, a 95-kg-plus Maori bloke in his early twenties. 'Good meeting you, Wally. How'd you get on at Placemakers?'

'Piece of piss, mate. All under control. Everything should be delivered any time, so we'd better move all the tables and chairs into a corner. Wanna give us a hand?'

As it was now nearing four, and the café was exactly as

15

it was when we first arrived that morning, I was grateful we'd finally see some progress. We stacked the tables and chairs into a corner. It took five minutes, so we also moved the pie warmer, the shelves for the sandwiches and a couple of other bits and pieces.

'Wonder where that stuff from Placemakers is?' queried Mal. 'It should be here by now. Lend us your cellphone and I'll chase the buggers up.'

He called. He spoke. He roared with laughter. He gave me back the phone. 'Bloody funny one, mate. They've had the stuff on the truck all set to go for the past hour. Only trouble was, apparently I forgot to tell them where to deliver it. Simple mistake. It'll be here it the morning. What the hell, let's go across the road and down a couple of brown ones. Look at Wally . . . the poor bugger looks like he's dying of thirst.'

We locked up and crossed the road. 'Three beers darling — and make them big bastards,' commanded Mal to the young lady behind the bar. The beers came. He handed over the eftpos card and keyed in the pin number.

'Hey Mal, that's my card.'

'Oh yeah, magic little thing. Got some receipts for you from Placemakers somewhere. Must be in the ute.'

I retrieved the card and stayed for three rounds. Mal had shouted the first with my card, I shouted the second, and, as Wally's dole payment wasn't due until the next day and he was broke, I lent him money for his round.

'Whacker, have a sleep-in tomorrow,' called Mal as I was leaving. 'Wally and I'll get cracking first thing and if you come in late morning, you'll see some real progress. We always work a bloody sight better if the boss isn't hanging around. See you at lunchtime.'

3

The following morning my cellphone shrieked into life about nine while I was still at the bach. It was Mal, phoning from the real-estate office next door. 'Goin' like a rocket here Whacker, but we need a plumber fast. Bit of an accident but nothing serious. Just need your OK for me to call Sid, the best plumber on the island. He's an old mate of mine, but we have to get him pronto. OK?'

'What's happened?'

'Nothing really mate, just a slight problem with the dunny. Wally sat on it and the bloody thing collapsed. Water's pouring out and we can't stop it. Luckily it's going straight into the real-estate place next door — that's where I'm phoning from, so the café's all right.'

I gave him my OK to contact 'the best plumber on Waiheke', then got on the bike and peddled like buggery to Oneroa. It's always nice to meet your neighbours, but when there's 5 cm of water through their premises, caused indirectly by you, the first meeting isn't perhaps as cordial as it should be. The plumber hadn't arrived. The water was still pouring in — for some reason the water couldn't be stopped.

'Dreadfully sorry about this,' I said to three real-estate people in bare feet. 'I assure you we're getting it fixed just as soon as possible.'

I asked Mal where the plumber was. 'On his way, mate. Be here any minute. Wally's gone down to see the quack.'

Wally. Big Wally, the cause of the current problem. 'Is he all right?'

'No mate, he's got pieces of porcelain up his arse. Cut to buggery. Bloody lucky he didn't castrate himself. They'll probably have to helicopter him to Auckland. He'll be on compo for weeks, poor bugger.'

I shot into the café, shoes off, pants rolled up, in search of the elusive water main. The dunny was flowing like crazy with water pouring out. I tried a couple of taps on the wall. No luck. I went into the kitchen and played around with some taps under the bench. The first two were off but the third one was on, and I tightened it up.

Mal called from the dunny, 'You've found it! It's turning off.'

I finished tightening it up. The crisis had been stopped. Why nobody had looked under the sink until I did was beyond me — that's where water taps are. Perhaps only Willie Woofters from Queen Street know things like this?

I went back to the real-estate office and told them the good news, and took the liberty of introducing myself. I also said I could be looking at buying a house. Well, that changed the icy atmosphere in a hurry. Suddenly, there we were, standing in the water in our bare feet happily discussing Waiheke Island property.

The damage didn't look too bad. The floor was tiled, thank god, and the water was draining out fast. When I said I'd pay for the place to be cleaned they were amazingly decent about the whole thing and almost seemed to be enjoying the crisis. 'Don't worry, we'll dry it out. Give us something to do. Why don't you go down to the medical centre and see if Wally is OK?'

I left Mal mopping up in the café and walked down to the nearby medical rooms, looking skyward for the rescue helicopter, and expecting to find Wally lying face down, with umpteen bandages round his backside. Instead of which, Wally was on the point of leaving when I arrived. 'Are you OK Wally?'

'Yeah. Just a couple of little cuts, nothing to worry about. Sorry about your shit-house though. That's never happened to me before.'

We walked back to the café. As we passed the bar we'd been at last night, Wally expressed his opinion that a medicinal beer would go down well and help to soothe his rear end. I expressed the opinion that modern medicine has yet to prove the soothing effect of alcohol on cuts and bruises.

When we got to the café, the plumber had arrived and Mal was filling him in on the situation. Walking in with Wally was like walking in with the Holy Ghost. Wally was meant to be flat on his stomach in bed. Wally wasn't meant to be walking into the café. 'Jesus Wally, how are you feeling?' asked Mal. 'Thought we wouldn't see you for a while.'

Sid, the plumber, who obviously knew Wally well, thought it a great joke and said the council should appoint him chief shit-house tester. 'If a dunny can support you, it can support anyone. What did you do — fart and blow the thing up?'

Wally assured him it just collapsed.

Sid surveyed the scene and gave us his report. 'You'll need a new dunny.'

An observation any brain surgeon would have been proud of.

'Must be your lucky day. I've got one in the van. I was going to install it down at the wharf later today but I'll get another one. It's a heavy-duty job as well.'

'Fair enough. Just one question. Can you move it back

from where it is now? That's a beautiful view and I'd prefer to have a table and a couple of chairs there instead.'

'No way mate, that's a big, big job — and with permits involved, it's not worth it. You'd be better off to keep it as it is. Nothing wrong with a shit-house with a view for us blokes, you know.'

Mal got into the act then. 'Sid, while you're here, can you do another minor plumbing job for us? We want to move the sink from the back to the side, so we just need the waterworks changed around.'

'As long as you've got a permit, I don't see any problem. Remember what happened when you changed Harry Turnbull's house around without getting that permit?'

'Jesus Sid, of course we've got a permit. When can you do it?'

'Well, I'll do the dunny today and come back later in the week to move the sink.' Sid then turned to me and asked if it was a cashie. 'Won't do it any other way mate. Let's make it a hundred bucks for me labour — cash, and three hundred and eighty for the new dunny. You can pay for that with a cheque.'

I wanted the dunny installed pronto. It was now lunchtime on day two of the renovations to *The Glorious Ocean View Café* and little progress had been made. Wally's dole money had come through, so the three of them went across the road to the bar for lunch. I was asked, but declined. Instead, I went to the liquor shop, bought a couple of bottles of wine and took them into the real-estate office, as a small gesture of apology.

They were very decent about everything — nothing major had been broken or put out of working order, which was something. One of the girls wanted to know if we'd be having an official opening of the new lavatory. If so, could she come?

I waited a full hour, then walked over to the bar and dragged my enthusiastic workers back to the coal front. Sid got me aside. 'Whacker, if you wanna get that joint finished, just let Mal and Wally get on with it. They're the best team of builders on the island, and they'll do you proud. But leave them to it — don't stand over them. But you have to understand they're both chronic pissheads. When they've got a couple inside, their metabolism works much better. They can't work sober. Give 'em a beer for morning tea and you'll have your bloody alterations finished by lunchtime.'

In all my years of business and study, I'd never heard of this method of increasing productivity. I don't believe it's taught at Harvard, Oxford or Otago. The things you learn on Waiheke Island. I went over what we had to do with Mal. 'Don't worry mate,' he told me. 'I know what the plan is. We'll get stuck into it this afternoon. The stuff from Placemakers is here now. May even stay a bit later tonight. I'll make sure Sid puts in the best dunny in Oneroa. You just piss off and leave us to it. The phone's on in the café now, so if there's a problem, I'll give you a call. See you tomorrow afternoon.'

I decided to leave them to it.

The next day I kept busy in the morning at the bach making a checklist of what we were going to need for the café — plates, pots, décor, food and so on, filling in time before going back up to see whether Mal and Wally had made any progress. The phone didn't ring, so I assumed either they'd removed a supporting beam and the place had collapsed, or no news was good news.

I got to the café at midday. What a transformation! The old kitchen had practically gone and the new one was making rapid progress. Even more impressive, Sid had decided to stay with our job and had not only installed a wonderful new loo, but was busy moving the sink and other waterworks over to the side. A carton of beer was on the floor, with some full ones in it and a few empties beside it. The secret ingredient.

'What do you think, Boss? On the right track?' asked Wally.

'Looks great guys. Most impressed.'

'We did a tenner last night,' commented Mal.

'What's a tenner?'

'Jesus, you're a dopey shit. We worked until ten o'clock. Felt we owed it to you.'

'Very impressed. Hey Sid, does the dunny work?'

'Course it does. A real credit to Mr Crapper, that one. Wally christened it, reckons he had the greatest shit of his life. Only trouble is, all the shit-house paper got wet. There isn't any. Just don't get too close to Wally's arse, it don't smell too good. Perhaps if you have time you could hop out and buy some.'

I walked up the road, made the most important purchase of the day, and dropped it back at the café, before leaving them to it.

Another day dawned. It was very wet so I ordered a taxi and picked up Peg, who was coming to show me the ropes. When we got to the café it was unlocked, but there wasn't a sign of life. I heard a grunt, followed by a semi-snore, from behind the counter. I walked around, and there was Wally, sprawled on the floor. I gave him a good shake. 'Wally, Wally, wake up. Are you OK?'

'Jesus, where am I? What's going on?' he groaned, trying to sit up.

'You're in the café, mate. Didn't you go home last night?'

'Oh, G'day Boss. Whoooo. The ol' head ain't too good. What's the time?'

'Just after nine. Did you have a couple last night?'

'Just a couple. Remember now, it was pissing down so we decided to stay here for the night. Mal's here somewhere.'

I found Mal around the corner, absolutely out to it. I gave him a gentle kick. No reaction.

'He might be dead,' said Peg, kneeling down beside him. 'No, he's breathing.'

I went over to the new sink, grabbed a bucket and filled it up, then threw it over his face.

'What the fuckin' hell? Where am I? What time is it?'

'It's a new day in your wonderful life. Peg's here and she's going to make you and Wally a nice strong cup of coffee. You had a few last night eh?'

'Oh, wow, yeah, yeah. It was the rum. That's right; it was

raining. Pouring. So when they threw us out across the road, we bought a bottle and came back here to wait for the rain to stop. Must have flaked.'

'By Christ I feel crook,' Wally said, coming alive on his way to the loo. 'A good chunder might make me feel better.'

I left Peg to make the coffee and walked up the road to buy some fresh bread. Hopefully a bit of food and hot coffee inside them would bring the dynamic duo back into the world again. When I returned a few minutes later, they were sitting at the table, drinking coffee and laughing away with Peg, as if they were on a normal morning-tea break. I put the bread on the table and they grabbed a few slices.

'We're really making progress,' said Mal. 'Today we'll build you the divider to separate the kitchen. I'll have to go to Placemakers to organise some more timber. OK if I borrow your card? What's the pin number again?'

'Bit of luck, Mal. Peg and I are going down there soon for a few bits and pieces so you can share our taxi.'

'Might be a bit of a problem.'

'No problem, you're more than welcome to join us. Besides, if you got picked up driving by Mr Plod, you'd make the bloody bag explode.'

'It's not that. It's the taxi. They won't take me. None of them will.'

'Why?'

'Well I've had the odd chunder in the odd taxi or two.'

'C'mon Mal,' said Peg, 'everyone knows what happened to poor ol' Percy Bishop's new Jap import. Not only did you chunder all over him and the car, you shat yourself too. It was disgusting.'

'It was an accident. And I did try to clean it all up.'

'Try? The stink was so vile nobody could sit in that car for two weeks. It was Percy's pride and joy too.'

Mal was a bit embarrassed. Once again progress at *The Glorious Ocean View Café* had ground to a halt. 'Tell you what,' I said. 'I'll drive your ute, you and Peg come with me, and that way we can get things cracking. There's no point in risking your licence.'

'Haven't got a licence, so you don't have to worry about that.'

I pretended not to hear. It was soon time to go shopping, which meant it was also time to drive Mal's ute. The three of us climbed aboard. 'Mal, is it registered?'

'Yep.'

'Does it have a current warrant of fitness?'

'Yep.'

'Is it legally yours?'

'Yep.'

Away we went and it seemed to go all right. Until we came to the first intersection. I put my foot on the brake. No reaction. I put my foot down harder. No response. I grabbed the handbrake. It worked.

'Mal, the foot-brake doesn't work.'

'I know.'

'Well why didn't you tell me?'

'You didn't ask.'

I drove very, very slowly to Ostend, using the gears and handbrake. We parked outside Placemakers and went inside. Mal went one way, Peg and myself the other. Forty minutes later, the ute was loaded up and then it was a slow drive back.

'Lunchtime, Whacker. Wally and myself might just pop across the road. You and Peg want to come?'

'No way.'

'We'll just have a couple and then we'll fly into it.'

'Well have something to eat as well.'

'Sure, Whacker. Er, you couldn't give us a little advance could you? Say fifty bucks.'

'Yeah, same for me if possible,' piped up Wally.

'Ten bucks each. Be back in half an hour.'

Five minutes later they were back, eating meat pies. 'The arsehole — he's fuckin' banned us for a week. Accused us of being right royal turds last night — that's what he said. What's a right royal turd anyway? He's insulted our royal family. Stuff him. We're not going back there again are we Wally?'

'No way. We'll come and drink in the café every night.'

'Now just hang on guys, we're not going to be licensed. And the last thing I want is a couple of pissheads like you sitting around. The place is going to have a bit of class. So you got yourself banned for a week — that'll teach you. Love to know what you did last night!'

'You'll never know mate. Nor will we — can't remember a bloody thing. Right, we'd better get into building this room divider. Bit of work involved and you want to have a few shelves and a decent workbench. Couple of days, and we'll have to get Sid back. The dishwasher has to be fitted properly. Then we'll be adding a few finishing touches. I reckon we'll be done within the week.'

'Mal, we have to get the walls painted. Do you know a professional, experienced painter? Not a Waiheke cowboy though — somebody really good.'

'You're looking at the best painter on the island. Any silly bugger can whack a bit of paint on a wall.'

5

By the start of the following week, progress was being made. The room divider was taking shape and the kitchen was starting to look like a kitchen. I bought a can of CRC from the gas station and got to work on the windows. With the help of the dynamic duo, we got them all open. It made a big difference — fresh ocean air poured into the café. Then on to the massive job of cleaning the windows. It hadn't been done for a decade, so that was a challenge and something to keep yours truly occupied all morning.

In the afternoon I caught a taxi down to Placemakers to get some paint, telling the taxi driver to wait. I had a bit of luck, as the guy who served me knew *The Glorious Ocean View Café* well. 'Peg used to have great pies, nice pink lamingtons too.' Besides describing the cuisine, he roughly knew the size of the place, so was able to tell me how much paint I'd need.

When I brought it back to the taxi, the driver asked if I'd mind if we collected her mum on the way back. 'She has to see the quack in Oneroa.' I didn't object. 'I'll just charge you a flat fifteen bucks if that's OK.' That was fine by me.

Mum lived out towards Rocky Bay, which was quite a detour. Cheryl, the driver, chatted all the way about this and that. When we arrived, her mum was still in her nightie so I was invited in for a cup of tea while she got changed. It was a lovely cuppa, made with real tea leaves.

Finally, dear old mum was ready. 'So sorry to keep you waiting. I thought it was tomorrow I had to see the doc. Isn't Cheryl marvellous the way she looks after her old mum? Would you like some silverbeet? Cheryl, go and pick this nice man some silverbeet.'

Five minutes later I had a plastic supermarket bag full of silverbeet. I hate silverbeet. Always have. Always will. 'Thank you so much. I really appreciate that. I do love silverbeet.'

'Get this nice man some more, Cheryl,' called out Mum.

'No, no, this is fine.'

'Don't be silly, there's plenty. Cheryl's getting more for you now.'

Five minutes later, I had two plastic supermarket bags full of Cheryl's mum's silverbeet. I said my thanks again, but with less enthusiasm.

Back in the taxi, I insisted Mum must have the front seat and when we got to the doctor's rooms, I felt obliged to get out and help Mum inside. Cheryl left her with the nurse, and drove me on to the café.

'Anyone want some silverbeet?' Two faces looked as me as if I was a lunatic. 'I've got plenty from the taxi driver's mum's place. You're more than welcome.'

'You can stick your bloody silverbeet right up your arse. But, if you're feeling generous, we're as dry as a couple of camels marooned on a deserted island.'

'Would you like a cup of tea?'

'Tea? Drinking tea in the afternoon is what fuckin' grannies do. Besides it's nearly knocking off time.'

Point made. Five minutes later we were sharing a six-pack, while Mal told me a little more about his personal life. 'Can't stay long tonight, gotta get home. Promised the missus I'd take her to look at a new pup. Bloody dog got run over a couple of weeks back and she's been pestering me for another one.'

'You didn't tell me you had a missus.'

'You didn't ask, mate.'

'Got any kids?'

'No sign of any yet. She's no ravin' beauty, my Bets. Big girl. The only way I get into her pants now is if I'm as pissed as a chook.'

'But when you get pissed and don't go home — doesn't she worry?'

'Why should she? I'm a big boy. Besides, when I come home pissed, she knows she's goin' to get it. Ha, ha, ha!'

'Does she work?'

'Well, she's had a few jobs, my Bets. At the moment she cleans out a bed and breakfast up the road. Quite likes it because she doesn't have to start till ten, so she can have a good lie-in. Plus, it's a cashie.'

Wally added more intrigue. 'Bets is me sister, Whacker.' Mal and Wally were brothers-in-law. I should have known.

'Well mate, better go. Wally, wanna come too?' Mal called out.

Riding my bike home, my cellphone rang. I ground to a halt. Number Three was calling. 'How's the café going? It must be quite exciting for you because I know you love challenges.'

'Yeah, you're right there, darling. That's why I married you.'

'Oh, cut it out Whacker, we've been through all that. We agreed we'd be friends. I really want to help you feed those poor island weirdos.'

'Darling, your Herne Bay attitude to my customers is really appreciated.'

29

'Sorry. How about I come over in the morning so we can sit down and work out a menu?'

I already had a pretty damn good idea about what I wanted for a menu, but I also knew Number Three was going through another bust-up and probably needed some occupational therapy. As a rich bitch, having done the essential three years with a used-car importer, she had untold time on her hands.

'OK, come over. You haven't been to Waiheke before have you?'

'Of course I have, when George had the gin palace. We used to hide from the wind in those little bays when it got rough. Whacker, why do men like boating?'

'That's simple — to get away from their wives. If you want to come over, catch the ten o'clock ferry. I don't have a car, so I can't pick you up, just walk up to the shopping area — it's only a couple of hundred metres. I'll shout you lunch. Pie à la Waiheke and coffee. See you tomorrow. Oh, and I've got a great guy to introduce you to — single, name of Walter. Wally for short.'

Tuesday wasn't a nice day. Number Three hadn't arrived by eleven so I go decided to get on the black bike and look for her. About fifty yards from the café I saw a drowned rat. I recognised the drowned rat and spun the bike around. 'Want a double?'

The look said it all. 'You fuckin' arsehole! You said the shops were just a couple of hundred metres up from the ferry. I've walked for miles. No cabs went by, nothing. I'm drenched — I've got water in my shoes and down my back — look at me.'

'Yeah, you do look pretty horrible. Want a double? Sit on the bar.' The drowned rat glared at me before sportingly climbing aboard. We went a short distance and stopped.

'We're here!'

'You mean I was nearly here under my own power?'

'Yep, but not quite. Much more impressive to roll up on your ex-husband's two-wheeled limo.' My humour wasn't appreciated. I had a feeling we might not be agreeing on menus.

'This is it. What do you think?' I asked the third big love of my life, as we entered my new pride and joy. There was no sign of my two illustrious helpers.

'Good god — it's a coffee bar! I thought it was a café. Where can I dry off? My dress is soaking.'

'Look, take it off and I'll put it through the dry cycle of the dishwasher. Put these old curtains on to keep you warm.'

'Are you sure nobody else is here?'

'Well, the Invisible Man's over there, so you might be lucky.'

Number Three removed her very wet dress and wrapped herself in an old frilly curtain. I took the dress to the dishwasher, put it in, and turned it on to the dry cycle.

A couple of minutes later, the door opened, and Mal and Wally came in with a six-pack while I was endeavouring to make the ex-love of my life a cup of tea. 'Whacker, you kinky bastard! Do you want us to piss off and come back later?' Mal asked.

'Into it, Whacker!' enthused Wally.

Number Three gave me a look that would have stopped a turd in mid-flight.

'Gentlemen, gentlemen,' I said, trying to inject some class into the situation. 'I'd like to introduce an old acquaintance of mine. Number Three.'

'Hallo, Number Three,' they both said together. Nice manners.

'Darling, two very close colleagues of mine, Malcolm and Walter.'

'Hallo.'

'Would you like a beer, Number Three?' Wally asked.

The kettle was whistling, so I moved to make the tea, leaving a very pissed-off woman dressed in a frilly curtain to make conversation with my illustrious colleagues. For some reason she wasn't interested in sharing a beer with them. Face to face with an attractive woman, Mal and Wally weren't exactly gifted conversationalists, and after the offer of a beer, the conversation dried up.

'Is my dress getting dry?' asked the ex-love of my life.

I checked. I shuddered. I had a problem. The dishwasher had gone on to full cycle. The dress was absolutely soaked. I lied. 'Nearly ready, just another few minutes.' I handed her a cup of tea. Meanwhile, as one would expect, Mal and Wally were thriving on the unexpected free entertainment and work ground to a halt.

'Now, would you like to sit down and go over the menu?' I asked.

'You've got to be joking! If you think I'm going to discuss menus while I'm dressed in an old curtain, you obviously don't know me very well.'

After five years of marriage, she was right on that one.

Sid arrived to complete the installation of the dishwasher

that was in the process of having a premature run. I introduced him to Number Three and discreetly explained my predicament. 'The thermostat's fucked in that thing. You won't get any heat. That dress is wet for the night — you lucky bastard!'

The shit hit the fan. Number Three had heard part of our conversation. 'What was that about my dress?'

Sid was marvellous. 'Won't take long to fix, just an hour or so and we should be in business.'

'An hour or so? I'm not sitting here for another hour, dressed in a curtain in front of three strangers and a dork. That's you,' she kindly said, pointing at me. 'I want out of here. Whacker, call a cab.'

'And my Herne Bay princess, just where do you think your golden carriage is going to deliver you to, dressed in that beautiful attire?'

'We'll go to your place. I want a hot shower and you can lend me some clothes.'

Sid kindly offered to drive us home in his van, and while the look Number Three gave me made it obvious it was most definitely not her choice of transportation, I accepted.

A little later, I had a slightly happier ex-wife. She'd showered and was wearing a pair of my jeans and a sweatshirt. I made coffee and a toasted sandwich with leftover spaghetti, and she actually ate it. We were nearly friends again.

'Now Whacker, what about your menu? What do you have planned?'

'I don't want poofter food, it won't work in the kind of place I'll be running. I want good, basic food. I've spent a small fortune eating poofter food at umpteen Auckland restaurants, but what I've enjoyed most is the kind of food I was lucky enough to have as a kid. Would you like a glass of wonderful Waiheke wine?'

Normally ex-wives aren't entitled to top shelf — it's basement if they're lucky. However, I felt that Number Three had had a rough morning, so I opened a magnificent bottle of Waiheke red. She knew her plonk and it was good. We sat around discussing food but it quickly became obvious we'd never agree. With the sun appearing, we decided to walk back to the café. A considerable hike, but I knew this particular ex enjoyed a walk — except when it was raining.

'Who is this Walter you were talking about last night? What does he do?'

'You met him. Mal's mate.'

'That's Walter?'

'Yeah, great guy. Mal's partner is his sister.'

'Thanks Whacker. Why the hell did I ever marry someone like you?'

'Because you had your brains between your legs,' I replied as quick as a flash. She laughed. I liked that. I always admire people who can laugh at themselves. Even ex-wives.

Grubby looks were cast at us as we entered the café. Mal and Wally were ninety-nine per cent sure we'd hopped home to have a nooner. 'Well guys, it's looking good. I'll get Number Three back on the ferry then come back and get stuck into some painting.'

'Would you like me to help you paint?' asked Number Three.

'We'd never agree on the colours, my old darling. No, you get back to the mainland. I'll send your dress back when it's dry.'

'Like hell. There's no way I'm going back on the ferry in your old gear. I look like a tramp.'

'You haven't got a choice, your dress is still soaking. Besides, dressed like that you look like a real person. You should try it more often.' I walked her up to the taxi rank.

'I always knew you were crazy, but what you're doing looks like fun. If you do need any help, just give me a call. Oh, and don't send the dress, it gives me an excuse to come back to collect it. Bye.'

As the taxi roared off, I told myself to remember to send the dress back by the end of the week. Ex-wives hanging around curb progress, as they have to be entertained. I hadn't achieved much today.

'Jesus, Whacker! That was a good lookin' sort,' commented Wally as I re-entered the café. 'What the hell did you give her the arse for?'

'Didn't. She met a Yank on a shopping trip with the girls in Sydney. He had a penthouse in New York and an apartment in Acapulco. Rich bastard.'

'Is she still with him?'

'Shit no. He got pissed one night, drove his car into a crowded Burger King and ran over half a dozen Mexicans. Had to sell everything and went bankrupt. When the money went, so did Number Three. She came back, married her used-car importer, did the three years and flicked him. Now she's sniffing around again. I tried to line her up with you. A bit of older woman could do you a world of good.'

'Thanks, Whacker.'

7

On Wednesday morning I was enjoying a second cup of tea in my new café, when an extremely large woman entered the café. Big. Fearing she'd break one of my not very robust chairs, I got up before she could sit down.

'Hallo. Look, we're not actually open yet, probably in another week.'

'Are you Whacker McCracker?'

'Yes, that's me.'

'I'm Mal's partner, Bets. Wally's my brother. I need your help. The cops have locked them up. I've just spoken to Mal on the phone and he told me to come and tell you.'

'Are they all right?'

'They're coming right. Bit crook earlier on. It seems they drank all night and got into a bit of trouble walking home.'

'What did they do?'

'The Carters up the hill use a goat to keep the lawn mown. Wally told me Mal thought it was a big lamb. It was dark, Mr McCracker.'

'Call me Whacker, Bets.'

'Thanks. Anyway they decided to take it home. Just borrow it like. Well, there was a hell of a battle. The goat let fly at them. They let fly at the goat. It woke up the neighbourhood and Jack Koster, the local sergeant, lives just two houses down from the Carters. He comes running up in his undies, sees what's going on and arrests them. His missus, in her nightie, drives the police car up. Jack bundles them in the back and she drives them down to the cop shop where they get thrown in a cell. God knows what'll happen to them now. They're not exactly squeaky clean.'

It was all I could do not to roar with laughter, but Bets was upset, so of course I didn't. I sat her down and made her a nice cup of tea. The chair didn't break. We had a nice chat and I told her how impressed I was with her husband and brother. I'd do all I could to help.

Minutes later I walked up to the police station. Being mid-morning, it wasn't exactly booming. I explained the reason for my visit to a constable. A sergeant joined us, introducing himself as Sergeant Koster. I heard the full story and asked what would happen to them now.

'Justice, Waiheke Island-style, Mr McCracker. They're bloody lucky Clem Carter doesn't want to press charges. He knows them both so we're just scaring the shit out of them at the moment. So far, we've told them they could be facing attempted rape of a sheep or goat. Not the nicest charge to face on an island of animal lovers. We'll let them stew on that for another couple of hours, and then, after a bloody good ticking off, and, hopefully, a good kick up the bum, they can go home. Poor buggers are in for hell from the locals. Everyone will be baaing and bleeting at them for weeks! Bloody characters those two.'

I went back to the café, where Bets was waiting. 'It's all OK. They're not pressing charges. They'll be out soon.'

'Thanks a million Whacker. They said you'd be able to pull a few strings.'

'I assure you Bets, I pulled no strings. The cops were pretty decent about it.'

☕

I painted for the remainder of Wednesday, Thursday and Friday on my own. Mal and Wal simply didn't turn up. The real-estate girls from next door came in and were most impressed. The chemist said he couldn't work out why the view hadn't been utilised before. The guys who ran the second-hand shop on the other side came in for a look and a chat. And so did the bloke from the booze shop. It was nice to meet the neighbours.

When I made my plans to come to the island, I decided against bringing a car over with me. However, I quickly realised Waiheke was bigger than I thought, and quite hilly. To enjoy the place, I was going to need a car. Nothing flash, just something practical.

In between painting, I phoned up an old schoolmate, Jim Morran, who was in the bottom class with me and with whom I used to vie for bottom place of that particular class. He was into cars. Big into cars. I told him I needed a shit-heap for Waiheke.

'We don't normally worry about that end of the market, we just send them straight to the auction. But there's always a few floating around. When do you want it?'

'Sunday.'

'We'll find you something. I won't be in, I'm going to the farm for the weekend. Why don't you come along?'

'Haven't got time. Got this café to open next week.'

'Heard about it at the golf club. Everyone reckons that

after all those bloody wives, you've finally flipped. I'll give you until Christmas, then you'll be back.'

'No way, Jim. The island life is starting to suit me.'

'I'll wait and see. Anyway, come to the showroom and ask for Jackie. I'll make sure there's something for you to drive away in.'

'Thanks Jim. You must bring Sandy over for lunch one day.'

'We'll do that. Next time we're out on the gulf, we'll drop anchor and come up. Cheers.'

I caught Mr Fuller's ferry on God's day of rest. After only a couple of weeks downtown Auckland seemed different — big! From there it was a taxi up to Jim's car emporium. Jackie was indeed expecting me. 'Jim's selected a car for you. He told me it will fit in on Waiheke Island perfectly.'

It wasn't on display in the new-car showroom. It wasn't on display in the used-car yard. It wasn't on display in the service department. It was on display around the back where nobody could see it. A Skoda. A lime green Skoda.

'Is this a joke?' was my first question.

'No, Jim personally selected it for you. He had to phone several places to get it. A mechanic spent a couple of hours on it yesterday and it's got a new warrant.'

'I don't want a bloody Skoda.'

'It's only nine hundred dollars.'

It was Jim's idea of a joke. He'd be down on his farm roaring with laughter. I could also imagine him telling everyone at the golf club about what he sold the loony from Waihehe Island. 'What else have you got?'

'Mr McCracker, this is it. Mr Morran insisted this was the car for you. Ideal for the island, built like a tank and it won't rust like some of the Japanese cars. He really felt it would suit you — and he went to quite a bit of trouble to get it. Plus, the price is really good; it's registered and has a warrant. Jim wouldn't sell you a moving disaster.'

I'd known Jim for many years. In his earlier days he would and did sell moving disasters. Many. He made his initial fortune from selling moving disasters. I hoped he really had stopped doing it by now, especially to an old schoolmate.

'Does it go?' was my next question. That prompted Jackie to get in and start the thing. It took some choke, but it did start.

'Take it for a drive, Mr McCracker.'

I did, and it drove surprisingly well for nine hundred dollars. Perhaps it could be OK for the island — it certainly qualified for the shit-heap category I'd specifically requested. I returned to Jackie and told her I'd take it.

When we completed the transaction, I asked if it would be possible to leave Jim a note of appreciation on his desk and she showed me his office. I went and found his diary on his desk, opened it to the next day's page and wrote one extremely rude word across it.

I drove the Skoda, with great caution, to my storage garage in Mt Wellington. After all my marriages, it was my own little piece of heaven. My Aladdin's Cave. Nobody else knew it existed. I sorted out numerous bits and pieces I could use in the bach and café. The back seat of the lime green Skoda was soon full, as was the boot and the front passenger seat.

The vehicular ferry left from Half Moon Bay at five. Not one person on it gave the car an admiring look, or asked how fast it went. They could have at least asked about the radio. It worked, but didn't have FM — only AM.

9

Monday morning saw me puttering up the hill to the café, after the Skoda had started the fifth time. Mal was there. 'Don't you say a bloody thing. Don't bloody baa me or bleat me for Christ sake. I've had a weekend of it.'

'Morning Mal. Been a tough few days huh?'

'Have had better Whacker, have had better. Can't go anywhere without someone taking the piss out of me. Wally's done an abo so we won't see him for while.'

'What do you mean?'

'He's gone walkabout. Like the abos do. Christ knows where he's gone or when he'll be back. He really got the piss taken out of him at the footy club. Bets had a long talk with him and reckoned she'd never seen him so upset. Silly bugger should have stayed at home. He's done it before.'

'How long was he away last time?'

'Well, he hit the mainland and got the bus to stay with a mate in Gisborne. Got into a bit of trouble the day after he arrived. He got locked up for six months and then they sent him home. Trouble is, he knows some bad bastards on the mainland and he can be easily led. Bets is really worried.'

'He could be still be on the island. Has anyone checked his friends?'

'The Maori network on this island is magic — if they want to find someone they find 'em. The word is out, so let's hope he's around. If he does suddenly appear, don't take the piss out of him. He's bloody sensitive.'

Mal wasn't himself. I thought taking him outside and showing him the car could cheer him up. 'A fuckin' Skoda. What a beauty!' It won his approval.

A truck from the council went by. The driver saw Mal, and yelled out the window, 'Hey Mal, hear Wally's fallen in love with a sheep and run away with her. Hope I get an invite to the wedding!'

'Arsehole!' yelled Mal. 'Whacker, I could really go a bloody beer. I'm just not myself at the moment.'

'Too early Mal. A little later.'

'Promise?'

'We'll see. Depends on progress. You slowed us down a bit by not fronting up for half of last week. Today, you finish off your bits and pieces and I'll get stuck into the painting. Another job we have to think of is the floor. It needs sanding and staining.'

'No trouble with that. We can hire a floor sander from that place in Ostend, then just stick some polyurethane over it. Sorry about last week. We both really got stuck into the grog.'

I got painting and Mal got carpentering. Mid-morning I went out to see a man about a dog and returned with a six-pack. Mal drank two in five minutes. Sam, a local signwriter I'd spoken to a few days earlier, called in with a layout for signs. We agreed on the sizes of the blackboard, the signage above the café and the one at street level. I'd given a lot of thought to the name and decided the café had to be repositioned. The old name was quaint, but a bit too old-fashioned. The café needed some vibrancy so I decided to give it my name.

'Whacker McCracker's Café is a great name, Mr

McCracker. Everyone will remember it. I'll get the signs up later in the week. Is that OK?'

'That'll be fine.'

The floor sander and a set of earmuffs were delivered to the café at eight the following morning (Mal's ute was finally off the road. The handbrake had packed up too, so even he wasn't too keen on driving it.) The floor was cleared and given a final sweep.

'OK Mal. Crank 'er up and let's get into it.'

'Do you know how these things work?'

'No.'

'Nor do I.'

'Well, let's have a cup of tea and see if we can work it out. Any word on Wally?'

'Oh yeah, forgot to tell you. He's fine. He phoned Bets last night.'

'Where is he?'

'Raglan.'

'What's he doing in Raglan?'

'Staying with a friend.'

'One of his mates from jail?'

'Probably. You meet a lot of people in jail, gives you a good network if you want to use it. Especially if you're on the run. Not that Wally is.'

'What are you going to do?'

'Not much we can do. Wally's a big boy.'

'Has he got money? I owe him some. If he hasn't got any, that's when he'll get into trouble.'

'No, he probably hasn't. But if we send any, he's so

43

bloody generous he'll be stony broke again by the end of the day. He'll sort himself out and be home soon.'

'I suppose Bets is worried.'

'She is and she isn't. She's got a cousin down that way so she called her to keep an eye out for him. Now let's see if we can get this bastard working.'

It took some experimenting and getting the right setting, then away it went. The dust! The noise! With only one set of earplugs I left Mal to it and found a bit of peace outside.

The screeching brought us close to our neighbours again. The real-estate girls and the antique-shop couple commented about the noise level, but in a very nice way. No rude words or anything. I apologised and said it wouldn't be long but it had to be done. Unfortunately, it was long. It took most of the day. The hire firm picked it up just before five and we'd only just finished. The floor looked good, but the place was full of dust.

Bets phoned Mal to say her cousin had located Wally. 'He's with a friend all right, a lady friend. He met her on the island. I assume it's Pong.'

'Pong?'

'Well that was her nickname. Wally and her had quite a thing. Bet it's her.'

'Nice girl?'

'Yeah, not bad. On the DPB, she's got a couple of little kids. No dad around when she was over here, that's why Wally was getting into her knickers. Feel like a beer? Me week's up now. I can go back across the road.'

'Good idea.'

Mal was greeted with a few baas and bleats but he took it in good humour. The guy behind the bar thought he had another day to go on the ban, but wasn't too worried. We had a couple and called it a day. Mal didn't want to stay by himself, so we left together. I had the bike, and Mal was walking.

'Give us a double down the hill will you, Whacker?'

Mal climbed on to the bar and away we shot.

'Thanks mate,' said Mal as we got to the bottom of the hill. 'See you tomorrow.'

We cleaned up all the mess from the sanding the next morning. Peg phoned to say the curtains and tablecloths were ready, and I told her to come up in the afternoon when we would be finished. Bets called in soon after she arrived and I had the feeling it was a jack-up so she could chat to Peg about getting a job. Anyway, she was more than welcome and we all sat around having a very nice cup of tea and some fresh scones Peg had brought along. Bets said she'd help her hang the curtains. Mal and I left them to it, and drove to Placemakers to get the polyure-thane, some brushes, hinges, a dunny-roll holder, towel racks, hooks and a few other bits and pieces needed to finish off the kitchen.

An ambulance was double-parked outside the café when we got back, and a police car. Our neighbours were all looking at the café. The shoppers and the school kids were looking at the café. We parked in the no-parking zone across the street and ran to the centre of attention.

Bets had fallen out of the upstairs window and was sprawled on the veranda. Peg was most upset. 'We had a spare curtain so we decided to put it upstairs in the storeroom. She just leaned out a bit to get the end of the curtain up and fell out. The language when she landed! It certainly brought the neighbours in to help. Trouble is, she's a big girl and we can't get her back. Luckily she doesn't seem to be badly hurt.'

Mal called out to her. 'Is the veranda all right Bets? Bloody lucky you didn't go through it and drop another few metres. If you did, you wouldn't be cooking me tea tonight.'

'You're an arsehole Mal. You bloody well help me,' replied the love of his life.

An ambulance officer and the constable had reached her by lowering themselves out the window. Mal felt obliged to join her, so he went up and lowered himself out the window as well. I called up to see if they needed me too — I wanted to do something, but the constable told me no way. Any more weight and the whole veranda could collapse.

Mal spoke to his beloved then shouted down to me, 'She's all right Whacker, just a sore arse and a couple of bruises.' A domestic started between husband and wife on the veranda. The constable intervened.

We now had one heck of a problem. Getting her back. A fire engine arrived, along with another police car and two officers. The street was crowded and the café packed, with everyone wanting a look at poor Bets. I recognised one of the new cops to arrive as Sergeant Koster, from the goat incident. One of the firemen went back outside and got a ladder to make access easier from the upstairs window to the veranda. The local doctor arrived and was all set to climb down when the constable below yelled at him not to. 'We shouldn't have any more weight on this than we need to. Wait until Mal goes back in, then you come down.'

Mal climbed back up to the window and the doctor went down. The sergeant was beside me weighing up the situation. 'Lucy,' he said to the constable beside him, 'can you run down and see what kind of support is under that veranda?'

The firemen decided to clear the café, so gradually the observers, thoroughly enjoying a good dose of live drama, were pushed out to the street. The reporter from the local paper arrived and pleaded to be let in to get his story of the year, and was soon taking photos of everything.

Mal called down to the doctor, 'Hey Doc, is she all right?'

The doctor called back as quick as a flash, 'Mal, living with you she'll never be all right. But you're damn lucky. I can't find anything broken, but we can't take any chances. She must get to hospital.'

Lucy came back from under the veranda to report it was very flimsy and in her opinion there was no way anyone else should be on it. Sergeant Koster's initial summing-up had been right. She couldn't be raised up to the café in a stretcher and she couldn't be lowered down from the veranda because of weight problems. It was a crane or a helicopter, but there was no mobile crane on the island.

Within twenty minutes the rescue helicopter was hovering overhead. The pick-up was very professional and she was on her way to Auckland five minutes later. Then, it was a matter of getting the café back to normal. Sergeant Koster took control and gradually the café started to empty. The reporter, who was a stringer for the *Herald* as well as working for the *Gulf News*, briefly interviewed me about the café.

'Anyone own an old Skoda parked in the no-parking zone across the road?' called Constable Lucy.

'Oh, that's mine. Sorry. I'll go and move it.'

I went out to the car, opened the door, and just as I was getting in, the reporter, who'd followed me out, took a photo. I didn't think anything of it, and re-parked the car. Back in the café I did the thanks bit again. As it didn't seem as if Bets was badly hurt, everyone could see the funny side. It was now after five. 'Would anyone like a beer?' I called out.

'Good idea,' replied the doctor and a couple of others.

I got Mal to pop down the road and get a couple of dozen. He was back in a few minutes and we all sat around, discussing the day's events. How she actually fell out was still a bit of a mystery. Peg hadn't seen her depart, she only heard the landing.

Mal was pretty impressed with the doctor because he told him he didn't think there was any advantage in him going over on the ferry to spend the night in Auckland to be nearer Bets. She'd be better off without him around. 'I feel like having a few beers tonight Whacker.'

'What about the polyurethane on the floor of the café? We were going to do that.'

'C'mon Whacker, the bloody missus just about croaks it hanging your fuckin' curtains and you want me to work tonight?'

'Just kidding Mal, just kidding. I feel like having a few too. What say we get a taxi to the pub, have a big steak, and get stuck into it?'

'You've got me, mate.'

It was the least I could do for the husband of such a willing curtain hanger. Doc said he was coming to the pub too. So did Mark from the real-estate office next door. And Terry, who worked for the council. Mark and Terry had just sort of come in during all the action, and stayed.

The cab rank was just up the road, with only one small Jap import cab. We all piled in. 'Hey, I'm only licensed for four passengers. I can't take the five of you,' the driver advised us, in a most un-Waiheke manner.

Terry from the council introduced himself to the driver. 'Hi mate, I'm Terry Verson from the council. I authorise cab licensing on the island. As of this moment, your cab can take five. Promise.'

'Bullshit Terry. But, seeing it's dark I'll take you all.'

It turned into quite a session.

The phone in the house rang for the first time at about seven in the morning. I let it ring. My cellphone shortly afterwards. I let it ring. The house phone went again. I got up and took it off the hook. The cellphone went again. I turned it off. I awoke again about nine, feeling dreadful. I put the phone back on the hook. It rang within minutes. It was Number Two. 'I've been trying to get you for ages.'

'Look, can I phone you back? I feel like death. Yesterday was quite a day and I still haven't recovered.'

'Yes, yesterday sounded like quite a day — a fat lady

49

falling out your window, a helicopter rescue . . . and Whacker McCracker driving a Skoda.'

'How in hell do you know all that?'

'Simple. I read the *Herald*. Front page. Haven't you seen it?'

'What does it say?

'Pretty much what I told you. Plus, a magnificent photo of you and your new set of wheels. It's hilarious. You must get the paper and have a read. When's the opening party?'

'No opening party. It's just been cancelled. Look you old fart, I'm not feeling the best. Can I call you later?'

'Sure, Skoda boy.'

The shower was pure bliss. When one has a staggering hangover, a nice hot shower works wonders. So did the cup of tea afterwards. And the toast. I phoned for a taxi, and there was a *Herald* on the front seat. I glanced down at it and nearly chundered. Bets' accident had happened on a no news day. It was the headline story — *Large woman falls from Waiheke Island café. Helicopter Rescue*. There was a photo of Bets being hoisted up to the chopper and one of me with the Skoda. I cringed as I read the article. The taxi driver said it was a nice photo. I thanked him and asked if he knew how Bets was. He did. The radio news had reported she was bruised, but looking forward to her husband coming to collect her. I didn't feel it was my business to tell him that from my last sighting of said husband, I doubted very much if she'd be seeing him until well into the afternoon. The driver insisted on giving me his copy of the paper.

When I arrived at the café, Sam had just finished putting the sign up above the café. He'd already done the smaller one at street level. 'Good timing, Mr McCracker. I've got the blackboards in the van. I'll bring them in.'

'Looks good, Sam. Many thanks.'

'Had a bit of excitement here yesterday? I saw the chopper from the workshop and wondered what was going on. Nice photo in the paper — one of the ladies in the real-estate office showed me. Your phone's been ringing like crazy.'

'Sam, it was like a circus. We supplied the entertainment and everyone came to watch.' The phone was ringing again as I opened the door. It was Mal. He'd heard from the hospital that his beloved seemed to be all right but they wanted to keep her in for another day for observation. When Mal said he didn't see the point in rushing over to see her, I said I'd like to send her flowers.

'Flowers — what's the point of sending her flowers? She'll be home tomorrow.'

I told him I felt obliged, after all, it had happened in my café. 'Are you coming in today, or do you want to take it easy?'

'I'll be in. We have to do that floor. See you shortly.'

Across the road and up a little bit was a florist. After all the drama yesterday the young woman in the florist shop knew who I was, and I explained that I wanted to send some flowers to Bets at Auckland Hospital. 'Send her a stack of pink carnations.'

'Why pink carnations?'

'Because I've never met a woman who doesn't like pink carnations. It's all I ever send.' I think she was impressed. She assured me they would be there later in the afternoon. 'Just one other thing. Put on the card: "Bets, love you, Mal".

Oh, and half a dozen kisses.' I'd won a friend for life with Cynthia the florist. She was a real romantic.

Back at the café, Sam was hanging up the phone. 'Can you phone back your ex-wife.'

'Which one?'

'Which one? Just your ex-wife . . . that's what she said. Oh, and some radio station's going to phone you back in ten minutes. They said they'd been trying to get through to you all morning.'

'Thanks.' I removed the receiver from the phone because I didn't want to speak to the media. I also knew heaps of friends and business colleagues back in Auckland would be trying to contact me to take the piss over the Skoda photo. Plus an ex-wife or two.

After all the people in the café the day before, our beautifully sanded floor was a mess. I piled up the furniture on the benches and the room divider, then out with the broom, the bucket and the mop for another good clean.

Mal came in early in the afternoon. 'Bets is fine. Spoke to her on the phone. She'll be home on Saturday. Wally's on his way up to Auckland. Someone in Raglan showed him the paper and he's going straight to the hospital. He phoned me. Upset too. He loves his Bets, there's only the two of them and they're bloody close.'

'Mal, if it's good enough for Bets' brother to come up from Raglan to see her, surely you should go over. She is your wife.'

'Been thinking about it, especially with Wally coming up. If I go over, we could both get on the piss. Might just do it. Could you lend us a hundred bucks? Oh, and Wally might need some of his wages.'

'Why don't you stay over and bring Bets back with you on Saturday?'

'I guess I could do that, Whacker.'

'I'll go to the hole in the wall and get you both some loot and then drive you down to the ferry.'

Twenty minutes later, I dropped the patient's husband off at the wharf, then went back to the café to put the polyurethane on the floor. It was thick and sticky stuff and took a while, but I was determined to get it done and take advantage of nobody being around for three days so it could dry. By eleven the job was finished. I locked up and went home, determined to have a very quiet long weekend.

I caught up with Bets on the phone on Saturday afternoon. She was home and very much on the mend. Absolutely nothing broken and just a few bruises. The specialist reaffirmed what we all knew — her size had saved her

'You will think of me for a job, won't you Whacker? I'd really like to work with you. It's going to be a great success, that place.'

'Bets, you'd have to promise me you'd keep away from the windows. I don't want you falling out again!'

The café looked more and more like a café should when I got to it on Monday morning. The floor was looking good and the wood grain really stood out. The first thing I did was to put out some of the tables and chairs. Wow! Then I made a cup of tea and did what you do in cafés — read the morning paper.

Peg arrived and joined me over a fresh cup. 'Do you reckon I should employ Bets? She really wants a job here, and after what happened, I'd like to help her.'

'Whacker, she's a big, big girl. Bigger than Wally. Getting around the tables, especially if it's a bit crowded, could be a bit of a problem, and while the new kitchen's nice, it's not very big.'

'You know, she could actually be good for business. She's a bit of a celebrity now. Not too many people on the island make the front page of the *Herald*.'

'Where's the arsehole who sent my missus pink fuckin' flowers?' Mal had arrived.

'That was nice, I bet your Bets liked them,' said Peg.

'Never been so embarrassed in my whole life. Somehow, someone down at the footy club found out about it and they all started calling me Pinky-Winky.'

'Morning Mal. Good weekend? How was your night in the big smoke? Wally behave himself?'

'Bloody Wally. Did you hear what happened?'

'No.'

'Well, I get over there and Wally is with Bets at the hospital. Plus bloody Pongy, and her two little kids. We all ended up staying in a place just across the road. Since leaving the island, Pongy's become a Mormon. She's got Wally off the piss. He reckons he hasn't touched a drop since he reached Raglan. When he got there he told her about the goat bit. She said it was Divine Intervention that brought him to Raglan and she would save him. The silly bugger's fallen for it — and her.'

'Might do him a world of good. Where is he now? Gone back to Raglan?'

'On Saturday they went to stay with her auntie in

Otahuhu. Don't know for how long or where he'll go next. He's sick, Whacker.'

'But also a big boy, Mal. Now, let's get our mind on the café because I'm aiming to very quietly open next Friday. No big opening party, nothing. I want it to be quiet for the first couple of weeks so we all know what we're doing. Right Peg?'

'Well yes, but you don't want it too quiet. People like to have people around them. Besides, I'll be here to help. And Bets is available if we want her.'

'We could put Mal in an apron,' I suggested.

'Actually, all joking aside, I wouldn't mind helping out. I know Bets is keen.'

'It's only ten bucks an hour to start with — and you'll have to pay tax. You'd be better to stick with your carpentry. Speaking of which, we have to get cracking. We need more shelves in the kitchen; there are towel racks to hang; a dunny-roll holder to fit and other bits and pieces. And I reckon we should shove a bit of paint on the front outside. It looks a bit shabby.'

At the bach that evening I wrote down what I liked to eat most of all. Mashed potato. Meat pies. Bacon and eggs. Steak. Fresh fish. Mince on toast. Muffins. Scones. Toasted spaghetti or baked-bean sandwiches. Baked beans and spaghetti on toast. Vegetable and tomato soup (separate — not mixed.) Pink lamingtons. Ice-cream slices with pink biscuits. Banana toasted sandwiches. Good genuine Kiwi tucker. My café would only serve what I liked. I was pretty excited about my new menu.

Snacks
Muffins
Lamingtons (pink)
Scones

Brunch
Bacon and eggs (fried) with toast
Banana toastie pie
Spaghetti/Baked Bean toastie pie combo (Oak)

Soup
Vegetable (Watties)
Tomato (Oak)

Meals
Meat pie, mashed spud and gravy
Chicken salad
Savoury mince on toast
Spaghetti on toast (Watties)
Baked Beans on toast (Oak)
Freshly caught Waiheke Island fish with
mashed spud and peas
T-bone steak (medium rare only) with
mashed spud and peas

Whacker's Daily Special
See the blackboard

Dessert
Ice-cream slice between pink wafer biscuits
Banana toastie pie

Drinks
Tea
Coffee (filtered only)
Coke
Orange juice
Milk

●●●●●●●●●●●●●●●●●●●●●●●●●●●●●●●

When I showed Peg the next morning, she thought it was nice and said she'd bring Al along for a meal. Without meeting Al, I believed he was a man who was not into poofter food. Mal reckoned it was great. 'Exactly my kind of menu. No bullshit.'

Peg's only concern was the fish. 'We have trouble getting a regular supply of fresh fish. Most of it comes across from Auckland.'

'Can't we buy it fresh on the island?'

'Well there's a tiny bit, but it's very popular and hard to get. If I were you, I'd take the fish off. The trouble with fish is that it doesn't keep like meat and it's not the same if you freeze it.'

It was great having a local like Peg to tell me about the odd problem like this. As a fish lover, I could see a challenge looming: how to serve fish, caught in the waters around Waiheke Island that very morning, to café patrons at lunchtime.

'Are you going to hire Bets?' asked Peg, when she joined me in the Skoda to go shopping.

'I think we should. She really wants to do it. Apparently the bed and breakfast is quiet at this time of the year. She doesn't have to give notice.'

'So on Friday and for the opening weekend we'll have you,

Bets, and myself. My daughter could help in an emergency but she's getting bigger. Al isn't the best with the little ones. We should have one or two more on standby.'

'I told Mal he could help.'

'Whacker, Mal would be a handicap . . . he's drunk all the time for starters. If I were you, I'd keep him right out of it.'

'Let's give him a chance. I've got a couple of ex-wives back in the big smoke who have trouble filling in each day. They'd help, but I'd prefer to keep them out of it.'

'You seem to get on with your exes. That's nice.'

'Well, at the moment, only four of them. They've become better friends over the years than they were wives. All remarried, and all divorced again. The funny thing is, they get on well together. Number Five, the youngie, is going through a strange stage, but no doubt one day I'll be friends with her again.'

'Well, if you haven't got anything sorted out by Thursday, I'll get on the phone. Between you and me, I'm not sure how much Bets will be able to do. I don't think she's ever been too keen on work. If we don't watch it, there'll only be the two of us and if it gets busy, it'll be a shambles.'

'Peg, it won't be busy. We're doing no advertising, and it's late winter. Look how quiet all the other places around us are right now. We'll be able to handle it standing on our heads.'

We got to the supermarket and filled up a trolley with bits and pieces. Peg made a point of showing me just what the place stocked. 'If you run out of anything, you can always come down here and get it. I know I used to.'

Mal was waiting for us when we got back to the café.

'Hey, you know that bloke from the paper? Well he came over and interviewed me. He'd seen the opening notice in the window.'

'What did you tell him?'

'Nothing much. He said he might come back and have a yarn with you.'

I was just a wee bit concerned about Mal's interview, and hoped the reporter would come back. In the meantime, I busied myself helping Peg put things away on the clean, newly painted shelves.

Bureaucracy was expected at nine-thirty on Wednesday morning, two days before we planned to open, in the form of the health inspector. I wasn't worried because the place was very clean. My lawyer had assured me that as long as the place was spotless and had no bugs, there wouldn't be a problem.

'Double clean the dunny,' he advised. 'Any stains in the bowl and you could be in deep shit — excuse the pun.'

I'd warned Mal about the inspector coming. 'Best behaviour mate — and don't use the dunny until he's gone. And for God's sake don't crack a beer while he's here.'

The health inspector from Auckland turned out to be a very shapely woman in her early thirties. Blonde. And a lovely laugh, but unfortunately handicapped with an engagement and wedding ring. Her name was Belinda Worth. She looked around the café for fifteen minutes and pronounced it fine. Including the dunny. Mal had managed to withhold his daily constitutional, which he always insisted on doing during company hours.

Her next appointment was Ostend, so I offered her a lift, as I was going out that way to get some printing done. She accepted. 'So is this the car I saw in the *Herald* last week? The famous Skoda?'

The famous Skoda wouldn't start. Here I was trying to impress the young lady and the bloody car wouldn't go. I cursed the Eastern Europeans. I cursed Jim Morran. But, luck was on my side. I was parked on a hill. On a rolling start, it caught straight away. Perhaps Eastern Europe has lots of hills?

Belinda thought the car was wonderful, ideal for Waiheke. I seized this opportunity to enquire about her husband. 'So Belinda, what does your husband drive? Something sporty?'

I expected her to say, 'No, a Corolla actually.' But she didn't. Because she didn't have one. She did have one. But she didn't have one now.

'But why the rings?'

'To keep people like you out of my pants. In my job I visit six food outlets a day. Some men I have to deal with are only after one thing. To them, everyone is fair game. The sad thing is, most of them are married with four kids. The rings stop a lot of problems.'

I assured her I wasn't married, but she'd read the *Herald*. 'The paper said you'd been married three — or was it four times? Quite a record.'

I didn't like to say five actually. I'd found out previously that it isn't always a good way to impress members of the opposite sex. We were coming up to the takeaway shop she had to visit, but I didn't want to see her disappear. 'Listen, how about a bite to eat afterwards?'

'No time. I've got two more places to inspect after this one. Besides, you're opening the day after tomorrow. You must have a million things to do.'

'I have, but one of the million things I'd like to do is let you sample the cuisine of the new café.'

'Tell you what. If I finish earlier than planned, I'll call in on the way back to the ferry. If you're around, you can make me a cup of coffee. Fair enough?'

'Deal. See you this afternoon.'

Belinda took off into the takeaway bar. I took off to the printers, not daring to stop in case the car wouldn't start again. When I got back to Oneroa, I parked it facing down the hill.

'Did you give her one, Whacker?' Mal cheerfully asked when I returned.

I chose to ignore him. 'Any calls or anyone visit?'

'Just that reporter joker. He wanted to clarify a couple of things. I handled it for you.'

'What did you say?'

'Nothing of any interest. He took a couple of photos.'

'Does he want to speak to me?'

'No. I said I was your spokesman. You should be bloody grateful.'

I went inside and tried to phone him. His phone was on cellular secretary. I left a message for him to phone me. The call was not returned.

'Sam delivered the menu. It looks shit hot.'

I agreed. It was very pinchable. Hopefully lots of patrons

61

would take it home and show it around. That was the best type of advertising on earth. 'Any word of Wally?'

'Nothing. Poor bugger must be dying of thirst. Bets is worried. She told him to phone in every day. She's not too sure he'd be the best Mormon missionary.'

I was busy soaking the labels off some empty wine bottles when the health inspector returned. 'What are you doing with the wine bottles?'

'Converting them into water bottles.'

'Oh.'

'Speaking of wine, would you like a glass? We've got some here in the fridge.'

'You're not going to sell it are you, Mr McCracker? You're not licensed.'

'Look, please call me Whacker. And, no, we're not going to sell wine. This place is just a glorified coffee bar. Twenty years ago that's what all these places were called. Then someone improved the food a little bit, upped the prices a hundred per cent and cafés were born. Now, is it tea, coffee or wine?'

'A glass of wine would be wonderful thank you. I've just missed the three o'clock ferry. Make sure I get the next one please.'

'Hot date tonight in Auckland?'

'No, nothing like that. I just like to get home for the TV news.'

'Wow, that sounds exciting. Where are you living?'

'Slap in the middle of downtown. Fourteenth floor. One bedroom facing the wrong way, with distant views of Australia on a fine day.'

'Well I guess living in the middle of town you must get

a lot of free feeds from all the restaurants. There must be a few perks being a health inspector."

Downtown isn't my territory — and I don't eat out much. Living by yourself in town is expensive.'

'No kids?'

'No kids. You?

'Yeah, three. Scattered around the world.'

'And *five* ex-wives the lady at the Ostend takeaway told me.'

'Jesus, have they been gossiping about me?'

'She saw me being dropped off in the Skoda and put one and one together.'

'I didn't know they read newspapers in Ostend.'

'Five is a lot.'

'It wasn't my fault. It was God's.'

'God's?'

'Yes, he just kept on creating more beautiful women. Unfortunately, due to the business I was in, I kept meeting them. What about your ex?'

'A nice guy. I really loved him, but he couldn't have kids and wouldn't adopt. I wanted kids. So, we split. He's remarried now.'

Belinda was upset as she told me this, so I asked if she wanted another wine. 'One for the road please. You know, you're very easy to talk to — I don't usually tell people I've only just met what I've just told you.'

Brian and Bruce, the couple from the antique shop next door, came in, and wanted to have a talk with me. I thought it might be over something we'd done to upset them, so I excused myself and went over to the other side of the café.

'Look, it's not that important,' Brian said. 'We didn't mean to drag you away from the young lady.'

'No trouble. What's the problem?' I was a little concerned.

'No problem,' replied Bruce. 'It's just that we've watched what you're doing and we don't think your café will be big enough. Well, to be quite honest, we're on the bones of our bums. The shop is a disaster and the rent is killing us. If we could find someone to take over our lease, we'd walk. There's no way we can sell it as a going concern. Brian and I thought, before you open, you might like to think about it.'

'Guys, I came over to Waiheke to take it easy, to run a little café. I reckon what I've got is plenty big enough. It comfortably seats thirty-four. Forty at a squeeze. I really don't think I'll need any more room.'

'Well,' said Brian, 'something to think about is there's a big lav in our shop — much bigger than the one in here. Why, I don't know. You'd easily fit a wheelchair into it. If you shoved a hole in the wall, you'd have two lavs — one with wheelchair access. That's all you really need to get a liquor licence. Plus, you'd double your size.'

'I'll think about it, but at this stage I haven't even applied for a BYO licence. I don't think people are going to linger here. Let's leave it for now and I'll see what happens over the first few weeks.'

'Well, if you need a hand, we're only next door. We've both worked in food before — and swore we'd never do it again. It's hard work.'

'Not for me. The hours are only going to be from ten till four. We may even close on Mondays and Tuesdays if there's no demand. Take care.'

My two neighbours had a good look around, said their farewells, and went back to their disaster.

'What was all that about?' asked Belinda when I got back to the table.

'My neighbours from the junk shop next door. Poor buggers are going down the gurgler. They want to know if I'd be interested in taking over their lease.'

'Would you?'

'No way. This place is big enough. We could be empty or nearly empty fifty per cent of the time. The only advantage if we shoved a hole in the wall is that we'd get a second loo.'

'It'd help you get a liquor licence,' commented the health inspector.

'We won't sell booze. We're going to sell coffee, tea, cokes and fruit juice. This is only a lifestyle business for me. I don't want boozers like Mal and his footy-club mates hanging around here all day. As soon as you start flogging booze you get a different clientele.'

'Perhaps a more interesting clientele.'

'Well, I'll see. It's coming on for four o'clock. Do you want another drink and go on a later ferry?'

'No. I'll be getting back. Thanks for the wine. I have a feeling you could be on to something. I bet next time I come over you'll have moved into the antique shop.'

'No way. Hey, why don't you come across in the weekend and see the place in action? Come across for lunch on Saturday.'

'Well, as my social life isn't exactly booming, perhaps I could. Give me a call on Friday.'

I drove her down to the wharf and the very presentable health inspector returned to the big smoke.

13

Thursday dawned — the day before opening. The Skoda started on its sixth attempt. I drove it to the garage to see if they could fix the problem. The mechanic knew who I was and I let him know I needed it fixed for the official opening the next day. It was needed to transport visiting dignitaries. He thought that was hilarious and assured me he'd get on to it pronto. 'I'll drive it up to your café when it's ready.'

I walked back from the garage feeling pretty good. Everything was coming together well. It was a sunny day. There was the prospect of a new lady on the scene. The car was being fixed. My five ex-wives were separated from me by a considerable stretch of water. I wasn't experiencing the stresses of Auckland.

Arriving at the café, Mal was painting the left front windowsill yellow. 'Morning Mal. Hey listen mate, you'd better stop what you're doing.'

'Why? What's the problem?'

'Well, you've painted the other windowsill red and they should be the same colour.'

'Oh. Sorry about that. Just as well you arrived when you did.'

Peg and Bets were inside pottering around the kitchen and there was a delicious smell of something baking. 'Making a few muffins, Whacker. Easy as anything to make, you just use a packet. Customers love the smell of fresh baking. They're very profitable too — the more you can make yourself, the more money you'll make.'

'Smells fantastic. Do you know if you can buy any fresh baking sprays? We should get some to spray around the place.'

'I've organised practically everything we need in the kitchen,' Peg advised me. 'The hardest thing is to know how much to get. Wastage is expensive. You don't want to order too much, but at the same time, you don't want to run out. After a couple of weeks we'll have a better idea. Most of the deliveries will be coming in daily. The stuff from the greengrocer, bakery and butchery is all local. They'll either deliver it or we can pick it up.'

'We have a couple more helpers if we need them. The gay guys next door said they've said worked in food. I spoke to them yesterday.'

'Kettles boiled. Cup-of-tea time,' called Bets. She waddled over to a table with a big plate of warm buttered muffins and some cups and saucers. The tea followed. We called Mal.

A couple of minutes later he came in. 'I've got a surprise for everyone!'

We looked. It was Wally! Bets was up in a flash and moved at a speed I didn't think possible, to hug her brother. They stayed clutched together for a good minute. Even my eyes were feeling a bit misty. Wally came across to me. It wasn't a handshake he extended to me. It was a hug.

'Hi Whacker. Good to see you.'

'Great to see you too Wally.'

Mal sat down beside me and leaned over. 'He's OK. Back on the piss.'

'Whacker, it's really good to be back on the island.'

'How long are you back for?'

'I'm never leaving again. They're all bonkers over on the

mainland. Finally managed to sneak away for a couple of beers last night and they bloody well went apeshit when I got home.'

'What about Pongy?' asked Bets. 'Is that over?'

'Damn right it's over. She got her cousin to drive me to the ferry this morning and to wait and make sure I caught it. Those Mormons are strange people.'

Mal was smiling from ear to ear. 'Knew you'd see the light, Wally.'

'Need a hand around here? I'm raring to go.'

'Well, I guess you can help us over the opening weekend. Mal's going to. Something else team, before I forget and that's what you wear tomorrow. Nothing grotty please. Casual smart — or, as Mal would no doubt delicately put it, semi-poofter. We probably should have got some T-shirts printed up. I'll get on to that next week.'

'What about some decent music? That radio's pretty clapped out,' Bets commented.

'I'm bringing my CD player in from home. Any other suggestions?'

'Don't forget the change from the bank. The eftpos seems to be OK,' said Peg.

The mechanic from the garage drove the Skoda back. He came in to give me the keys, get paid and have a look around. 'Jesus, Peg,' he called out. 'What have they done to your old place? Didn't even know you had those windows. Is that where the fat sheila fell out?'

Bets glared at him.

'Now don't you be so damn rude, young Brian Henry,' said Peg. 'You're sounding more and more like your father every day. You apologise to Bets right now.'

'Sorry Bets. Didn't realise you were here.'

68

The first person to tell us about what was in the *Gulf News* was Doris from the real-estate office next door. She came flying in around lunchtime. Bets had made the front cover! A dramatic photo of the helicopter swooping low over Oneroa, with Bets dangling on a stretcher below. *'Drama at new Oneroa café'* was the headline. Inside, the article was an extension of the one that appeared in the *Herald*, plus a brilliant photo of the café with the new sign. I couldn't have asked for better publicity. That is, until I came to Mal's contribution. *'A spokesman for Whacker McCracker's Café, Mr Malcolm Scudd, advised that the café would open this Friday at ten. He added that Mr McCracker did not propose serving any wog, chink, curry-munching or poofter food.'*

'Jesus Mal,' I yelled to him. 'What the hell did you say that for?'

'I only told him what you told me.'

'I never said anything about chink food.'

'No, fair enough. I added that.'

'I love Chinese food.' I shook my head. And slowly said, 'Mal, sometimes we say things within these walls that I don't particularly want the great unwashed to read or hear about. That is an example by the way — the great unwashed. It's a private joke. We don't go telling reporters. For god's sake mate, if you ever talk to a reporter again, think very carefully what you say. They love anything a bit different — like the wog and poofter thing.'

'Sorry mate. I was only trying to help.'

'I know you were. Still, it probably won't do us too

much harm. At least we'll be talked about on the island. Tell you what you can do, stick a menu up in the window so people can see what we'll be serving. They can judge for themselves.'

Brian and Bruce from next door were in next, roaring with laughter. When I explained how it happened they laughed even harder. 'Well let's hope our Western Oriental Gentlemen, Indian, Chinese and gay friends take it the same way!' I gave them a copy of the menu and they started laughing again.

'Looks absolutely delicious, Whacker. We'll be in with lots of our poofter friends!'

I wasn't too sure if they were being serious or taking the piss, so I told them the spaghetti was from The House of Wattie and the baked beans from The House of Oak. They both roared with laughter again.

'How's the staffing situation? Anything we can do?' asked Brian.

'Well, Wally's arrived back from Raglan to help. So with his sister Bets, Mal, Peg and myself we should be able to manage.'

'Who's actually worked in a café before?'

'Only Peg.'

'Oh boy, are you in for some fun!'

'You don't happen to know where we could get some T-shirts screened on the island do you? We'll need some big ones too.'

'Our friend Cyril down in Surfdale — I'll give him a call if you like.' Brian got hold of his friend who said he had heaps of T-shirts, but the only ones he had in extra large were red. 'He said he could do them this afternoon. He's got nothing else to do today. Let them dry overnight and you can pick them up in the morning.'

'Tell him I'll bring over some artwork right away.'

Cyril was waiting when I arrived and showed me the red shirts. They were fine. 'Cyril, an idea came to me while I was driving here. On the front, could we put: *I enjoyed the most shambolic meal of my life at Whacker McCracker's Café!* and our logo on the back.'

'You're kidding me.'

'No way. Look, this weekend four out of the five café staff have never worked in the food business before. In all probability things won't be all that wonderful. The customers are bound to bitch and moan a bit. By wearing T-shirts like this, it'll mean we're laughing at ourselves. People like that.'

'Nice strategy.'

'If you have the time to do it, could you print up thirty in assorted sizes and I'll see if we can sell some. They could be quite a hit in Los Angeles, Paris, Tokoroa or Rome. Could be a money spinner for both of us.'

After leaving Cyril's I called in at home to pick up the CD player and some CDs, then made my way back to the café. Our neighbours had been calling in to find out more about not serving wog and poofter food. They seemed to have got as good as they gave from my café team! Thank heavens for a sense of humour. Peg was happy with progress and even happier that Al hadn't phoned her all day. Obviously The Immaculate Conceptor was more capable than she thought.

We finished the day by finalising the roles everyone would play on the opening day. Mal brilliantly summed it up by saying, 'It's going to be a piece of piss.'

Opening day was a glorious late winter's day. I wanted to be at the café by seven-thirty, because we were expecting early deliveries. Peggy and Bets were going to be there at eight, to get things fired up. The Skoda started third time and foot flat to the floorboard, I chugged my way to Oneroa. My cellphone went. It was Number Three, roaring with laughter. I knew that was a bad sign — she never roared with laughter at that hour of the morning. 'You've made the headlines again! Have you seen the *Herald*?'

'No. What does it say?'

'Heaps. You've only made page three this time. Another photo of you and the Skoda — much smaller this time — plus a photo of your spokesman, Malcolm Scudd. Who on earth is he?'

'That's Mal. You met him when you came over. What does it say?'

'The headline is *Controversial Waiheke Island plain food café opens today*. It goes on about Bets falling out the window last week, then starts quoting your colleague Malcolm. I like the no wog, chink, curry-munching or poofter food comment. That'll go down well with the island's ethnic and gay communities. What's even more impressive my darling, is the simply awful menu you're offering. They've printed it in full.'

'We stuck it in the window. That reporter must have got hold of it.'

'Want me to go on? It's brilliant. I can just imagine your business colleagues back here sitting on the loo right now reading it and roaring with laughter!'

'No. Don't read any more, I'll go and buy a copy myself. And disconnect the phone so no more lowlife like you can phone up and take the piss.'

'I might come over for lunch — I adore mince on toast. See you darling.'

A quick visit to the gas station to buy a copy of the *Herald* confirmed the news. It wasn't very happy reading. My team of co-workers had all arrived by eight o'clock, looking remarkably respectable. Waiheke Island respectable, that is.

'It's a sign of good luck when you open a business on a nice fine day,' Bets advised me.

'Thanks Bets. Is that old island folklore or something you learnt when you did your Bachelor of Commerce degree?' Much laughter. Peg went to put the kettle on, while Bets got cracking on the muffins.

'Just a minute guys, there's something here that may be of interest to you all — especially Mr Malcolm Scudd. Had your photo in the *Herald* before, Mal?' I placed the article on the table. There was silence as four sets of eyes looked at the pictures and skimmed through the article.

'Nice they included the menu, that should bring a few people in,' Peg commented. 'Are you happy with it?'

'Well, like I said yesterday, I just wish the spokesman had been a little more cautious about what he said to that reporter. We don't want to upset anyone. If someone takes this article seriously — which I don't think they will, we could get some flak. The race relations people could give us a bit of a roasting. Please, if the media sniffs around here again, don't make any earth-shattering comments. Let me be the official spokesman from now on. OK?'

It was agreed.

Bets put some cups and saucers on the table and Peg brought over the teapot. I went through a bit of a review about what had to be done before opening. Mal had to peel the potatoes for the mashed spud. Wally had surprisingly neat handwriting, so he was responsible for writing on the blackboard that as our fishing boat hadn't been able to get out last night, due to a storm, we didn't have any fresh fish. 'Wally, you be the wordsmith on that one. Now, we need a special. Let's make it sweetcorn on toast, I love sweetcorn. Put that on the blackboard.'

'We haven't got any sweetcorn,' advised Peg.

'I have to go to Surfdale to pick up the T-shirts. I'll go to the supermarket and get some.'

I switched the AM radio on in the Skoda as I chugged towards the supermarket. The announcer was talking about a restaurant opening on Waiheke Island, serving no wog, chink, curry-munching or poofter food. Roaring with laughter, and quoting the *Herald*, he proceeded to read out our menu. He wasn't saying anything bad — just making a big joke out of it. I was pleased when he went on to discuss the weather.

Cyril had the T-shirts ready. They looked great. 'Try to get up and see the place.'

'I will. Your cuisine sounds intriguing. I was talking about it last night. Us poofs going to be allowed in, are we?'

'Yeah,' I laughed. 'But we don't have none of that poofter food!'

'I can't wait. I love baked beans. I might come along tomorrow with my friend Johnny,' Cyril grinned. 'See you then.'

The Skoda started on the third attempt and I made my way back to the newest eatery on the island. I gave the health inspector a call. Belinda answered her cellphone on the second ring. 'Hi health inspector.'

'Hey, you're famous again,' she laughed. 'The article in today's paper was hilarious. That won't do you any harm. How's everything going?'

'Nearly there. Half an hour to go. I just hope we have some customers. Otherwise, I'll be joining Wally and the café's spokesman, Malcolm Scudd, for an early liquid lunch.'

'Wish I could be there. I'm doing Henderson today. Several of your so called wog, curry-muncher and chink places.'

'Hope you can come over tomorrow. I'll give you a call later to tell you how the day went.'

It was coming on for the magic hour of ten, so I made my way back to Oneroa, parked the car, and walked to the café. There were about a dozen people outside — locals waiting for us to open! I said my good mornings and advised we'd be opening in ten minutes. 'Any problems?' I called out to the team, as I came in the door.

'Sweet as,' reported Mal. 'All going like clockwork.'

'Have the pies arrived Peg?'

'Yes, they came just after you left.'

I then presented each member of the team with their T-shirt and told them the reason for printing *I enjoyed the most shambolic meal of my life at Whacker McCracker's Café!* on the front. That got a laugh. The ladies disappeared into the loo to change. Mal, Wally and I did it in the café. A couple of minutes later we were a real team in our bright red T-shirts. I also told them that if customers wanted to buy one, they could.

'OK, team, lots of smiles. I'm going to open the door in a minute. Positions as discussed. Good luck!'

I walked over and opened the door. People poured in. 'Good morning, good morning, welcome to Whacker McCracker's Café,' I called out. 'Just go up and place your order and we'll bring it to you.'

Our first patron wanted two coffees and two muffins. Peg asked her first name, and wrote it down on the order. It was Sally. This was my way of getting around the dreaded number scheme. We'd call our customers by their real names.

The second patron wanted two teas — and could she try two banana toastie pies? Her name was Bronwyn. The third patron was our first gentleman. He was by himself and wanted a cup of tea and savoury mince on toast. Mr Jackson, he told Peggy. Patron number four wanted three coffees, that's all. They were the girls from the real estate next door. Cathy's name was used. Peg's next order was for two teas, one spaghetti on toast and one baked beans on toast, for Catherine. The sixth customer requested three teas and three lamingtons for Mrs Simpson.

Peg caught my eye so I went over to see what was what. 'Whacker! You get behind here fast and take the orders. I've got to help Bets and Wally. They're already in trouble.'

I joined the workers in the kitchen. The first order was ready and Mal was called over to do his bit. 'It's for Sally — two coffees and two muffins. Take the muffins first then come back for the coffees.'

Mal took the muffins. A few seconds later, a loud voice shouted out, 'Sally? Got some tucker here for you! Where are you?'

I don't very often go red. I think I went burgundy. The customers all laughed and I felt a little better. Sally gave Mal a wave, and over he went, smiling from ear to ear at the attention he'd created. Then, back to the counter for the coffees that were right beside me. Before I could say anything, he quietly said to me, 'Piece of piss,' and off he went with the coffees.

Somehow we made it through the first hour, thanks to unflappable Peg, who held us together. The other surprise was Mal. He just walked around the café calling out the person's name and the patrons loved it.

Wally was quite happy on the tea and coffee. Bets was going flat tack and seemed to be in her element. By eleven-thirty, the place was packed and the next hour was chaos. Tables weren't being cleared, water and the slices of complimentary, white, buttered bread weren't being given out; the dirty dishes were mounting, and patrons were waiting.

Right in the middle of the shambles, a television crew arrived. The producer came over and introduced himself. 'Hi Mr McCracker. I'm Pete Morosey from *One News*. You're a bit busy I see.'

'Flat stick Pete. I can't leave my post at the moment I'm afraid.'

'That's OK. We'd like to do a bit for the news tonight. Have a brief interview with you about your ingenious menu and café.'

'Look, you're more than welcome to film. Just go ahead. It should get a bit quieter soon and then we can have a yarn. If you need any help finding power points or anything, Mal will look after you. We'll give you and the crew something to eat when we can see some daylight here.'

Daylight miraculously appeared. Three well-dressed women had joined the queue. I looked up from serving Angus, who wanted two tomato soups and saw them. Numbers Two, Three and Four. Sixty per cent of my ex-wives club.

'Come this way,' I called out to them. 'Now, give me your handbags and put these T-shirts on. I need help fast.'

'Aren't you going to say hallo?' said Number Two.

'Hallo my salvationists. Look, it's a shambles here and we've got the television news filming. We have to get things sorted out. Please help.'

'And what's in it for us?' asked Number Four.

'A tantalising free luncheon.'

'Yuk. Don't worry Whacker, of course we'll help. That's why we came over, we knew you'd stuff it up,' said Number Three.

I went over to Peg and Bets to say we had more help. They had noticed. 'They're my ex-wives.'

'I beg your pardon!' exclaimed Peg.

'They're Numbers, Two, Three and Four. Surprised Number One isn't with them. Good ladies, the three of them . . . except of course when one is married to them. They'll help.'

One o'clock and all tables were occupied. 'Now, you'd like a meat pie; a spaghetti and baked-bean toastie pie combo and two lamingtons. Two teas, Mrs Caple, won't be long Mrs Caple. One of our magnificently trained staff will bring it to you.'

Number Three came over and asked if I want to be

relieved on the till. She'd had the hobby shop in Parnell, so knew how everything worked. We had the simplest of systems anyway. I said a million thanks and slid out.

'Mr McCracker,' asked *One News* Pete. 'Which was the window the fat lady fell out of?'

'You should go and ask her. That's Bets, working flat out in the kitchen. Actually, it was upstairs, the second one from the left. Her brother Wally, another big boy, is working the coffee and tea department.'

'Oh, so you're keeping it in the family eh,' said Pete with a laugh.

'Well I guess you could say that. Mal over there is Bets' husband, Wally's brother-in-law. Three of my ex-wives are helping at the moment too.'

I caught up with Numbers Two and Four. After thanking them profusely for what they were doing, I asked if they could do a stint in the kitchen. Peggy and Bets had been in there all morning and I wanted to give them a break. They both liked cooking, and agreed, with surprisingly little fuss. It was a little after one, only halfway through the lunch hour.

Pete came to ask if he could do the interview. 'OK. I'll be there in a couple of minutes. I just want to put my other two exes in the kitchen for a while, to relieve the other two.'

'So you'll have three of your ex-wives behind the counter?' asked Pete.

'There would have been four if Number One hadn't been in Sydney for a dirty weekend.' I'd found out that bit of gossip when Number Three had taken over the till.

'I've got to get a shot of them together. Not too many guys could do what you've managed,' he laughed.

Bets and Peggy didn't really want to be relieved but I insisted they had a short break. Pete grabbed the opportunity to get the three ex-delights of my life together. I yelled out to them to smile! A couple of silent rude words were mouthed at me. The cameraman then moved upstairs to the window from which Bets had taken her famous tumble.

Brian and Bruce from next door came in, along with a whole stack more customers. 'Whacker, it looks like business is booming!' exclaimed Brian, stating the obvious.

'You're not wrong there. I tried to find you guys earlier to give us a hand.'

'Bruce and I had an appointment with the accountant. Otherwise we would have been in sooner,' he replied. 'Things aren't looking good in the finance department. We hope you'll be looking into taking over our lease. Now, what can we do?' I gave them a couple of T-shirts and they started to clear the tables.

After my interview, I asked Bruce and Brian if they could see a table that would be emptying shortly, so we could give the film crew some lunch. 'I've got a better idea,' replied Bruce, 'move them in next door. We've got a few old tables and chairs we've been trying to sell for ages. We may have room for a few more too. Brian and I'll go next door and do some rearranging.'

Off they went and I told Pete what we were organising. As the next ferry back wasn't until three, they had time to kill. Then I went over and got Number Four out of the kitchen. I asked if she would mind giving waitress service to the *Stratford off Avon* antique shop next door. She said of course she did, but would.

Bruce came back to tell me they'd cleared some space.

There were three tables and fourteen chairs. We got the film crew and took them in and I told Number Four there were ten more spare seats next door. She found five Auckland businessmen on the island for the day and took them in there. A few minutes later, four ladies from Parnell, celebrating a birthday, also found themselves next door.

I went in to see if everything was OK and noticed the ladies had wine and explained we weren't licensed or BYO. Bruce overheard me and said not to be silly. He'd just pour it into one of the teapots they'd been trying to sell, plus four dainty matching cups with saucers. Pete thought that was a good idea and said he'd go and get a couple of bottles down the road for the crew. The businessmen seemed to have similar thoughts. I left our new extension with Brian and Bruce retrieving old teapots and cups from their stock and Number Four explaining she would take their food orders for the 'simply dreadful selection of food'.

I had my first accident when I got back into the café. Helping Mal carry some food over to a table, I got bumped and an order of spaghetti on toast went straight into the lap of Mrs Carter from Onetangi, a local pensioner, out on a treat with her niece. I apologised and went back to get a cloth from the kitchen.

Number Three had seen it happen. 'You always were a clumsy arsehole. I'll look after it.'

I took over the command post from her. 'No fish today, I'm sorry. Big storm last night. Our boat couldn't leave port. But I do recommend the sweetcorn on toast. No? Two vegetable soups, two lamingtons and two teas. And your name? Clara. Thank you Clara.

'So that's three spaghetti on toast. Plus one baked beans

81

on toast. Two coffees, one milk and one Coke. Christine. Thank you. Won't be long. We'll bring it over.'

Number Three came back and said she'd put me out of my misery by taking over, on condition I didn't try to be a waiter again. 'Throwing spaghetti over little old ladies on opening day isn't the best way to attract repeat business.'

Time was ticking by and soon two-thirty was looming. I went to the carpark to get the Skoda fired up, to take the television crew to the ferry. They were reluctant to leave, but somehow we got the four of them, their gear and myself into the Skoda and away we chugged to Matiatia. There was a bit of time up their sleeve before the ferry went so Pete got the cameraman to get some footage of me and the Skoda.

We advanced our closing time from four to three o'clock, and it took another half an hour to get every one out of the café and the junk shop. Then Bets, Wally, Mal, Peg, my three exes, Brian, Bruce and myself sat around two tables. 'Wine tea' from the teapot was consumed with enthusiasm.

'Whacker, you're going to have to cut a hole in the wall and take over our shop. It's just sitting there waiting for you.'

'I'll have a good think about it. Actually, tomorrow I have the health inspector coming over for lunch. I might take her in to have a look and get her opinion.'

'Is that the good-looking blonde sheila who was here on Wednesday?' asked Mal.

I kicked Mal under the table. Quite hard. 'Who the fuck's kicking me?' He saw me glaring and realised he'd put his foot in it.

Ex-wives love comments like that. Adore them. Thrive

on them. Three pairs of Piranha-snapping, Pauanui-loving eyes stared at me. With that *we want to know more* look.

'So, the good-looking blonde health inspector is coming over tomorrow, is she Whacker?' asked Number Three. 'Is she bringing some rat poison?'

'Have you caught some vile disease, darling?' asked Number Two.

'Health inspectors replacing models now? You must be ageing,' sneered Number Four. 'And how old is she? I hope she isn't a child like your last wife. That was disgusting.'

'Delightfully disgusting,' I couldn't resist replying. It had always been a sore point. 'Bruce, Brian, are you sure you're OK to work tomorrow?' I asked, wanting to change the subject.

'No trouble, we'll be here,' replied Brian. 'If we can keep on top of it from opening, we should be OK. That was your problem this morning — everyone arriving at the same time.'

I indicated to Peg that I was ready to drive her home. Bets wanted to come too, so I told my three exes that when I got back, the limo would be ready to take them down to the wharf. When I returned, it took a bit of effort to drag them away and get them seated in the Skoda.

'Lovely car Whacker. Is it brand new?' Number Four asked sarcastically as we were finally driving down to the wharf.

'I bet the health inspector is impressed with it,' commented Number Three. 'The back seat's nice and comfortable. Have you tested it?'

'I guess the Waiheke dog catcher will be next on your list of conquests,' suggested Number Two.

'Already playing that role, Number Two. Taking three old dogs down to the ferry to get them off the island.'

'Arsehole,' chorused my three passengers.

Naturally I thanked them all again for what they'd done and, in a round about way, invited them back when we were a little more organised for a proper lunch. They said they were in no particular hurry.

I phoned Belinda that night. 'You're famous, I've just seen the news! How did it go?'

'Absolute shambles but somehow we did it, thanks to the three ex-wives and the two poofs from next door. We were packed all day.'

'Well, after the coverage on the news tonight, you're going to be packed over the weekend. The weather looks good too.'

'The guys next door are really keen for me to take over their lease. I still feel it's a little early to be expanding. We've only been open a day.'

'You strike me as the kind of person who loves a challenge. Bet you do it.'

'Will you come over tomorrow? I'm afraid it isn't going to be a quiet lunch. It's all hands on deck. We're really short-staffed.'

'Yes, that would be nice. Thanks.'

'Get the ten o'clock ferry. I'll try and be there to meet you, but if I'm not, you'll know we're having a drama, so grab the bus. Oh, and I might get you to have a look at the shop next door. See you then, health inspector.'

'OK, you absolutely mad Waiheke Island café proprietor!'

Saturday was busier than Friday. I was the first to arrive, only to find the remains of forty-eight pies scattered all over the pavement. Bloody dogs! Two cartons of pies, along with the bread and milk, had been delivered and left on the doorstep.

Job number one, after carrying in the milk and bread, was grabbing a broom and cleaning up the mess. The team arrived in Mal's ute shortly after I'd finished. 'Meat pies are off the menu,' were my first words of the day.

'Got your special worked out?' asked Peg, as she busied herself in the kitchen.

'Same as yesterday — sweetcorn on toast. Not one person ordered it. Perhaps today we'll have someone with a bit of class.'

Soon the smell of fresh muffins was in the air. When the first batch came out, we sat down, enjoying them and a cuppa. The television news report was discussed in detail. Everyone seemed delighted with their appearance on the little screen. We all agreed the café urgently needed more seating. There was room for a couple more tables and I thought we might be able to borrow some from next door.

We needed a few bits and pieces at the supermarket and Placemakers, so I left Mal peeling a big stack of spuds, Wally writing on the blackboard and Peg and Bets preparing food in the kitchen.

When I arrived back, after detouring to Matiatia to pick up the health inspector, the café was already open. Brian and Bruce had arrived early. As there were people waiting, and the team was all fired up ready to go, they threw open the doors twenty minutes early.

Visitors to the island and residents all seemed to want to try the new place they'd seen on the television or read about in the paper. As it got nearer midday, the place was getting so crowded, I decided we'd have to control entry from the door like all the flash nightclubs. Cyril arrived just as I started doing this, and introduced his friend Johnny. 'Do you need a hand?'

'Cyril, would you mind? It's another shambles. Some extra hands would be really appreciated. At the moment nobody's getting a break.'

'Johnny and I used to own a restaurant in Paihia. Went bung three years ago, but we learned a lot. We'd love to help.'

'Really appreciate it. Look after the door for a minute and I'll get you both a T-shirt.'

Cyril and Johnny saved us on the Saturday. It just got busier and busier. With four gays, four island characters, Belinda and myself, everyone seemed to be getting fed, coffee-ed and tea-ed. The biggest problem was booze. The patrons were bringing in bottles of wine and every second table had a large teapot.

It wasn't until just after half past two we finally had nobody waiting, and we closed at four. While waiting for the last of the customers to go, I took Belinda into the *Stratford off Avon* antique shop. The loo was given the seal of approval, and just needed a couple of alterations to the door to make it suitable for someone in a wheelchair. She could see no major problems. 'Just cut a big hole in the wall and you'll practically double your size. Two loos means you'd probably get that booze licence.'

We went back into the café and soon all the customers had emptied out. A couple of tables were pushed together and Peg was loading it up with goodies. Teapots of wine tea were produced. It was time to relax and talk about the day's activity.

'We should open earlier tomorrow,' advised Bruce. 'Nine o'clock. It's Sunday morning and you'll have a lot coming in for breakfast and brunch.'

'Sunday is a big muffin day,' said Peg. 'Bets, we'll need to make lots more tomorrow.'

'Belinda, what did you think of next door?' queried Brian.

'Great potential, but I guess it all depends on whether Mr McCracker wants to expand his empire.'

'How about it, Whacker?' asked Wally. 'Mal and I could shove the hole in the wall on Monday and we could be in there by next weekend.'

'No building permit or resource consent?' I asked.

'Wouldn't worry about it,' replied Wally.

'Well I'm sorry, but this is quite a big job and I think we'll need one. What we did in here was borderline.'

'No mate, clean as a whistle in here. We didn't do anything structural. That's the key word.'

Everyone pitched in and did their final chores. Peg was on the phone to place the orders for the next day while I cashed up and by five, everyone but Belinda and myself had gone. The hours of daylight were drawing to a close.

'I think the health inspector should be given a nice walk along the beach before it gets dark. Then we could go and try one of the restaurants in downtown Surfdale or Ostend. Take in a nightclub or two afterwards.'

'We've both been stuck in a café all day. Why don't we

just get a bit of food and cook it up back at your place? See what's on TV.'

I thought all my Christmases had come at once.

We were open by nine on Sunday morning and the first of the hoards came in soon after. And they kept on coming, just like the first two days. I made the special of the day scrambled eggs on toast. Fish was off again because the allocation for our café had been sent to Japan by mistake. We changed delivery instructions and the dogs didn't eat the pies. Naturally, behind my back, Belinda reappearing first thing with me was the gossip. After five wives, one gets used to gossip, and as long as it isn't offensive, it doesn't really upset me.

Sunday was also the day several of my friends from Auckland came across to see the café for themselves. I couldn't even give them preferential treatment in the actual café, where seating was very democratic. So we did what we did on Friday — put them into the *Stratford off Avon* antique shop. The teapots were soon working overtime.

The drama started about two-thirty. A middle-aged male patron went to the loo. After about fifteen minutes, his daughter became very concerned because he hadn't returned. She went to the loo and asked the three people waiting if they'd heard him trying to get out — or had he called out? He had not. She banged on the door and got no response. She banged a lot louder. By now people were looking across to see what the problem was, so I went and thumped like hell on the door.

Wally came over and told everyone to stand back; then charged. It took three charges to break down the door. The daughter followed him in and let out a shriek. The room was silent by this stage. Everyone heard it. I poked my head around her and saw the problem. Dad was still sitting on the loo with his pants around his ankles, with his top half leaning against the wall. He wasn't moving. Daughter rushed to his aid. I called out, 'Is there a doctor in the café?'

A woman in her early twenties came over and said she was in her fourth year at medical school so I quickly let her in. There was nothing she could do. A patron had passed away. Dead. Sitting on the loo at *Whacker McCracker's Café*. On only its third day.

Belinda went off to phone the nearby accident and emergency centre. When she came back she took control of comforting the daughter. I asked Johnny to go and close the front door, and tell the people waiting to order that we had to close, due to an emergency. We couldn't very well keep the place open with a corpse on the premises. Plus, nobody could use the loo. With special tea being so popular, a working loo was essential.

The doctor arrived quickly and confirmed the fourth-year medical student had made a correct diagnosis. He was dead. A couple of minutes later, two police constables also arrived and confirmed that the doctor and the fourth-year medical student were right in their assessment.

I got on a chair and advised the patrons that due to a terrible tragedy we would have to close the café. They understood. I then went next door to tell the terrible news to my friends in the *Stratford off Avon* antique shop. They were having a lovely time. The special tea had been flying from the teapots into the teacups like there was no tomorrow.

'Whacker,' Bob Hendrew, an old neighbour, called out, as I entered. 'This place is fantastic! We'll be back.'

I raised my hand and got them to shut up. 'Look guys. We have a serious problem. We're going to have to close the café. One of the patrons has just dropped dead in the loo. You can stay here for a while, but please be respectful of the dead. And don't go into the café. I'll come and have a drink with you soon. I need one.'

Someone started to laugh. Soon the whole lot of them were laughing. I told them they were a bunch of disrespectful arseholes and went back next door.

Belinda said the daughter wanted to talk to the owner. I introduced myself and gave her my deepest condolences. She asked if we could talk privately, so I took her around the corner, away from the action.

'Mr McCracker, my name is Karen Blomfield and he's not my father. He's . . . er . . . a friend. He's also very well known. We were over here for the weekend.'

From past experience I immediately understood. 'Who's your friend?'

'I thought someone might have recognised him. He's on television and in the paper. He's Sam Hankle.'

'The lawyer Sam Hankle?'

'That's the guy.'

'He's big. A QC.'

'I know. His wife thinks he's gone fishing in Taupo with the boys for the weekend. Is there any way we can handle this so she won't know? Take the corpse to Taupo or something? Perhaps we could switch it.'

I'd never actually been confronted with a situation like this before. We needed advice fast. We had it, sitting right next door. One of my friends, Tom Brookler, was a lawyer.

I caught Belinda's eye and asked her to look after Karen. Then I went next door, got hold of Tom and asked if he'd come with me. 'Tom, the stiff in the dunny is Sam Hankle.'

'Holy shit!'

'And the babe he's with ain't his wife.'

'Holy shit!'

'His wife thinks he's fishing in Taupo.'

'Holy shit!'

'Tom, is there any way we can work it so that he died on the fishing trip? Helicopter the corpse to Taupo?'

'You can't do that. Too many people know.'

'Could you do me a favour and explain this to his young lady friend.'

'Sure.'

I introduced Tom to Sam's last bonk and went back to the scene.

The undertaker arrived. He lived in Blackpool and kept his hearse at home so he could go straight to the job when necessary. Within half an hour Sam Hankle was on a stretcher being carried out. We helped. Wally had one corner, Mal another one, Cyril on the third and the undertaker the fourth. By now most of the customers had gone and my friends from next door came out on the footpath as the body was put into the hearse, just to make sure I wasn't having them on.

Tom discussed the situation further with the doctor and the police constable. He then came over to me and said not to tell anyone else Sam's name. His wife and family must be told first. The police had already phoned Auckland and a car was being sent to the Hankle home in Epsom to give them the sad news.

The doctor and the police left soon after. The young constable couldn't help but ask what entertainment the café would be putting on next week. Sarcastic bugger. Karen was very upset and wanted to get back to Auckland as soon as possible. Belinda said she'd go with her so Tom suggested they return with their party as they were leaving as well. Two minivan taxis were called and fifteen customers and one pending girlfriend departed for the mainland. I thanked Belinda and said I'd give her a call a little later.

'You certainly have an exciting life, Whacker,' she whispered as she left.

Peggy and Bets left together, but Mal, Wally, Johnny, Cyril, Bruce and Brian were still around, cleaning up. We hit the teapot.

'Well, Whacker,' said Mal, 'we need a new dunny door. Wally fucked that one up.'

We laughed, and it felt good after all the drama we'd just been through.

'We're not opening tomorrow,' I announced. 'Or Tuesday. I think it would be disrespectful. And I don't think people would want to come here while the corpse is still warm.'

'More publicity, eh Whacker,' said Johnny.

'Yep, but not exactly the kind we need.' I didn't tell him that I suspected the publicity this time could be larger

92

than Bets falling out the window. I just hoped like hell that tomorrow wouldn't be another no news day. A good plane crash, parliamentary embezzlement, earthquake, murder . . . anything would do.

'Let's not linger too long. The media could turn up. If there's nobody here, we can't say anything. Wally, do a sign for the window saying the café will be closed on Monday and Tuesday for personal reasons.'

'No trouble, Whacker.'

Bruce was sitting beside me. 'You know, things were going smoother today, until our friend snuffed it. We were ploughing through the customers and most of them seemed pretty happy.'

I agreed. The next wine was even nicer than the previous one, but we had to leave. 'C'mon guys, let's get out of here. If anyone wants another drink — or something to eat, I'll shout you something at Gulfies.' This was a bar up the hill from us and we all ended up there. By the time the bar closed, we were very nicely. With very good reason, I should add.

Disaster. Monday was an absolute no news day. The lead story in the *Herald* was *Top barrister drops dead in new Waiheke Island café*. The full story. Karen Blomfield had been elevated from companion to mistress and the radio stations were having a field day. I hid from the world. On the evening news, it was the lead story, using Friday's footage of my café. They'd also dug up a bit more filth. Karen wasn't his mistress. She was an escort, working for a very upmarket escort agency.

When I reached the café on Tuesday morning, I made myself a nice pot of tea, and read the paper. The *Herald* had more coverage on the bottom half of the front page, with inside information on the escort agency Karen worked for. It also said it was believed I'd left the island for a few days. That was good. The funeral was to be on Wednesday at two o'clock at the cathedral in Parnell. Naturally I felt an obligation to attend.

I phoned up Bruce and Brian to see if we could have a meeting about expansion. Twelve o'clock was agreed upon. I then phoned my landlord, who owned the three shops in the block, to see if he had any problems if I took over the lease of the antique shop and knocked a hole in the wall. As long as he didn't have to pay for it, he was quite happy.

Brad, my lawyer, was contacted next, to arrange a suitable time for us to get together. 'Killing the legal fraternity in that loo of yours, Whacker? Safer to fall out the bloody window!'

I couldn't resist telling him the learned member of the bar had actually suffered a heart attack, probably caused by too much shagging over the previous twenty-four hours and perhaps lawyers, as they age, weren't up to doing things like that. We agreed to a meeting at his office the next morning at eleven, to discuss the lease and perhaps a booze licence.

When Bruce and Brian arrived, the first thing we discussed was the death in the café and the resulting publicity, along with our progress after only three days in business. 'You must expand next door into our disaster,' said Bruce.

'If I did, what would you two do? Stay on the island?'

'We'd love to stay on Waiheke. Our friends are here. We have a nice home and Brian's dear old mum has just bought a house in Onetangi to be near us. But, it depends if we can get a job.'

'If I took over your shop, would you both consider working in the café?' I asked.

'We most certainly would,' replied Bruce.

It had become obvious to me very quickly that if we did expand, I'd need more help. Professional help! Wally, Mal and Bets were great but they weren't management material. Peg was only temporary. Bruce loved people and had good organising skills and Brian was good with food, having done a catering course a few years ago. If I could get them on board to look after a lot of the day-to-day running, the purchasing, staffing and whatever else, I could try and use my marketing skills to get bums on the seats, and play host. It would be a great combination.

'Well, I reckon it could be a bit of fun enlarging this place and getting a licence so the patrons could enjoy a glass or two of wine. I may just take you up on your offer and bang that hole in the wall.' I went on to tell them I'd already spoken to the landlord and I was seeing my lawyer in the morning to talk about that, and about going for a booze licence. They agreed to contact their lawyer to arrange for their lease documents to be sorted out with my legal beagle.

Money was discussed and we agreed on base salaries rather than hourly rates, with a performance incentive. In effect, they'd be responsible for the day-to-day managing of the café. Many years ago I'd learned that was the way to succeed in business. Find people who can do the job better than you and pay them to do it.

'You're off to the big smoke first thing tomorrow?' asked Bruce.

'No, I'm going over this afternoon and I'll stay the night.' I'd arranged to stay at Belinda's.

'We can take command now and open tomorrow?'

'If it's OK by you. Just a couple of things though, and it may piss you off a bit. I don't want Mal, Wally, Bets or Peg ever fired without discussing it with me first. They're part of the original team and give enormous character to the café. Two fatties and colourful Mal. I don't think Peg will stay long — she wants to look after her Al. But who knows?'

'Let's hope they stay for years,' said Brian. 'Too often cafés are full of beautiful people who really shouldn't be working in food. Don't worry, we'll look after them.'

I got on the phone and called the team together for a late lunch. When everyone arrived, after discussing the latest in the death in the dunny saga, I went on to say we'd be expanding next door as soon as possible. Plus, we'd be having a crack at a booze licence. Bruce and Brian would be joining the team on a permanent basis and be responsible for the day-to-day running. Bruce would look after administration and Brian the food. Everyone agreed it made good sense and seemed happy about it.

'Right team, you're opening tomorrow. I'll be in the big smoke. Mal, that dunny door has to be fixed before then.'

'I'll do it this afternoon. Piece of piss.'

'Can you also do me a favour and do some plans for banging the hole out so we can move in to next door? Whether you like it or not, we will have to get a building permit. I'll speak to Terry at the council to see how fast we can push it through.'

I left shortly afterwards. On the ferry I phoned Terry at the council, whom I'd met thanks to Bets falling out the window, and talked to him about the building permit. He said to give him the plans as soon as they were done. As long as no supporting beams were affected, it wouldn't take long.

Brad Crocker, my lawyer, had excelled himself. When I arrived at his office the next morning he'd already spoken to Brian and Bruce's lawyer about taking over the lease for the *Stratford off Avon* antique shop. There was a clause allowing them to sublease, with two years to go, with a right of renewal. I told him I'd spoken to the landlord about doing alterations and it was fine by him. Next we discussed the booze licence. I told him about the current teapot situation. He already knew. Tom Brookler had told him — warned him. He agreed the sooner we were legal the better!

'Brad, I'd also love to supply fresh local fish, caught that morning. At the moment if I want to buy fish, due to limited quotas, there's not much available. If I wanted quite a few fish every day, I'd have to buy it through the Auckland markets. By the time it gets out to the island it's about a week old.'

'You're living in New Zealand now, not some Third World country.'

'But in Third World countries the fish is always fresh and delicious. The resorts and beachside cafés just row out, catch it, bring it back and sell it. At the end of the day what they don't sell they give to the cat and then row out and get some more.'

'Quotas, Whacker, quotas,' my legal man said. 'Plus there are regulations galore. Third World countries don't have all that crap. New Zealand does.'

'So there's no way I can get in a tinny, row out from the beach, come back and serve the fresh fish I've just caught to my very grateful customers?'

'Well you could buy a quota.'

'How much?'

'Megabucks, if you can even get one. Tell you what. I'll have a bit of a dig around in the regulations and see what the story is. I'd like to know myself, because I love a bit of fresh fish and you do raise a good point.'

Brad was going to the funeral and said most of the legal fraternity in town would be there to pay their final respects. We decided to have a bite to eat in Parnell and go on together.

The cathedral was packed. Sam's eulogy, presented by Judge Arnold, was brilliant. A gifted man, who had achieved so much. Unfortunately our café didn't get a plug, nor did the escort service. Watching the coffin being carried down the aisle was moving. To think that only three days before, the person inside had been enjoying my café's cuisine and ambience. After the service I didn't feel it was the right moment to introduce myself to the family.

I got a lift into town with Brad, who told me Sam Hankle was known for his philandering. 'He was worse than you, and you've got a bloody good record.'

'Think of the fees you've made out of my five divorces.'

'I'm not thinking about your wives. I'm thinking about

the other problems you've caused with that bloody dick of yours. Remember that mad bird jumping up and down on your new BMW in her high heels and that husband who came into your office with the axe. Then there was . . . '

'Brad, that's all in the past. Besides, I've got myself a new lady. The local health inspector.'

Brad roared with laughter, made the expected rude comment about my health and dropped me off outside his parking garage.

'Thanks for the ride and don't forget to look into the fresh fish situation!' I called out as he drove away.

Arriving back at the café on Thursday morning, I found the team very pleased with how things had gone on their first day without the proprietor. Nobody had died. Nobody had spaghetti thrown over them. Nobody had fallen out the window.

'How boring. Now I'm back, I'd better put some life in the place!' I told them the funeral was big, and the corpse was a mad shagger, exaggerating slightly to make him sound even more interesting than he really was. Sam would have loved the eulogy I gave him.

'Won't be doing too much shagging now,' commented Brian.

Mal, amazing Mal, produced a rolled-up sheet of A3. He unrolled it and showed me the plans for the expansion next door. With the help of Brian and Bruce, he'd worked out exactly what was needed.

Late morning, Mal and I went to the council in Ostend to see Terry about the permit. I'd phoned first, so he was expecting us. I hadn't been able to work out exactly what Terry's role was at the council, but he seemed to be terribly important. However, he wasn't directly in charge of building permits, and introduced us to the bloke who was, Joe Blakely. He also knew Mal.

Mal quietly managed to tell me that Joe, like Terry, was a pisshead. On Waiheke, being a pisshead is a bit like being a Mason, a Lion or a Rotarian, only even more illustrious. All the pissheads know and help each other. I was so pleased I'd brought along a fellow pisshead.

The plans were examined in detail. Joe seemed to think it was pretty straightforward. 'Just a matter of inspection really,' said Joe. 'When do you want me to do it?'

Mal answered for me. 'Why don't you come over for lunch today and do it then? We'll shout you a feed and a few bevvies. Bring Terry.'

'Don't know about that soon, I've got a few other jobs in the pipeline,' replied Joe.

'Bullshit, Joe,' said Terry. 'Let the other bastards wait. I could go a good feed at the new café. And, knowing Mal, he'll have something nice to go with it.'

They came. They briefly inspected. They ate. They drank heaps of special tea. When I drove them back at four o'clock, they informed me the building permit would be ready late the next day. The secret brotherhood of Waiheke pissheads had worked wonders. I told myself that as long as I'm in business on the island, I must always retain a pisshead on the staff.

Back at the café there was much excitement over the permit. Mal was the hero of the day. He'd been the one who sat and entertained his brothers, keeping them well refreshed. I phoned my lawyer to see when we could start bashing the hole in the wall. The answer was as soon as all the documentation was signed. The landlord had signed and returned his. It just needed Brian and Bruce's signatures, plus my own, in front of a JP or lawyer. 'But it's going to take you a week or two to get that building permit. You know what councils are like.'

'We've got it. I can pick it up tomorrow.' I briefly described the events of the day.

'I don't believe it! Listen, there's something else I want to talk to you about — that fresh fish situation. When can we catch up?'

'Why don't you bring Barbara over for lunch in the weekend and see the place for yourself? Preferably Saturday. We expect Sunday to be really busy.'

'Deal. As far as I know we're clear. Just make sure Brian and Bruce are around to sign the forms in front of me. Once they've done that you can bang your hole in the wall. I suggest you show me the permit too, I just want to make sure it's the real McCoy. Also, you need to sign the booze application forms.'

'Right Brad,' I replied. 'There's a ferry at twelve. One more thing — should we send the invoice for the new dunny door to the escort agency or Sam's estate?'

'The escort agency. The escort probably was the cause of death. Don't like your chances of getting it paid though!'

For the second week in a row the café made the front cover of the local *Gulf News* with the stiff in the dunny story.

They'd managed to get a photograph of the stretcher being taken out of the café. Mal, Wally and Cyril, with the undertaker, were on the front page. Cyril was most excited. He hadn't been on the front cover of the *Gulf News* before and bought five copies to send to family and friends.

'We may have found a loophole in the fresh fish situation,' Brad told me, not long after he arrived with his wife for lunch on Saturday. 'I'll tell you about it after you've signed your life away on the lease and booze application forms. And got the other guys to sign.'

'Well, you're going have to wait a while. It's a shambles here again. All hands on deck.'

The café was chocker. Johnny had to go on door duty, and Brian and Cyril were in the kitchen with Bets. Peg had stayed home because the Immaculate Conceptor was unwell. Bruce was at the command post, Wally on his drinks and Mal and Belinda were trying to keep up with things on the floor.

'What can I do to help?' Brad's wife, Barbara, asked. She was quickly given a red T-shirt and flung into topping up glasses of water on the tables and handing out slices of freshly buttered white bread.

The lawyer and I fled next door. I wanted to show him the antique shop. He'd been surprised at just how busy we were and realised why I wanted to expand. 'This old junk shop will be ideal, there's heaps more room.'

'Looks like we may need it, although the initial novelty factor is bound to wear off and and all the publicity will soon stop.'

'Knowing you, you'll crank it up again. Now, about the fresh fish. On Wednesday afternoon I had a yarn to one of our firm's bright young things and she got interested. To cut a long story short, she went into our library and did some research. There could be a loophole you may be able to use, until they change the legislation and stop you. It could take a year or two to do that — even more.'

'I'm all ears, mate. Go on.'

'Well, in 1884, legislation was passed that enabled a church minister of any denomination to obtain food for his parishioners or anyone in need. Our interpretation of this is that this food could be meat, honey, vegetables, fish and fruit. Anything the parishioners, and, the crucial words, *anyone in need*, could eat. As far as we can see, the legislation has never been dropped or changed. Probably because nobody realises it still exists.'

'Fat lot of use to me, I ain't exactly the local vicar!'

'I agree,' my learned legal man replied. 'But if you had a vicar catching fish for you and you gave him or her a donation, to supply those in need, the vicar wouldn't be breaking the law. The fish would then be served free to those in need of a good Waiheke Island fresh fish feed. Your customers.'

'Free? How could I make money doing that?'

'Serve the fish with that mashed potato you love so much, charge for that and very generously throw in the fish for free.'

'Come again Brad?'

'Simple. Charge fifteen bucks or whatever for the mashed potato and include the fish for free.'

'Would we get away with it?'

'For a while. Until our friends in Wellington change the

legislation, which could take a year or two, and with appeals we may be able to stall it even longer. The vicar — or vicars, also shouldn't be greedy and take too many fish. By only taking the day's recreational limit, that shouldn't cause a problem.'

'But that wouldn't be enough fish.'

'Have half a dozen vicars rowing out to sea every day. There must be heaps of retired fishermen on the island wanting to earn an extra buck or two.'

'There might be, but it's unlikely there are that many retired vicars!'

'These days you don't have to go to Vicar University to be a Man of God. You can do it over the internet, or by direct mail. People send fifty bucks to the States and get a vicar's certificate just like that. An awful lot of people just give themselves a title. There's nothing to stop you offering vicar courses at the café in the evenings to keen fishermen. Create your own church if you so wish. The Church of the Holy Whacker sounds good! Then appoint them to their own local parish on Waiheke Island.'

'Are you serious, or are you having me on?'

'We've found a loophole, now over to you. Do you want me to look into it further?'

'What do you reckon? You're the legal man.'

'I'd say you should. With your personality and entrepreneurial flair, you'd get away with it. You'll have the best restaurant in the whole of the Hauraki Gulf. Just one thing though, I wouldn't do it until you've got your booze licence. That won't take long, a few weeks. But there's nothing to stop you from finding some keen part-time fishermen. Or fisherladies. Great for somebody semi-retired, on a benefit or on the dole.'

'Mal will know heaps. We'd better get back next door and see how the lunchtime chaos is progressing. And get the guys to sign the documents.'

We went back next door. By the time I got there, my brain was going a million miles an hour. I was already the Archbishop of Waiheke, Mal was Canon Malcolm, Wally was the Very Reverend Walter and Bets, Sister Superior Bets.

Mal and Wally got stuck into the alterations and within a week the café had expanded next door. Seating was now available for seventy-eight. We kept some of the old junk from the antique shop for decoration and called the extension *The Stratford off Avon Room*. Brian and Bruce loved it.

The second dunny was most welcome. We had a plaque made and put it above the original loo. It read: 'This toilet is dedicated to Sam Hankle, QC.' It was the least we could do.

My love affair with the health inspector was glorious! The day we finished the alterations she came across to the island, inspected the premises and we received immediate approval to move in the next day. You don't get that kind of approval so fast these days unless you're bonking or bribing the local health inspector. The first is far more pleasurable, and a lot cheaper.

Mark Braithwaite, the manager of the real-estate office on the other side of the café, caught me one day as I was leaving and told me they were moving to new premises down the hill. Their offices, also owned by my landlord, would be vacant. He commented on the way we were expanding and told me I'd be mad not to move into their old premises as well. I wasn't so sure but said I'd give it serious thought.

Brad phoned me on a very wet, cold afternoon. 'Great news! Your booze licence has been approved. It certainly pays to know someone in the licensing department. You can legally start flogging beer and wine from the first of October.'

'Fantastic! No problems?'

'None. I think that health-inspector friend of yours may have also known the right person or two in the right place! Normally they take a bit longer than that. Whacker luck again. How's the fishing venture going?'

'I've kept quiet about it. I didn't want to do anything to jeopardise that booze licence. But, now we've got it, I'll get things cracking. Nothing like causing a bit of a stir.'

I was in the café when I got the call and told the team I wanted a short meeting at the end of the day. When the last customer had gone, and everyone was seated, I announced we'd got the booze licence. I told them this meant substantial changes to our operation and working hours. We'd be staying open in the evenings, as our licence stated we could serve wine and beer until eleven o'clock. 'One other thing. We could also be serving fresh Waiheke fish in the not too distant future.'

'Impossible,' said Peg. 'You can't do it. If you want enough for a good seafood café, you have to buy it from the markets in Auckland.'

'Brad's found us a loophole. All we have to do is find some good keen fishermen on the island who'd like to supply us with a few fresh fish every day, within the recreational limit.'

'If you can legally serve fresh fish caught the same day, this place will be jammed,' commented Brian. 'It's what everyone on the island wants.'

'We need up to a dozen recreational fishermen with their own boats, at least fifteen footers, to catch us fish every day. They must be reliable. We'll pay them a fair donation for the fish and expenses.'

'Cashies, Whacker?' asked Wally. 'Most important they're cashies. Otherwise you won't get any bastard working for you. I know heaps of people who'll do it, but only for cash.'

'Don't worry, they'll be fairly reimbursed.'

'When do you want them to start dragging in the fish?' Mal wanted to know.

'We've got to select the people who're going to fish for us properly first. We can't have people just arriving at the door. That's illegal and we'd be in deep shit. It would be good if they were spread out all over the island. We'll have to get a van or car to go around and pick up the fish every morning. Good job for you, Wally!'

'Sounds great.'

'Should we place an ad in the *Gulf News*?' I asked.

'No way,' replied Mal. 'If we do that we'll get a hundred replies. Wally and I know lots of jokers on the island with boats who'd love to go fishing every day. Good, honest, hardworking pissheads.'

'Something else,' I said. 'They must all have a good sense of humour and be reasonable communicators.'

'Why?' queried Bruce. 'That's asking a hell of a lot from Mal and Wally's fishing mates. Pissheads might be good for a laugh, but they might not pass a communication test.'

'Watch it,' replied Mal. 'Your fairy friends couldn't even pass a fish-catching test.'

I stepped in and stopped what could have been the start of a wonderful debate. 'OK, OK. Now, Mal, Wally, I want you to ask around and see if you can locate some reliable fishermen.'

'Sweet as,' replied Mal and Wally together.

'Right. I'll leave that to you two.'

'We'll have hoards of new customers pouring in with the booze licence. Even with the expansion, we're already full nearly every day. Where are we going to fit everyone?' asked Bruce.

'Oh,' I replied. 'Didn't I tell you? We're going to expand into the real-estate office.' That was a spur of the moment decision. Several holy shits were muttered. They kept on being muttered as the meeting broke up.

20

I met a number of potential fishermen and fisherwomen. Wally and Mal did a brilliant job in this particular recruitment area. Because of the vicar thing, which I still hadn't told anybody about, I knew I had to find not just great fishermen, but also people who were real characters. I also didn't want any stark-raving bible-bashers, and after meeting seventeen 'applicants' I narrowed the field down to eight.

I then called another meeting with my team and told them about 'Project Vicar'. They thought it most ingenious. It would definitely start on the same day as the booze licence — the first of October. A Suzuki Jeep had been purchased to pick up the fish. Wally was delighted to do that. I told him he'd have to be made a minister of the church too, as he was supplying the fish. Brad had told me to do this, and advised me to also follow God so I proudly grabbed the Archbishop of Waiheke title.

The ordaining of our new fisherfolk was planned for nine o'clock on the last day of September. I chose to call them fisherfolk because we were going to have two couples, giving us two women and six men. They'd be given more details of Project Vicar then, and be accepted into their respective churches. Brad was coming over from the city to explain the legal side and how they were within the law.

The ordinations were hilarious! The eight fisherfolk and Wally roared with laughter when I explained the scheme. Brad assured them they were within the law and, if there was any trouble of any type, the café would pay.

All they needed was a very brief religious course, the actual ordaining and the allocation of a respective parish, which had to be done in front of witnesses. All of the originals had arrived by this stage and enthusiastically agreed to be the other witnesses.

I stood up with a *Bible* in my hand and read a verse each

from the Gospel according to Saint Matthew, Saint John and Saint Luke. Each of the fisherfolk — and Wally — was asked to name one of the gospels I'd just read from.

A voice called out 'Saint John.'

'Correct,' I replied with enthusiasm.

The other eight all chorused, 'Saint John.' Wow, they'd all passed their course in religion. I asked them to come up individually and kneel before me to be officially ordained and receive their parish.

Heke Samuels was first. 'Heke, I appoint you Cardinal Heke of Surfdale. Go forth and catch fish for your flock.'

Tina Samuels, his wife was next. 'Tina, I appoint you Mother Superior Tina of Putiki Bay. Go forth and catch fish for your flock.'

'Hey Whacker,' called out Peg. 'You can't do that. They're married. You can't have a married cardinal and a married mother superior.'

'Too late now, Peg. They've just been ordained. We don't want to ex-communicate them already do we?

Blacky Black followed. 'Blacky, I appoint you the Reverend Blacky of Palm Beach. Go forth and catch fish for your flock.'

Bert Glander came up and knelt down. 'Bert, I appoint you Canon Bert of Ostend. Go forth and catch fish for your flock.'

Esky Bill Tohora was next. 'Esky Bill, I appoint you Rabbi Esky Bill of Onetangi. Go forth and catch fish for your flock.'

'Whacker,' interrupted Brian. 'You can't do that. Esky Bill isn't Jewish.'

'Too late. He's now the world's first non-Jewish rabbi.'

George O'Connell knelt down. 'George, I appoint you

Father George of Blackpool. Go forth and catch fish for your flock.'

Teresa O'Connell, George's wife, was next. 'Teresa, I appoint you Sister Teresa of Matiatia. Go forth and catch fish for your flock.'

'Did you get the Pope's personal approval for that married couple too?' interrupted Bruce.

The last of the fishermen, Fred Pinkley, came forward. 'Fred, I appoint you the Reverend Fred of Rocky Bay. Go forth and catch fish for your flock.'

Wally the fish picker-upper was the final person I needed to ordain. 'Wally, I appoint you Bishop Wally of Oneroa. Go forth and deliver the fish to your flock.'

'Bloody hell,' cried Bets, who was in tears. 'My brother's a bishop!'

'What about you, Whacker?' called out Bruce. 'Who's going to ordain you? You've got to be done too.'

I agreed I did indeed need to 'be done'. Wally was a bishop, so he could do it. I knelt down in front of him.

'Can't do that yet, Whacker,' called out Brad. 'You have to pass your religious exam. Wally, read out a verse.'

I passed the religious exam. My mother would have been proud of me. I knelt before Wally. 'Whacker McCracker, I appoint you Archbishop Whacker of Waiheke Island. Go forth and fuck your flock!' Everyone roared with laughter, and I was probably laughing the loudest. The respective certificates were handed out and refreshments served. It was the café's first religious event.

'Well Brad, that was a great success. Now let's hope it works.'

'It will, Whacker, it will.

Wally drove Brad down to the wharf in the Skoda as the

Suzuki was being signwritten and wasn't due back until lunchtime. Sam was also doing some new signs for the window.

I went over the final procedures with our eight new reverend fisherfolk. It was agreed they would all be back on the island by ten each morning and Wally would pick the fish up shortly after. I also really emphasised that they, and only they, could catch the fish.

Sam the signwriter delivered the Suzuki just after eleven. The secret was out for all to see in Oneroa. It was painted red — from the original T-shirts, with white signwriting down each side. *'Whacker McCracker's Licensed Café. Fresh Waiheke Island fish our speciality. Open daily.'*

The sign Sam did for the window announced we were now licensed and serving *Fresh Waiheke Island Fish*. He put it up, with a smaller sign we would remove in the morning saying: *As from tomorrow.*

Paul Masters, the local reporter, liked our café. It created news for him. He was seeking me out within half an hour of the sign going up. 'How are you going to serve same-day fish caught on the island? You won't be able to get enough from regular sources. If you think you can just get people to go out and catch them, you're making a big mistake.'

'Paul, I'm not a bloody idiot.'

'Well how are you doing it?'

'Loophole, Paul, a loophole. I'll tell you about it when we've started serving. Not before. Call in tomorrow, when hopefully it's all systems go.'

112

'You're an ingenious bastard. If you can pull this one off, you'll have people lined up from here to the ferry wharf. See you tomorrow.'

At ten o'clock the next morning, the first day of legal booze selling and borderline legal fresh fish selling, I opened a bottle of bubbles and we toasted the success of the new venture.

At twenty past ten, four well-dressed women arrived. Four exes. Wives One, Two, Three and Four. I didn't fancy having them hanging around, getting quietly, and then noisily, sloshed, spoiling what I hoped would be a wonderful day.

I knew that one of the joys of running licensed premises was that you could refuse entry to anyone and ask people to leave. I was fairly familiar with this law myself, having been ejected at the odd place here and there over the years. I told Bruce to go and eject the four ladies who had just come in.

'You're kidding! They're your ex-wives.'

'Kick 'em out. They'll just cause trouble.'

'Whacker, I'm not going to interfere in a hetro thing. Do it yourself.'

I knew better than to do it myself. I nicely asked Mal. 'No way. They're your exes. It'd cause a big shit if I threw them out.'

'Mal, it's an order. Chuck them out. I've been waiting

113

for this day for years! I'm going over the road to get the paper. When I get back I want them out of here.'

To cut a long story short, when I got back they were still there. Having a blazing row with Bruce. They'd already had a blazing row with Mal. (I found out later he'd told them to fuck off. Not the best way to handle the four ex-loves of my life.)

Number One spotted me sneaking in and making for the kitchen. 'There goes the arsehole,' she shrieked. 'You come over here this instant.'

Brian asked me to please go over and help Bruce. I think he was afraid they were going to take him upstairs and throw him out Bets' famous window. I reluctantly agreed. 'Now my darlings, what seems to be the problem?' I asked, when I arrived at their table.

'You,' four voices responded.

'It's a bit early for a drink, isn't it girls? Why don't you go for a nice walk first?'

'You bastard,' said Number Two. 'You tried to have us thrown out.'

'I wouldn't do a thing like that,' I lied.

'Yes you would,' they replied together.

'Would you like a cup of coffee?' I inquired.

'We came all this way to be the first customers to legally drink in your glorified coffee bar and we want a drink,' shrieked Number Two. 'Bubbles!'

'I'll shout you one glass each and then you can be on your way,' I generously offered. 'Are you over here to do the vineyards? Or perhaps a tour of the art studios?'

'No,' replied Number One. 'We're here to share a long leisurely lunch. Amongst the four of us, you're the only ex-husband with a licensed café — or whatever you call this place. We thought it would be nice to come over more often and keep an eye on you.'

I leant down and whispered in her ear that four letter word used frequently by divorced people to describe their ex, then went up to the bar and poured four glasses of bubbles. I asked Mal to take them back to the table. He refused. I asked Bruce. He refused. Bets was standing nearby and said she would.

Just after eleven o'clock, an historical moment in the history of Waiheke Island eateries occurred. Wally arrived in the Suzuki with fifty-four freshly caught snapper. By eleven-thirty, my four exes commenced their third bottle of bubbles and ordered mashed potato with free fish, for lunch.

At twelve o'clock a representative from the Ministry of Fisheries, who'd heard a whisper of what we were up to, arrived along with Sergeant Jack Koster. He announced he was going to seize the fish and I was to be charged for illegally acquiring them. Brad and I had expected that, so we'd had photocopies made of the legislation. I explained I hadn't done anything illegal; briefly described the loophole, then gave him a copy of the 1884 legislation. I also advised we weren't selling the fish. We were giving it away free with the very expensive mashed potato.

A flashlight went off and I looked over to see Paul Masters had arrived. His timing was perfect. He came over and joined us. 'Afternoon, Whacker. Entertaining the law for lunch?'

'Hallo Paul,' I replied. 'This gentleman from the Ministry of Fisheries has arrived to illegally seize my fish and I've asked the sergeant to arrest him for making false accusations.'

The café was now filling up and we were attracting attention. Admittedly, I did talk loudly so the patrons soon knew what was going on. Several came over and told the fisheries gent what he could do. With the bureaucrat telling me I'd be hearing more and to stop doing what I was doing, he left with the sergeant in tow. Numbers Two and Four walked by on their way back from the loo and expressed their extreme disappointment that the policeman hadn't taken me away.

By two o'clock we knew we had a success on our hands. Our customers thought it was a hoot to pay for mashed potato and get free fish. The atmosphere of a full, happy café rubs off on you and I was feeling pretty good.

Even the four exes behaved themselves and complimented the chef. Naturally I was still itching to throw them out, but decided to do it some other time. To get rid of them, I offered to drive them down to the wharf to catch the three o'clock ferry. When they accepted I got the keys for the Suzuki from Wally and drove them to the wharf. It was a squash and did smell rather fishy. The limo service I provided wasn't appreciated, and they let me know it. I think each of them called me that awful four-letter word. In parting they told me they'd had a very enjoyable lunch and would be back. I told them not to bother.

The café made the *Herald* on Saturday. Page five. *Controversial Waiheke Island café serves 'free' fresh fish*. It then went into detail about how we were getting around the law by using a cardinal, rabbi, canon, bishop, mother superior and other newly appointed religious leaders to provide fish to feed their flock. It went on to report that the café owner was now also the Archbishop of Waiheke Island. The paper had asked their legal firm to give an opinion on what we were doing. It advised the paper they believed we had correctly interpreted the legislation and weren't breaking any law. A photo of the fisheries inspector and myself was also featured.

Belinda and I read the article together in the trusty Skoda. 'Archbishop Whacker,' my beloved health inspector said, 'you're going to get the piss taken out of you by everyone who knows you. Did you tell your exes about your rapid elevation in the ranks of the Anglican Church?'

'I kept very quiet about it. I'm sure when they read this they'll all be very proud of me.'

My cellphone went. It was Number One. She was *not* very proud of me and wanted to know how an arsehole could be made an archbishop. I blessed her over the phone. She hung up. I put the phone on to wonderful cellular secretary.

The phone had rung hot at the café all morning. Friends, ex-wives and business colleagues had called and rude messages for the archbishop abounded. Strangers, wishing us all the best, had called. Customers had called. Radio stations had called. *Sunday News* was sending a reporter and a photographer across on the midday ferry. Television One and Three were coming over at the same time. I felt like running and hiding for the day but decided to face up to my responsibilities — and get some publicity to put those bums on my seats, especially as we were now committed to taking over the real-estate office. Another thirty seats.

Brian and Bruce also had a surprise for me. They sat me down for a coffee, told me to shut my eyes, count to three and open them. When I did, Cardinal Heke and Mother Superior Tina were there in full costume. They'd phoned a costume-hire place in Auckland and had them sent over. Heke and Tina looked very impressive, and I asked them to hang around until the television people arrived. In the meanwhile, would they mind going around the restaurant greeting and blessing the customers? They were a smash hit!

Lunch was a happy chaos. The café was full and people were prepared to wait for ages for a table, after all, now they could have a drink or two while waiting. The cardinal and mother superior made themselves comfortable in the bar and were delighted when the patrons insisted on buying them drinks. By three o'clock, when Mal and I frogmarched them out, they were both pissed out of their brains.

The media, I began to see, enjoyed coming out to the café, and even more so, now that we were licensed. They did their interviewing, got some great shots of the cardinal and mother superior and enjoyed our hospitality. Belinda and I went for a long walk when they'd gone. We wondered what the television news teams would do that night, to say nothing of the Sunday papers the next morning. 'It looks as if we're going to need more fisherfolk,' I told her. 'We need more fish. Last night we ran out early in the evening and tonight we'll do the same.'

'I don't think you'll have any problem there. I'm sure you'll have half of Waiheke wanting to do it for you. What are you going to do when other restaurants start doing the same thing?'

'Do more promotions and marketing. Most cafés and restaurants are owned by chefs, and chefs often ain't the best with marketing skills. There's the old saying I believe me ol' mate Aristole came up with — *You can serve the most wonderful cordon bleu meal in the world in your café, but if no bastard's there to eat it, it ain't the most wonderful meal in the world*. Smart bloke, that Aristole.'

'Even smarter than you Whacker, an ancient Greek who spoke French! So, what's next?'

'Well, I'm thinking of sponsoring a streakers' race. Start at Palm Beach and finish at the café. It may have to be done after dark. Perhaps we should also supply each contestant with a ping-pong bat for modesty, with our logo on it.'

'You're not serious!'

'Dead serious. Do you want to enter? There'll be good prizes.'

'Like a night in jail?'

'The race would be for smart people, Belinda. Smart people don't get caught.'

'What's smart about having an illegal race in the dark? Nobody will see it.'

'It only needs one reporter to hear about it, my dear darling health inspector. Just one.'

Back at the café we'd installed a television set behind the bar. Six o'clock arrived. News time. We flicked channels to try and catch our report on both. Three was first. They handled it in a slightly sarcastic way and for some reason didn't include shots of the cardinal or mother superior. I guess they didn't want to upset their bible-bashing viewers. One was brilliant! They chose to make the holy couple the centre of the story. It was great journalism. Even more brilliantly, the newsreader said she looked forward to coming to Waiheke Island for some of that nice fresh fish.

119

The *Sunday News* had a glorious photo of the papal couple on the front page and, in a smaller shot, the buggers had managed to superimpose me into a photo of an archbishop. The article was really fun and gave us lots of laughs. Sunday was an absolute boomer for the café, by far our best day yet. The sixty-eight fish had all gone by mid-afternoon, so in the evening only our original menu was available.

We selected two more fisherfolk early in the week — Bluey Blanchard and Poofter Pete McKenzie. Pete had nine adult children, but for reasons not known to me, has always been known as Poofter Pete. Mal had known them both since primary school. We gave them religious studies, then I ordained Bluey as Father Bluey of Stoney Batter and Poofter Pete as Monsignor Poofter Pete of Kennedy Point. We now had ten fisherfolk.

A major development occurred on Wednesday of that week. The landlord, Grant Mitchell, phoned me. After exchanging pleasantries, he explained that as he owned the real-estate office as well as the two premises the café currently occupied, would I be interested in buying the three of them? I let him know I'd think about it and get back to him.

Since wife Number Five, I hadn't purchased another house. I also had a few bob sitting around from the sale of the ad agency. On several occasions over the recent weeks, I'd thought owning the freehold of the café would be a darn good investment. If I did, perhaps I could build a big deck out along the front, which is what it really needed. I had a yarn with Greg, my accountant, then phoned Grant the next day and told him I was interested. It was agreed I'd get the property independently valued, and if it stacked up, I'd consider making him an offer.

This was all arranged and I went over to the big smoke the following week and finally met Grant. I made him an unconditional cash offer, with settlement within two weeks. He asked for a little more. I agreed. He agreed. We shook hands on it and then I departed to see Brad, to get the legal side tied up. Vacant possession too, as the real-estate office was moving the following week.

Brian, Bruce, Mal and I worked out how we should expand into the real-estate office. We planned to put the bar in there, by the windows. Booze was very profitable. The longer we could keep our patrons near it, the better for the bank balance. (I was getting commercial again — not what I came to the island for!) We could also fit in another eight tables, giving us seating in the three buildings for around 110, plus the bar. Yikes! Mal worked on the plans and got hold of his pisshead mates down at the council. He said we wanted the building permit on the day we took possession. After two long liquid luncheons at the café, it was agreed. Alterations would take a week. The health inspector would then inspect us, and as long as the proprietor played his cards right, the first weekend in November would be opening weekend. It was obvious this would be the ideal weekend for the streakers' race.

After the visit from the fisheries inspector, I started to get regular communication from the Ministry of Fisheries in

Wellington. I just sent them across to Brad and he'd fire a letter back, politely telling them to get stuffed. We were both surprised nobody else on the island, or anywhere else in New Zealand for that matter, had tried what we were doing. Brad reckoned they'd be waiting to see what happened to us.

There was such a demand for fresh fish that two more fisherfolk, the final two, were ordained. Tom Cookdale and Dago Daymon. These two retired pissheads became the Reverend Tom of Shelly Beach and Archdeacon Dago of Piemelon Bay. For the expansion into the real-estate office, we would have twelve holy fishers of men.

To spread the story about the proposed streakers' race, I told Mal. In absolute confidence. We'd be supplying table-tennis bats with the café's name on, but he wasn't to tell anyone. The secret quickly spread throughout the island. The *Gulf News* picked up on it, and in a small article, asked if it was on or off. And was a table-tennis bat sufficient coverage? When that issue came out, the race was the talk of the island.

Sergeant Jack Koster called in to see me. I'd got to know Jack quite well after the Wally and Mal goat incident. 'What's the story with this bloody race?'

'What race is that, Jack?'

'C'mon, mate. You know what I'm talking about.'

'Heard a few rumours have you? Sounds like a bit of fun. Do you want to enter?'

'Anyone caught running nude around these streets wi
have an indecent-exposure charge slapped on them. Serious
stuff.'

'C'mon, Jack. They'll be carrying a table-tennis bat.'

'Don't do it, Whacker. Or, if you do, make sure they
wear something down below. But no nudes.'

'Topless OK then, Jack?'

'You'd probably get away with that, but not bottomless.
You've been warned.'

'I'll get some entry forms up to the police station. The
girls would love to see a few of you guys participating.'

'Cheeky bugger. Get back to your illegal fish.'

Miriam Webber. Glorious Miriam Webber gave us publicity for the race I could only dream about. She spent
eight months of the year on Waiheke and four months
travelling to religious centres of the world. Miriam, pushing eighty, had inherited nicely from her dad, who was *the*
Webber in the Webber Biscuit Company.

The first I heard of Miriam was when she wrote a very
strong letter to the *Gulf News* about how we were 'defacing
religion by using spurious religious leaders to catch our
fish'.

With the rumours about the race flying, the day after
Sergeant Koster had been to see me, Miriam walked into
the café. 'Where's Mr McCracker?' she asked Screwzy Suzy,
one of our new waitresses, who'd had this rather unfortu-
nate nickname since becoming an adolescent legend
while attending Waiheke High School. She sat Miriam
down and came and got me.

'Hallo Miss Webber. Lovely to see you.' I turned up the
famous McCracker charm, fearing trouble. 'Would you
like a cup of tea — or a glass of wine perhaps?'

om your evil mind, body or soul, thank
m.

coming from our kitchen, Miss Webber.'

...gnored my comment. 'Mr McCracker, I am appalled to hear you are going to have a naked race around Waiheke. That is disgusting. Absolutely disgusting.'

'Miss Webber, you've been listening to rumours.'

'I've heard about it from several reliable sources. It's even worse than what you're doing with your shameful mockery of religion.'

'It could be a bit of fun, Miss Webber, and great publicity for Waiheke. Everyone likes looking at a nice healthy body. The Greeks used to run all their sporting events in the nude.'

'Thank goodness we are not living in ancient Greece, Mr McCracker. That was a disgustingly immoral era. Are you going to do it?'

'We might. But just from Palm Beach to here. If we did, you'll be very pleased to know we would supply each of the contestants with table-tennis bats for decency. Plus, we'd do it at night, in the dark. So nobody's going to see much anyway.'

'Mr McCracker, I might not be able to stop you doing it, but I believe I can make it just a little more acceptable. I am prepared to supply each of the contestants in the race with underpants.'

'Underpants, Miss Webber?'

'Underpants, Mr McCracker.'

'But if we did that, it wouldn't be a streakers' race. It would be an underpants race. Not the same thing.' But then, I had a thought. For a start, I knew darn well people are shy about displaying the partner's best friend in public. Plus there was the indecent-exposure problem with the police. As nobody had expressed any interest in actually entering, a nude race could be a fizzer. Miriam could save the day! A nearly-nude race could be a great success.

'G-strings, Miss Webber.'

'I beg your pardon, Mr McCracker.'

'If you donate G-strings for all the contestants, I'll cancel the nude race. Promise. G-strings are very in these days. The height of fashion.'

'I know what they are, Mr McCracker. Well . . . they're certainly better than nothing. All right, I agree.'

'We would of course like to acknowledge your financial support, after all, it's the least we can do. Something like *G-strings courtesy of Miriam Webber* on our promotional literature. Does that sound all right?'

'Yes, yes, that will be fine. If I can go to heaven having stopped nude racing on Waiheke Island, I may have a better chance of getting in.'

'Miss Webber, why don't we have a nice glass of wine to celebrate the fact that you're going to be the official supplier of G-strings to the great nearly-nude race from Palm Beach to the café.'

'That would be nice. Thank you Mr McCracker.'

'My pleasure Miss Webber. I'm very grateful for your generosity.'

Settlement for the real-estate office was mid-October, and thanks to the pisshead network we got our building permit on schedule. Once we did, there was much hammering and nailing to get it ready for the opening, which was going to be the same day as the nearly-nude race. Mal and Wally insisted on doing this because they wanted to keep their hand in, and hired a third local to help them, Harry Oslo. Born and raised on Waiheke Island. I had a fair idea where he'd learnt his trade.

A deck facing the ocean was what the café needed next. Now that I owned the freehold, I wanted to push ahead and do it. By replacing the windows with sliding doors, and having seating outside, it would not only make the café one of the best on the island, but also give us seating for at least another thirty on fine days. This project was too big for Wally and Mal so I contracted it out to a local architect, Cocky Hancock, to prepare plans and follow it through. He knew through the Waiheke grapevine how we'd got our previous building permits and recommended that this time it would be advisable to do everything very, very ethically. I agreed. He said it would take months to get resource consent and the building permit. Perhaps up to a year. I told him in that case, to give us the plans and we'd arrange these with our contacts. The permits we'd previously obtained were quite legal, and we expected the new ones, with our short-cut method of handling bureau-cracy, to be the same. He understood. He also estimated it would take a month for a reputable firm to build it.

The fishing situation was sorting itself out. Bruce had organised the schedule so that our fisherfolk got time off when they wanted it. He was also getting to know how many fish we'd need each day. On rough days when the boats couldn't go out and we had no fish, the patrons were quite happy to eat our normal menu, which was still very popular.

With Bruce being keen on computers, we also had a website. Now our patrons could check out the menu, meet the team, read what was happening on the island, and see photos of the café. We started to accept email bookings, but it was a problem because we didn't check them all the time. People would send them at eleven and arrive at twelve-thirty, to discover their email was still sitting unopened on the computer. We tried to get around that by saying bookings could only be made this way if they were made at least one day ahead.

A problem arose when Wally wanted the odd day off, and we needed another reverend person to pick up the fish. Mal assured me he now had his driving licence back. After passing the religious exam with flying colours, he was ordained Bishop Mal of Orapiu. Bets was beside herself with pride.

Cyril was working like a beaver to make all our religious leaders appropriate costumes for formal occasions. He was great on the sewing machine and had found pictures of all the appropriate clothing on the internet. The material was expensive so it was agreed the café would own them and lend them to our fisherfolk for 'formal' occasions. There was room to hang them in the loo in the ex-real estate's premises. It was a double cubicle job, so we arranged to take out one dunny and used that space for storage.

After Miriam's visit, I called in to the police station to have another yarn with Sergeant Koster. I told him what she'd so generously offered to do, and was it OK with the local law-enforcement officers now?

'Whacker, as long as they're not stark naked and exposing their privates, your bloody G-strings are fine with us.'

'The topless thing, Jack. What happens if some babes enter?'

'Can't discriminate these days, mate. If we arrested a babe for being topless while blokes are topless, we'd have every feminist on the island hammering on the door. There's heaps of them. Dangerous people to cross. No, we wouldn't do anything.'

'Good publicity for the café if you would, Jack. Front page of the paper probably. Sure I couldn't twist your arm?'

'Piss off, Whacker.'

'One other thing, Jack. We wouldn't have to have it in the dark now would we?'

'Have it any time you like. Remember also to only run on the footpath — and little old ladies and women with prams have right of way.'

Sam did a great poster for the window:

Whacker McCracker Café's nearly-nude race from Palm Beach to the café

2 p.m. on the first Saturday in November

Free G-strings for all contestants, courtesy of Miss Miriam Webber. Sneakers essential.

First prize $500
Second prize $250
Third prize $100

Plus spot prizes and free meal and a drink for all contestants.
Free entry, with entry forms available inside
or on the café's website.
Official entries close on the Wednesday prior to the race.

At the start of the week before the race, we had eighty-eight confirmed entries from gents and twenty-two from ladies. I phoned up and ordered one hundred and twenty-five gents and fifty ladies G-strings, in assorted sizes, to be delivered to the café the next day, Tuesday. Cyril needed a couple of days to screen on them, in very small type, *I ran from Palm Beach to Whacker McCracker's Café wearing only this.*

The extension was ready for us to move into on the Wednesday before the big race. The health inspector had given it the big OK the day before. It looked good, with a wonderful bar area facing the window. In the morning, everyone working that day celebrated its opening with a glass of bubbles. A piece of ribbon was stretched across when we banged the hole in the wall, and Archdeacon Dago of Piemelon Bay, who just happened to have called in, was given the honour of cutting the ribbon and declaring it open. He did it admirably. 'May every arsehole who drinks in here enjoy every glass of piss.' Such elegant words from a man of God.

When official entries closed we had one hundred and four gents and thirty-one ladies. I thought it would be nice if we could get a few more ladies so I got on the phone and called Numbers One, Two, Three, Four and even Number Five to see if they wanted to enter. I didn't know women could use such language, as they all they declined my invitation to participate in a little fun run.

We gave Paul Masters a pink Miriam Webber first thing

on Thursday. He'd arranged to interview her that morning and wanted to get a photograph of Miriam. Not wearing it, heavens forbid, just holding it.

We'd hired two university students, one of whom was Ted, a third-year commerce student. I told him to look after the logistics of the race. His helper was Amy, a second year design student.

On Friday, for perhaps the first time ever, the *Herald* had a page-three girl. They'd hired a model to wear one of our Miriam Webbers and ran the photo with the headline *Island Heiress gives 175 G-strings to Streakers*. The interview with Miriam, plus another photo of her holding the donated item, made delightful reading, and we were referred to as the 'infamous eatery'.

Saturday morning was one of those glorious early summer days Auckland sometimes gets in November, a real beach-weather day. Out of one hundred and thirty-five official entrants, by one o'clock, one hundred and eighteen had checked in. I left the chaos of a hundred-plus people all trying to get into one bus to take them to Palm Beach, each holding a large plastic bag to put their clothes in. Ted the academic was trying to get another bus on five minutes' notice. He didn't understand Waiheke all that well. As I was the official starter, I wanted to get down to the beach to make sure things were going to schedule. Amy, Mal, Wally and Screwzy Suzy had left earlier to get things organised.

It took a while to get to Palm Beach — I had to park and walk about a mile. The place was packed. Everyone on the island had come along for a perv, plus hundreds from the city. At the north end of the beach, the nudie end, my very busy team of organisers said everything was going fine. It was hard to tell who was running and who was there for a good perv, with several hundred people swirling around.

By two o'clock we were still awaiting for more of the official entrants to arrive, so we delayed the race half an hour. Through a serious bribe of alcohol, Ted informed me on the cellphone that he'd managed to get a second bus. I was impressed. He was learning about the world of commerce, and the second bus arrived ten minutes later.

I announced over the megaphone the race would be starting at two-thirty. All contestants, official and unofficial, must be ready in their running gear five minutes beforehand. The rules were then explained. Official entrants in café-supplied G-strings in the front. Unofficial entrants in the equivalent or similar gear, behind. Absolutely no nude streaking — they could be arrested if they did. As it was an unofficial run, the contestants must stay on the footpaths, give way to cars, little old ladies, women with prams, cats and dogs. There were water stops and if anyone felt crook, stop.

A starting line had been drawn over the width of the beach and we had flags at each end. Five minutes before starting, Mal turned on a siren and yelled out it was gear-off time and to get into positions. Well, holy shit, everyone who was milling around got their gear off. There were going to be hundreds of participants. Hundreds! The undie brigade, the unofficial entries, were about three times larger than the official entries, and about a third were women.

I raised the flag, called out three, two, one and then dropped it. The flag, that is. Away they went, running down the north end of the beach to the main beach and off up the hill in the direction of Oneroa. What a sight! The photographers had a field day. The sight of hundreds of very nearly bare bums isn't one they get every day.

The support team was working like crazy to get all the clothing back to the café before the contestants. But with all the traffic, and the number of participants, that wasn't going to be possible. I left them to it, as I wanted to get back for the finish. The traffic situation was bad. I took a couple of the back roads, but still didn't get there until just after the first runners had arrived.

As there were no showers, we'd bought two hundred towels and heaps of body sprays. But we'd only catered for two hundred, not five hundred. With the clothes arriving late, we now had hundreds of practically nude individuals standing around in the café and on the footpath outside. We obviously didn't have room for everybody, so only those in official Miriam Webbers would be allowed in the café.

An hour later, most of the runners had arrived. And some clothing still hadn't. The café bar was full of heaps of practically nude people and so were all the other bars nearby. Because it wasn't cold and there was no wind, everyone though it was a hoot. Everyone that is, except Sergeant Koster, who caught me congratulating two gorgeous topless and practically bottomless blonde babes.

'Mr McCracker, you're in deep shit.'

'Jack, standing here with these two lovely ladies I would say I'm in deep heaven!'

'You should have called it off. You told me it was only going to be a few people.'

'Gatecrashers, Jack. The buggers just turned up. We both know you can't stop people going for a Saturday-afternoon run. This isn't Cuba, mate.'

The two blondes came up to Jack, one on each side of him, and gave him a big cuddle. A flashlight went off. Brilliant. I saw who took it. Belinda!

Jack acted fast. He pushed the two gorgeous babes aside and looked for the photographer. Gone. 'McCracker, you're in even deeper shit!'

'Jack, think of the deep shit you'll be in when that photo appears in the *Sunday News* tomorrow. Your sons will be jealous as hell, but your missus might not be too happy.'

'If that picture appears, you're history, mate. History.'

'And if I can stop it?'

'Do you reckon you can?'

'I'll try, Jack. Now why don't you go and do some real police work like catching burglars and finding lost kids?'

'I'll get you cracking rocks one day, McCracker,' Jack called back, as he left the bar, followed by jeering from various nearly nude and other fully clothed patrons.

The last of the clothing finally arrived; the prizes were presented and gradually the official entrants were wined and fed. They had to dress before they could be served, so we had no nudies sitting at the tables. The unofficial entrants wanted to be fed, and so did the spectators. Sadly we had no room for them, and they mingled outside the café, half of them still practically naked. The other bars and restaurants in Oneroa boomed and the pervs had a field day.

Sadly it was the first and last race. Like Jack said, I was in deep shit. Constable Lucy tracked me down on Monday, to tell me I was to report to the police station at ten o'clock the following morning. I phoned Brad, my lawyer, and he agreed to come over and hold my hand.

When I got down to the ferry to pick him up on Tuesday

morning, he walked down the wharf with a cop — the Area Commander, Dick Dawson, with whom we were to meet at the police station. They'd done some papers at university together so knew each other well. In fact, Brad said he bought the coffee on the ferry.

At the wharf, Dick got into the waiting police car and Brad got into the Skoda, which despite initial teething problems was proving to be a fairly reliable car. Brad set my mind at ease. Once they realised they were both going to Waiheke for the same reason, they'd discussed the meeting. All I was in for was a bloody big blast and a promise not to do it again.

And that was basically it. I was told I'd broken this regulation and that regulation, brought shame to the island and blah blah blah. If I promised never ever to run another nude or nearly-nude race again, and behaved myself, the matter was dropped. I'd already realised a second one would be an almighty anticlimax, so I agreed, ever so reluctantly of course, not to do it again. We parted friends.

Going out through the main office, Constable Lucy Simmonds was just coming in. I called out, 'Hey Lucy, are you going to enter the nude swimming race we're having next year?'

Everyone roared with laughter, except Sergeant Koster. I don't think he trusted me. 'Don't even contemplate it, McCracker.'

The race gave us not just national press, radio and television coverage but extraordinary international coverage. In a report sent to me by a television executive two months after the race, on lineage and airtime for a New Zealand news story appearing overseas, our race was the fourth most highly covered story ever.

We'd been selling quite a few of our T-shirts, and heaps more Miriam Webber G-strings were created and we started selling them too. We edited the video footage we'd taken down to thirty minutes, and with a price tag of twenty-five dollars we sold over four hundred in the first month after the race.

We went through a consolidation period for most of November and December. We knew the summer would only get busier and we had to be prepared to cope with it. It was also, as my lawyer described it, 'a keep out of trouble period'. With all the hoo-ha over the fisherfolk and the nearly-nude race, a low profile was called for.

Cyril finished all the robes for the fisherfolk and they were truly magnificent. We kept them at the café, where everyone took turns to wear them and bless the patrons' fish, and many memorable photos were taken.

One new event I did announce was a Miss Fresh Fish beauty competition to be held on New Year's Day.

But the best news of all was when Bets announced she was pregnant. Mal was going to be a dad.

24

On Christmas Eve we were closed to the great unwashed, and had a private party for the café staff and the fisherfolk. Because it was Christmas, those who'd been ordained were requested to wear their vestments, and the evening was a happy and colourful one. With so many holy people present, the spirit of Christmas was really with us, although perhaps with the exception of Rabbi Esky Bill.

By eleven o'clock Belinda and I had had enough. The café was closing for Christmas Day and we were going over to the big smoke to have Christmas lunch with her sister and brother-in-law. I also felt the team would probably enjoy it more if the boss wasn't around. They'd all worked damned hard and deserved to let their hair down. We wished everyone a final Merry Christmas and left.

The phone rang. I looked at the clock. It was two o'clock in the morning. Christmas morning. 'Hallo, Whacker speaking.'

'Mr McCracker, this is Sergeant Koster of the Waiheke Island Police Force.'

'You're kidding me, Jack, I thought it was Santa Claus. What the hell are you phoning me for at this hour?'

'To advise you that as of this moment, we currently have in residence in our cells two bishops, one archdeacon, one cardinal, one canon, two priests, a mother superior and a rabbi. I have reason to believe this despicable mob belongs to you.'

'What have they done?'

'Let's just say this, Mr McCracker. You're not likely to have much fresh fish for a while.' He laughed. 'Unless they can catch fish in Mt Eden jail.'

'Jack, I'll be there in ten minutes.'

'Fine. We'll be waiting down the road with a breathalyser so hopefully we can throw you in there with them on a DIC charge. What a joyous Christmas that would be.'

'I'll ride my bike,' I told him, and hung up. I explained to Belinda and she said she'd drive me there.

As we walked into the police station, we heard joyous carolling coming from the cells.

Constable Lucy was at the front desk. 'Hallo Mr McCracker,' she said as I entered. 'Have you come to join the carol singing?'

Sergeant Koster had seen us arrive and came over. 'Your mob of no-hopers are in deep shit,' he said, ignoring Belinda.

A chorus of 'Silent Night' filled the police station. 'Christmas Carols in the police station on Christmas Eve, Jack. That's nice. I bet not too many police stations are lucky enough to enjoy that.'

Constable Lucy started to laugh, but Sergeant Jack was getting madder. 'Wipe that smile off your face, Constable. Having a bunch of lowlifes singing in our cells is no laughing matter.'

'Now Jack, what the hell have they done? Getting pissed at the office Christmas party isn't exactly a hanging offence.'

'It's what else they've done. For a start, are you aware that these drongos went down the road from your fish and chip shop . . .'

I interjected. 'We don't sell chips, we sell mashed potato.'

137

'These lowlifes walked down the road to the Catholic Church to attend midnight mass. Dressed in their fancy-dress costumes.'

'Religious robes, Jack.'

'McCracker, not only were they pissed as parrots when they got to the church, but they'd brought their own alcohol to drink during the mass. Which they proceeded to do.'

'Discreetly I'm sure, Jack.'

'Bullshit. It was totally sacrilegious. Miriam Webber nearly had a heart attack when she looked across the aisle and saw a rabbi with an arm around a cardinal sharing a bottle of whisky. Then to make it even worse, mother superior learnt over, grabbed it off them and took a swig.'

The chorus in the cells started singing 'Jingle Bells'.

'Do you know what happened during the silent prayer? You'll be so proud of that fat boy you employ.'

'What did Wally do?'

'The whole church was completely silent. Then. He farted. Loudly. And for a very long time. He disrupted the entire service. All the kids started to laugh, some of the adults started to laugh, and of course your bunch of bloody no-hopers nearly fell off the pews with laughter. Father Peter completely lost control of the service.'

'Jack, is there a law against farting in church? Or laughing in church?' I asked, roaring with laughter at the same time. So were Belinda and Constable Lucy.

Sergeant Jack was not. Most definitely not. 'It gets worse. One of your mob chundered all over Mavis and Harold Mountford sitting in the pew in front. All over them. Mavis just happens to be my mother's sister. My aunt. Nobody, but nobody chunders over my aunt when she's attending mass! One of the worshippers phoned us on his cellphone. A major emergency at the Catholic Church. I got dragged out of bed to attend this major emergency and saw with my own eyes my beloved aunt and uncle being washed down in the church hall!'

'Sorry to hear about that, Jack. Really sorry. Tell them to call in to the café with the dry-cleaning bill and I'll pay for it.' I felt it was the least I could do. I was also beginning to understand the sergeant's anger.

'That incident concluded the Christmas midnight mass at the church. Father Peter isn't a very strong man, and couldn't continue. When I left him an hour ago, he was also a very upset man. In all his years in the priesthood he'd never had an experience like that. He was already talking about having to go to a retreat to recover. And who'll take Christmas mass if he's not right?'

'Cardinal Heke of Surfdale will take it if you like.' I said it as a joke. From the look Jack gave me I don't think he appreciated my little joke. The chorus in the cells started singing 'Silent Night' again. A bit flatter this time.

'Look Jack, can I see my colleagues? And just what are you charging them with? Farting, chundering and being a little boozed? If you do, you'll be the laughing stock of the police force. Just about every Catholic I've had the pleasure of knowing has been a great pisshead, a great farter and a great chunderer. Yourself excluded, of course.'

Jack looked at me with daggers in his eyes. 'I want to know who the chunderer was. You can go and see them as long as you find out who the chunderer was. You can tell them all to make themselves comfortable because they're spending the night here. Waking up in jail with sore heads on Christmas Day may put some sense in their thick skulls.

There will, of course, be other charges. It depends on how far Father Peter and my aunt and uncle wish to proceed.' For the first time, Jack smiled.

Constable Lucy took me into the first small cell. There was Mother Superior Tina of Putiki Bay out cold, snoring gently. The action was in the large holding cell next door.

'Whacker,' they all greeted me. 'Merry Christmas!'

'You dopey bunch of bastards!' I greeted them in return.

Monsignor Poofter Pete of Kennedy Point and Canon Bert of Ostend had flaked, but the others were in fine form. I told them to shut up and explained that Jack had decided they had to sleep it off in the cells. As this was not an unknown experience for any of them, nobody was too concerned.

'Jack also wants to know who chundered all over the couple in front. Unfortunately they were his aunt and uncle. Who was it?'

Silence. Absolute silence.

'C'mon, who was it?'

Silence.

'An Act of God?' asked Bishop Mal of Orapiu.

'Divine Intervention?' queried Rabbi Esky Bill of Onetangi.

'You silly buggers. Well, I'll leave you to it. In the morning, when they let you out, I'm sure Jack and his team of happy coppers will drive you home. If you have any problems, phone me at home before ten-thirty. I'm catching the eleven o'clock ferry. Sleep well, and I hope you all have a happy Christmas.'

'Merry Christmas Whacker,' they called out. And started singing 'Silent Night' again.

'Well,' said Sergeant Koster when I came out. 'Who was the chunderer?'

'Apparently it was either an Act of God or Divine Intervention, Jack,' I replied.

'So they wouldn't tell you?'

'You could say that. Perhaps they can't remember. Sometimes when you've had a few you can't remember everything you did. Think back to when you last got pissed.'

'Nobody is going to be released until someone confesses. They can stay there all Christmas Day.'

'You know you can't do that, Jack. I've got to go. Busy day tomorrow. Just make sure you let them out in the morning, and please arrange transportation to their homes. After a nice home-cooked Christmas breakfast.'

'Fuck off out of here,' roared the sergeant.

'That's not very nice language, Jack.'

'Fuck off McCracker!'

Belinda and I fucked off. I got her to drive me to the Catholic Church. Not a sign of life, but I read that the first mass on Christmas Day was at seven o'clock.

'Do you want to come with me to mass at seven?' I asked Belinda.

'I'm not a Catholic,' she replied.

'Nor am I. But we're going. We might just be able to nip this thing in the bud.'

Next, we called into the café, where I went to the safe and took out a thousand dollars in cash. We finally got home in time for a couple of hours' sleep.

Belinda and I were the first to arrive for mass, not long after six. The only person at the church was a priest who

141

was setting out the altar. I walked up and gave him one hell of a fright. He looked pretty fragile so I asked if he was Father Peter. When he said he was, I introduced Belinda and myself, before expressing our most sincere regrets about what had happened.

'Father, I'd also like to make a donation to your church on behalf of those who caused the disturbance. They are very, very upset. Here's five hundred dollars.' I handed it to him.

'Why thank you, Mr McCracker. That's very generous.'

'Also Father, could you possibly give a further five hundred dollars in compensation to Mr and Mrs Mountford? I'm sure they'll be coming to mass today because of last night's cancellation.' I handed him another five hundred dollars.

'Thank you, Mr McCracker. I'm sure they will appreciate it.'

'Father, please be assured I will be most severely reprimanding all of my staff who caused the trouble last night. Perhaps they could also do some charity work for your church? As it's Christmas Day, I do hope they will have your forgiveness and you'll now let me handle this matter myself, both discreetly and effectively.'

'Thank you, Mr McCracker. I really would appreciate it if you could.' He shuddered. 'I don't want to have anything more to do with it. The sooner I can forget about it the better. I will pray today for your friends and ask God's forgiveness for them.'

Belinda was pretty impressed with the way I handled that one. I have to admit, so was I. Not a single charge was laid. Jack tried like hell to get his aunt and uncle to lay one but they wouldn't. I've often wondered if the church ever received any of the five hundred dollars. Father Peter was pretty keen to take it. Perhaps the Mongrel Mob was after him for a gambling debt?

When the Christmas Day morning shift arrived to find a jail full of religious leaders, they did the decent thing. After feeding them up on some Christmas tarts and a couple of cups of tea, they drove them all home.

Sergeant Koster called in to see me in the café on Boxing Day. 'What did you do, Whacker? I know you did something. Someone told me you were up at that church at sparrow's fart. What did you do?'

'Nothing Jack, it's all over now. Let's not talk about the past. Now listen, I've got a favour to ask.'

'No favours. Favours are out for you. Forever.'

'Just a small one, Jack. I'd like you to be a judge at our Miss Fresh Fish beauty contest on New Year's Day. All you have to do is look at a line-up of gorgeous babes and pick the most beautiful.'

'That's my day off.'

'Even better. Make an afternoon of it. Relax. Have a few beers. Enjoy yourself for a change.'

'Well . . . could be a bit of fun . . . Right. I'll be there. How many entrants have you got?'

'Fourteen so far. All gorgeous. All over eighteen.'

'Just one final thing. Who chundered all over my aunt and uncle?'

'Don't know, Jack. Buggers wouldn't tell me.' I did know actually. It was Mother Superior Tina of Putiki Bay.

25

In mid-December we'd hired Luigi, an Italian backpacker, as a chef for the holiday period. He thought our menu was hilarious, the cheeky bugger. Within a day or two he started preparing pasta for the staff, who loved him for it. I wouldn't budge. 'No wog food in this café. Let's stick to our initial menu, plus the fresh fish,' I told Bruce and Brian, who'd been at me to diversify a little. I wouldn't eat his pasta — that is, until one night, a few days before Christmas, when I was hungry, and in a hurry to leave. A big dish of lasagne was on the table and the staff was ploughing into it. I grabbed a plate and spooned myself a bit. It was good. Not that I said anything nice about it or showed I was enjoying it.

'That wog food must be profitable, Bruce,' I said the next morning. 'After all, it's only flour and water.'

'And easy to make. A seafood-based pasta dish would be a hit.'

'OK. Let's try one.'

When we opened after Christmas, due to that dish's immediate popularity, and the fact that we had a 'genuine' Italian chef, we had three delicious pasta dishes on the menu.

The peak holiday season really got under way from Boxing Day. The island was packed with holidaymakers. So was the café. The twelve fishing boats were going out every day, but we still couldn't get nearly enough fresh fish. Most days found us running out by early evening. However, it didn't worry the patrons. They simply selected something else from the menu, which I have to admit, due to the pasta, was gradually starting to change. Brian and Bruce were itching to make further changes to go more upmarket. I resisted it.

Our staff made the café. As the year was closing, I reflected on how lucky I'd been in this respect. The originals were still with me and had worked amazingly hard. We'd also added some new people and had great casuals. With all our publicity and efforts to put bums on seats, if the staff hadn't delivered the goods, everything could have backfired.

Bets' doctor had advised that she shouldn't work standing up all day in the kitchen now she was pregnant. She was already a big girl, and on top of that, being pregnant was a fair bit to ask of her substantial body. We made her our cashier, so she could sit down. To be confronted by a very large pregnant woman as one left the café was a memorable experience. We put a sign on the front of the till that said 'I'm not normally this large, it's just that I'm pregnant!' A great talking point. The patrons all loved our Bets and wished her well.

Mal and Wally continued to be Laurel and Hardy. Skinny Mal. Big Wally. When we got the liquor licence, we'd changed to full waiter service rather than ordering at the counter. Mal was made for it, but the surprising thing was, when we had to use Wally in a couple of emergency situations, he was darn good. So we made him a waiter. The only trouble was his substantial size meant he did get stuck the odd time between chairs and tables. But with his lovely laugh and grinning face, everyone would happily move to let him through. He took turns with Mal to do the fish-collection run in the Suzuki every morning.

During the peak holiday period they both dressed up for an hour or two in their bishop's robes. How the holiday patrons loved that!

The things you find in a junk shop! Brian and Bruce from the next door *Stratford off Avon* antique shop were the most wonderful find I could ever wish for. Brian was completely responsible for the food side of the business and Bruce for just about everything else. They complimented each other. Sure they attracted heaps of their poofy friends to the café, but that gave it a very cosmopolitan atmosphere. Good guys most of them.

Peg wouldn't leave us. She didn't want to stay at home looking after Al with his piles and incontinence. Or the new third granddaughter from the Immaculate Conceptor. Daughter was given the job of looking after her dad, who I still hadn't met. In fact I sometimes wondered if there actually was an Al. Had he passed on to the next life and Peg had ingeniously managed to keep his benefit going? I didn't like to ask.

Cyril and Johnny came in and replaced Bruce and Brian a couple of days a week — or when needed. Cyril had taken Johnny in as his partner in his screen-printing-sewing-T-shirt-and-you-name-it business in Surfdale. It wasn't the most profitable venture, so they appreciated the extra income they made from the café.

Screwzy Suzy was our first permanent after the originals. She was a tizzy brunette, early thirties with a couple of great kids who went to the local primary school. They would drop by frequently and be spoilt rotten. Suzy'd had a fair bit of hardship in her life — in more ways than one, and was one of the genuine deserving Waiheke DPBs. We were paying her well, so for the first time in years she wasn't on a benefit. She did such a good job we made her our maitre d' . . or as we described it, 'the Bum Sitter'. We got a little badge with that printed on for her to wear.

Harry Oslo, always known as Horse, came to us as a carpenter and stayed on, taking responsibility for the bar. A good mate of Mal and Wally, he was an ex-pisshead, and very involved in Alcoholics Anonymous. Horse, who used to work at the RSA, was the ultimate barman. He was extraordinarily articulate, and knew more dirty stories than anyone I'd ever come across, and could tell them so well that everyone roared with laughter whether they were funny or not!

Over the holiday period, all of the casuals were university students. We had two studying medicine, one law, one architecture, a couple in the arts, one accountancy and one doing engineering. Bright kids, who liked a bit of fun — especially dressing up in the robes. The accountancy student, who was Jewish, dressed up as a vicar on the last day of the year, and greeted a couple from behind. When they turned around he was horrified to see his aunt and uncle. Very strict Jews. They were not amused. Nephew apparently got into a wee spot of bother at home over that little incident!

What had happened at the Catholic Church on Christmas Eve had been the talk of Waiheke between Christmas and New Year. The story became more and more exaggerated and colourful. Wally's fart had already become an island legend, and some who heard and witnessed the event reckoned it was the most exciting thing to have ever happened in their little church.

26

New Year's Day arrived, the day of our Miss Fresh Fish beauty competition. From mid-December we'd spread the word via the modelling agencies in Auckland. We were advised to increase the prize money and have three prizes so that pretty young ladies would have three chances of getting something decent. We increased the first prize to seven hundred and fifty dollars, second prize to five hundred dollars and third prize to two hundred and fifty dollars.

The contest was promoted with ads in the *Gulf News*, signs on the café window and posters on the ferries. By the morning of the competition we had twenty-four official entries.

We were licensed for a maximum of one hundred and forty in the café, which included thirty in the bar. The pre-sold admission tickets at twenty-five dollars each were quickly snapped up, with all of the money donated to the Waiheke Island Women's Institute.

The competition was due to start at three, with people holding tickets to be admitted after two-thirty. That proved to be an almighty hassle, as we had patrons still eating, who had no intention of being thrown out. Half an hour later they were still firmly in their seats waiting for the free entertainment. There wasn't much we could do, so I just hoped Jack Koster and his merry men wouldn't try counting heads.

Mal and Wally had built a basic catwalk for the girls and erected a changing shed of types in the kitchen, as no meals were going to being served during the event.

To make things even more colourful, we planned to use the religious robes. (Mother Superior's cassock was back from the dry-cleaner's.) Mal and Wally, in their bishop's robes, were to escort the girls to the stage — as well as serve the tables. Brian, who was the DJ, was to be a priest. Bruce, on the door, became a cardinal for the occasion. Peg wanted a role so we arranged for her to be Sister Peg, in charge of the girls. Somehow, Cyril had enlarged the mother superior's cassock, and Bets became Mother Superior Bets. Cyril and Johnny pleaded to attend, so they were made a rabbi and archdeacon respectively. Horse was to be a canon, and the compere was yours truly, the Archbishop of Waiheke. The remaining robes were to be used by original fisherfolk. We had a shortage of female robes and Screwzy Suzy, who was helping Peg look after the girls, was most pissed off.

The judging panel was to consist of Sergeant Jack Koster, Monsignor Poofter Pete of Kennedy Point and Karen Blomfield, the young 'friend' of Sam Hankle QC.

Belinda wasn't impressed with the judging panel. We'd had quite a domestic about it a couple of nights before when I told her Karen had agreed to come. I regarded getting her as a bit of a scoop. After all, she'd been quite a celebrity for a day or two.

'What do those three know about judging a beauty contest? You should be getting people who know something about beauty. Does Jack know who he's judging with?'

'Well, I told him there would be three learned people.'

'He'll hit the roof when he discovers he's sharing the job with a hooker.'

'She's not a hooker. She's an escort. Much classier.'

'And Poofter Pete. What on earth would an overweight,

sixty-year-old, absolute no-hoper, whose only ability besides collecting the dole is catching a few fish, know about judging a beauty pageant?'

'Well, we had to have one of the fisherfolk, after all, it's the Miss Fresh Fish beauty pageant. Nobody else would do it. Don't worry, he's an old perv from way back. He'll be all right. Plus he knows Jack — over the years he's been one of his best customers.'

Belinda shook her head. 'And Jack Koster. What qualifications does he have?'

'He's a policeman, Belinda. A policeman. Nobody can accuse him of taking bribes or blowjobs from any of the contestants. A man above reproach, I believe is the term.'

'Yeah, and so was Bill Clinton. I feel very sorry for the girls.'

'Don't worry, I'll be helping. I'll position myself next to Poofter Pete and give him the odd nod when the right babe comes out. I've been married five times remember, I know something about picking female form.' I was winding Belinda up and she didn't like it.

'You can't do that.'

'Wanna bet? Anyway, don't worry. It'll be OK. It's only a bit of fun.'

'I'm not going to your Miss Fresh Fish competition. That name is dreadful and I don't think you're being fair to the girls.'

I tried for two days to get her to change her mind, even offered to make her a judge. But she refused to come.

Everything seemed to be going to schedule as we got

closer to three o'clock. We were all getting into our robes and to our arranged positions and the patrons were enjoying the colourful sight of the religious dignitaries and generous amounts of liquid refreshments.

Peg came out to tell me twenty-one out of the twenty-four girls had arrived and she thought some of the bikinis were far too small. I told her to let the patrons decide that one. I asked if she'd checked their IDs to make sure they all were over eighteen. She said yes, and there were a couple of surprises. I didn't quite know what she meant.

The young ladies would come out individually; their order of appearance drawn out of a hat. Bishop Wally and Bishop Mal would escort them, one on each side, through the café to the catwalk.

The three judges arrived. I welcomed them individually, and handed each of them on to a student who was to explain the rules. Poofter Pete went off and got changed into his robes. I could tell he'd had one or two on the way, but he seemed all right. Jack was given a beer in the bar. Karen was taken to a table at the far end of the café for a coffee with her student. I didn't want Jack and her meeting before I presented them to the audience. The students had instructions to keep them well apart and not say who the other judges were. I thought Poofter Pete might do a runner because of Sergeant Koster. I thought Sergeant Koster might do a runner because of Karen Blomfield. I thought Karen Blomfield might do a runner because of Sergeant Koster.

At three o'clock, on the dot, we were ready to go. To a roll of drums DJ Brian had organised, I strode through the café, dressed as the Archbishop of Waiheke Island, and up on to the catwalk. The patrons cheered, whistled and yelled!

I welcomed everyone to the very first Whacker McCracker's Café's Miss Fresh Fish beauty pageant. Twenty-one beautiful girls were participating.

'Ladies and gentlemen, please welcome the first of our judges. Representing the fisherfolk who catch our beautiful fresh fish, please welcome Monsignor Poofter Pete of Kennedy Point!' Pete came on to the stage to heaps of cheers and stood beside me.

'Our next judge is a highly respected gentleman known to a lot of you present. Please welcome Sergeant Jack Koster of the Waiheke Island police force.' Jack, not looking the happiest, came on to the stage to lots of cheers and quite a few jeers.

I moved on quickly. 'Please welcome our third judge, a woman of high integrity. From Kohimarama, please welcome Karen Blomfield.' Karen walked up on the stage.

A voice from the back of the café called out, 'Hey Whacker, she's the hooker who was with that lawyer who carked it in your dunny. Are you sure she's got high integrity?'

Roars of laughter filled the café.

Jack came up to me. 'There's no way I'm going on the same panel as her. I resign.' With that, he stormed off and left the catwalk to much jeering from the crowd.

Karen was next. 'I've never been so embarrassed in my life. I can't do this. No way.' She walked off the catwalk to even more jeering.

Poofter Pete came up to me. 'I don't think I want to do this either. Sorry mate.' And with that he left the catwalk.

Suddenly I had one hell of a problem — a beauty pageant all set to go, with no judges. I thought hard. Very hard. 'C'mon ladies and gentlemen. Can't you take a joke?'

'That bloody Whacker, he's having us on,' I heard someone yell. Now they all thought it was a big joke and everyone was smiling again.

'I'd like to introduce three of the wisest men on Waiheke Island. Please welcome to the catwalk, Cardinal Bruce of Surfdale, Bishop Mal of Orapiu and Bishop Wally from our very own Oneroa.'

I caught Mal's eye, then Wally's, as they looked at me in amazement. 'Clear a way for their excellencies, ladies and gentlemen.' Mal and Wally came forward in a wide-eyed trance and climbed on to the catwalk they'd built a couple of hours earlier. Cyril and Johnny were pushing Cardinal Bruce, who had a look of horror on his face.

'Now ladies and gentlemen, nowhere else would you find a more honest judging panel than a cardinal and two bishops. The young ladies are indeed fortunate! I thank you, reverend gentlemen, for finding the time to come here today. We will now give the judges a chance to take their seats and get themselves organised. We'll be starting our glorious pageant of island beauty in five minutes.'

I ushered the three off the stage. 'Don't say anything. We were in the shit. You've saved the day. Now just judge. We need a first, second and third.'

'Piece of piss,' exclaimed Mal.

Wally agreed.

'Whacker, I'm gay,' Bruce hissed.

'Just look for big tits and legs up to their ears.'

By this stage, a couple of the students who'd been giving the original judges instructions had arrived at the judging table, and I left them telling the new panel what to do.

I caught Cyril's eye and he quickly came over. 'Mate,

you and Johnny escort the girls through to the catwalk. Make sure everyone keeps their hands off them. And if Jack and Karen are still around, tell Horse to pour as much booze as they want down their throats, on the house. I didn't mean to embarrass them.'

'Just brilliant — and Bruce a judge! Thank God we came!' gushed Cyril.

I got back on to the stage and signalled to Brian to get things rolling.

The first five contestants were nice young girls holidaying on Waiheke. Three wore one pieces; two wore not-too-small bikinis. The patrons were generous with their applause, as I asked each of them their names, where they were from and what they did.

The sixth contestant came out wearing a sundress and hat. Short, plump and ugly would be the kindest description I could give. Naturally the crowd roared and gave her a hearty welcome. Well, we had specified beachwear — not just bathing costumes.

'And what's your name,' I asked.

'Helen.'

'And where are you from, Helen?'

'Auckland.'

'And what do you do, Helen?'

'I'm involved with the Women's Liberation Movement.'

I expected her to unfurl a flag, whack me and scream out that I was running a meat market. But no, she didn't do anything. Just went over and stood beside number five. I began to feel slightly uneasy.

Number seven was a stunner, wearing a tiny bikini held together by a few bits of string. The guys went crazy. The café shook with their cheering, yelling and screaming. I

154

looked down at the judges, caught a couple of eyes to say watch this one, and got on with the job.

The next two were locals so they were made to feel really at home. One was particularly attractive — and she also had on a bikini designed to excite the guys.

Number ten. Number ten. Oh god. She was solid. Wearing a bikini. The crowd went ballistic!

'And what's your name?'

'Stiffy.'

'I beg your pardon?'

'Stiffy.'

'And where are you from, Stiffy?'

'Originally Te Kuiti; now Auckland.'

'And what do you do, Stiffy?'

'I'm involved with the Women's Liberation Movement.'

My uneasy feeling grew.

She went and stood beside number nine. The next three were very attractive girls, all working as part-time models in Auckland. Very sexy, two in teenie-weenies, and one in a slinky one piece. The crowd loved them.

Contestant number fourteen. She looked all right in her one piece. 'And what's your name?'

'Well, some people call me Alana, and others call me Alan,' she said in a husky voice.

A bloke. A transvestite. The patrons roared. Never had they had seen so much diversification in a beauty contest!

'And where are you from Alana — or, if you prefer, Alan?'

'Wellington.'

'And what do you do in Wellington?'

'I'm an entertainer.'

That brought another roar from the crowd.

155

The next two girls were sweeties. One was a very pretty Maori girl from Takapuna and the second a slim Indian girl with a lovely smile, from Warkworth.

Contestant number seventeen, a solid, muscular, non-feminine-looking thirtyish woman, wearing a singlet, shorts and of all things, boots.

'And what's your name?'

'Ms Atkins.'

'No Christian name?'

'Ms Atkins.'

'And you're from Auckland and involved with the Women's Liberation Movement. Right?'

'Yes.'

She went and stood beside the young Indian contestant.

Major uneasy feeling by now.

Eighteen and nineteen were two more very attractive local young ladies from Onetangi and Palm Beach.

Contestant number twenty, in an old-fashioned one piece, was perhaps the skinniest, dorkiest women I'd ever seen. She wore glasses so thick you could hardly see her eyes. Her hair was cut in a classic number one. The crowd, well lubricated by this stage, gave her a tumultuous island welcome.

'And what's your name?'

'Nina.'

'And, Nina would it be safe to say you're from Auckland and also involved with the Women's Liberation Movement?'

'Yes. My sisters from the movement and I have participated to show that all women should be treated equally. Beautiful women should not be separated from those who don't have the same physical qualities. Beauty is within! Sisters unite!'

With that the four women started chanting, 'Sisters unite!'

After a few minutes of that they stopped and took their places in the line-up. The other contestants looked stunned, and the audience bewildered.

Number twenty-one did a runner. After the chanting she was too petrified to come out. We had twenty contestants to be judged. Fifteen, if you took out the four libbers and the transvestite. I gave the audience a few minutes to settle down and for the judges to complete their judging, then went over to the three religious leaders to see if they'd made their decisions.

'Whacker, is it definitely the two-against-one rule?' asked Bruce. 'If two vote for a girl and one doesn't, that girl still gets the vote?'

'That's what we agreed on, Bruce. Very democratic.'

'Well in that case, we've finished. But I don't think you're going to like it.'

Mal handed me the envelope with the number of the first runner-up.

I asked for absolute silence from the audience. 'The first runner up is number seven.'

Colleen, from Hamilton, in the tiny bikini held together by a few bits of string, came forward. I gave her a big kiss, placed the sash Cyril had made around her and handed her a cheque as the crowd cheered.

The second runner-up was number eighteen, April from Onetangi, a very popular choice. Class written all over her. I gave her the sash, a big kiss and her cheque.

'And now ladies and gentlemen, the moment you've all

157

been waiting for . . .the winner of Whacker McCracker's Café Miss Fresh Fish beauty pageant!'

I opened the envelope Mal handed to me, grinning like a Cheshire cat. 'And the winner is . . . number ten!'

I'd lost track by now and wasn't sure who was number ten. I would soon find out. And will never forget. Number ten was Stiffy, the big Women's Libber. Previously from Te Kuiti; now from Auckland. I glanced down at the judging panel for confirmation. Mal was smiling from ear to ear. Wally was smiling from ear to ear. Bruce was not smiling from ear to ear. I leant down to them and asked quietly, 'Are you guys fucking serious? What was the vote?'

'Two to one, Whacker. I said you wouldn't like it,' replied Bruce.

'She's gorgeous. Reminds me of Bets. Don't like them skinny tarts,' said Mal.

'Right on,' said Wally. 'They've got to have a bit of meat on 'em.'

I stood up and announced, 'Ladies and gentlemen. The judges have confirmed that Miss Fresh Fish is Stiffy, previously from Te Kuiti; now from Auckland.'

I went over to Stiffy. The crowd were beginning to realise it wasn't a joke. Stiffy had won. They started to boo, heckle and abuse her. The other contestants couldn't believe it. They looked stunned. Then, before I could even present the sash and the crown, also made by Cyril, they stormed off. Only the four women's libbers and the transvestite remained on the catwalk for the crowning of Miss Fresh Fish.

Stiffy herself looked in a state of shock. She hadn't expected to win and take all the glory that goes with winning such a prestigious event. She stood there, her large

158

bikini-clad body quivering. Gallantly I somehow managed to get the sash over her head, then, as Brian in his DJ capacity, raised the drumroll so it could be heard over the not at all happy patrons, I proceed to place the crown on the head of Miss Fresh Fish and hand her the cheque.

Cameras were popping left, right and centre as the moment was captured for posterity. A cameraman came up on the stage for a close-up. He came a bit too close to Stiffy, who let fly and bonged him one. He went flying one way, the camera another way. Miss Fresh Fish then proceeded to give the fingers to the entire jeering crowd and her three sisters did the same. She stormed off the stage, with the others following and made it to the changing room. There, she faced another riot from the other participants who were all getting changed as quickly as they could to get out of the madhouse.

Pete Morosey climbed on to the catwalk, checking to see if the camera, rather than the cameraman, was OK. 'Brilliant, Whacker, brilliant. Just wish we had a second camera going to catch that old dyke whacking Mike one!' Mike had got up by this stage and seemed to be all right.

I pleaded with the patrons to calm down. After a while they did and I thanked them for attending our first beauty contest and looked forward to seeing them at the same event in a year's time. Then, with my archbishop's robes flying, I headed straight for the bar and asked Horse for a double Scotch.

Propping up the bar was Sergeant Koster. 'Whacker McCracker,' he slurred. 'One day, I'm going to fuckin' get you.'

When I got home, Belinda was waiting for me. 'How did it go?' she asked.

'Great success. You should have come,' I lied.

'Who won?'

'An interesting young lady previously from Te Kuiti; now from Auckland.'

'And the judges. No problems there?'

'Not really. We did make a couple of changes.'

'Really? Who ended up judging your pageant of beauty?'

'Er, Wally, Mal and Bruce.'

'You're not serious. At least, I hope you're not.'

Belinda caught the pageant coverage on the news. We had our second domestic. I tried to avoid showing her the Sunday paper, but it's hard to hand the paper to someone with the front page missing. They get a bit suspicious. She eventually saw it. We had our third domestic.

I'm not the type to hold a grudge. But, I have to admit, for the first few days of the New Year Wally and Mal were not exactly my best friends. I took a lot of flak from the patrons, locals, family and friends. To say nothing of the exes. They all phoned, even Number Five.

But, like most things that happened at the café, we moved on and by mid-January, along with the Christmas Eve incident, it was old news. The café was going flat tack.

The fishing boats were out every day. Because of Luigi and his popular pasta, we found that most days there was now almost enough fish to get us through the evening.

Cocky Hancock, the architect, had organised the deck to start in the first week in February, and an Auckland construction company had the contract. We'd have to get a mobile crane and some big steel beams around to the seaward side of the café and needed to get access from the empty section facing the beach below us. I'd made some enquiries about who owned it and found out it was the same bloke who owned the property next door. He wasn't in residence over the peak holiday period, but later in the month I saw some life in the bach. I went down and knocked, and a guy of about thirty opened the door. 'Hi. I'm Whacker McCracker from the café above you.'

'Hallo. Good to meet you. I've heard a fair bit about you and your café over the last month or two. I'm Terry Downing.'

He was indeed the owner, so I explained the purpose of my visit. 'Any chance of renting your empty section for a few weeks so we can have access to build the deck?'

'Don't see any problem with that. You don't want to rent it for longer do you? And this bach? I'm going to be in Oxford for most of the year doing a post-graduate course, so I won't be coming out here for a while. It's been in the family for a million years, so I don't want to sell, just rent it. Interested?'

'I'd be a mug if I said I wasn't. We could whack a staircase down from the café so my patrons could come down for a swim between courses.'

'What about the bach? Interested in that too?'

'Well, I guess that depends on how much you want. I'm

161

renting at the moment, near Palm Beach. Probably paying a lot less than you want for this place. Got a price in mind?'

'If you signed a year's lease and promised to look after the house — it's fully furnished, and the section, how about four hundred a week?'

I could see opportunity written all over this place. The empty section could be further utilised in some way, the patrons would love the beach access, and the bach, although basically an old dunger, had location, location, location. I could live in it quite nicely.

'Terry, it's a deal, though I'd like a longer lease on the section. Come up to the café and I'll shout you lunch and we can go over a few things.'

By the end of the month, I'd moved into a waterfront bach on Oneroa Beach and had a three-year lease on the house and the section. Mal and Wally gave me a hand to clean up the section, and with the lawn nicely mown, you could practically play bowls on it. Terry told me years ago it'd been a tennis court, and there was still a big old hedge totally hiding it from the next-door neighbour, who lived in Hong Kong.

Harry changed the plans to incorporate a staircase so we had access to the beach via the section, and on the second day of February, construction of the deck started.

When the local secondary school opened after the holiday break, there was a minor problem with some of the kids. After school, the café was the in place to come to for a Coke or a coffee. Nothing wrong with that, but the little monkeys would stay for hours. I read somewhere that you get rid of them by playing Frank Sinatra. So we did. They loved Frank. We tried Bing Crosby. They loved Bing. Classical. Loved it. A friend of mine, two years previously, had purchased a Thai bride by mail order. Part of her dowry was a vast collection of Buddhist chants. When he returned her to Bangkok after the novelty wore off, he was stuck with all of these CDs. Generously, he sent them out with his Christmas cards to friends with a sense of humour. An hour of Buddhist chanting is pretty hard to take. We tried it when the kids arrived and played it continuously for a week. It worked. They stopped lingering.

For some reason the thought of a farting championship had always appealed to my sense of humour. I thought it would appeal to others too, and be a great promotion to open the new deck in March. When I first mentioned it to the originals there was general agreement that it would be a unique event. Fearing there could be problems, I phoned my legal man. 'Bit of advice Brad. We're planning a new competition.'

'Not another beauty pageant I hope — you couldn't possibly upstage the last one. Jesus, that winner was beautiful!'

'No, it's a different kind of competition.'

'What kind of competition, my great impresario?'

'Well actually Brad, feel free to enter. It's a farting competition.'

'A what?'

'A farting competition. A world championship!'

Brad roared with laughter. 'You're not serious are you?'

'Of course I am. It could be a bit of fun.'

'But why a farting competition?'

'Publicity, Brad. We've got a big new deck to tell the world about. Plus, it appeals to me.'

'When are you planning this momentous event?'

'First Sunday in March. In the afternoon. So the contestants can all go to church in the morning.'

'Well, I just hope nobody chunders all over them!'

'That won't happen again. Are there any legal problems with running a competition of this nature? Is it against the law or anything?'

'Farting in your café is not against the law. And, as Wally knows, nor is farting in church. You shouldn't have a problem. Just make sure they keep their clothes on. Don't have them exposing a bare bum to the audience. If that cop friend of yours is there, he might take offence and try and charge the contestant with indecent exposure. You probably should go and see him and tell him what you're up to. He'll find out sooner or later.'

'Thanks, Brad. Can I put you down for two tickets?'

'Please do, I wouldn't miss it for anything. Barbara will love it. Give her something to talk about for weeks at the tennis club.'

I had my legal clearance. Just one more hurdle to get over and done with . . . to hopefully gain the support of Sergeant Koster. I knew he'd tell the others in the station and they'd not be able to resist passing it on. To start people talking, you can't do better than to start the story from the local cop shop.

I phoned Jack and made a time to visit the station. When I got there, the bugger kept me waiting for twenty minutes. I'd expected that and brought the paper. Finally he came out of his office and called me in. 'You've been keeping a very low profile over the last few weeks. In fact, there was a rumour going round that you'd become a Buddhist. Chanting has been heard coming from your fish and chip shop.'

'Mashed spud, Jack, not chips. Please get the facts right.'

'OK Whacker, what do you want?' Jack asked, sounding more like himself.

'I'm planning a new promotion. A competition, in fact, a world championship.'

'And you want me to be a judge again? Last time it was with a hooker and the biggest no-hoper on the island. Who've you got planned this time? A mass murderer and a serial rapist?'

'Nice of you to volunteer, Jack.'

'Like hell, I wouldn't judge a colouring competition if you had anything to do with it.'

'Always nice to know you have such confidence in me. Wally, Mal and Bruce handled the beauty contest beautifully after you let me down.'

'Ha! You nearly had a riot on your hands when that big dyke sheila won. Two of the constables had to put her in the squad car and take her to the ferry for her own safety.'

'That's all in the past, Jack.'

'Nothing is in the past with you, mate. You're collecting the biggest file on the island. What kind of world championship have you got in mind? Tennis? Golf? Fishing?'

'Farting.'

'Farting?'

'Sergeant Koster, I'm delighted to tell you the Whacker McCracker Café is the proud sponsor of a world championship farting competition.'

'You have *got* to be joking.'

'I'm not joking. I'm telling. It's going to be a beauty.'

'Now listen to me McCracker — there is absolutely no way you can run a competition of this nature on Waiheke Island.'

'Jack, you're sounding more like Fidel Castro every day. Since when did Waiheke become a dictatorship?'

'It used to be a peaceful place until you arrived. In six months you've done more to disrupt this island than anyone who's lived here for years.'

'I've also helped to bring a lot of money onto the island, Jack. Everyone benefits. Besides, it needed waking up a bit. I love it here, especially in the new bach down by the beach. Call in for a beer sometime when you're out chasing burglars.'

'I'll get you one day, mate. I'll get you.'

'Jack, it's going to happen. I've already checked it with my legal man. There's no law against it. We live in a free country.'

Jack was starting to realise I was serious. 'Mate, you're not fair dinkum about this are you? A farting competition isn't the right image for the island.'

'What *is* the right image for the island? It's only going to last a couple of hours. It'll be great fun and quite legal. I just thought it was a courtesy to come and tell you first, before you start hearing rumours.'

'So that was the only reason for this illustrious visit?

'Well actually no. I'd like to formally invite you to be

the first official competitor. Representing Waiheke Island. And of course, Her Majesty's Finest.'

'Piss off out of here, McCracker.'

'I take that as a no then?'

'Piss off.'

Jack showed me to the door. As I was leaving he called out, 'What about Wally? After nearly blowing the church apart, perhaps he'd be the one to represent the island.'

'Thanks Jack. Good thinking. I'll ask him. Cheers.'

I felt that calling the event a farting competition didn't have enough class. Remembering back to my awful history lessons at school, for some reason King John signing the *Magna Carta* at Runnymede in 1215 gave me an idea. We could adapt the name to *Magna Farta*. Much classier. An executive decision was made. The competition would be known as *The Magna Farta*.

Sam did a great sign for the window announcing another momentous event at the café at three o'clock on the first Sunday in March.

The Magna Farta, a World Championship Farting event

First prize $1,000!

Second prize $750!

Third prize $500!

Entry forms in the café or on the café's website.

A poster was prepared along the same lines. This was sent to the media and backpackers' lodges on the island and in Auckland.

I wanted this event to be a little better organised than the beauty contest, so a farting committee was formed. It was a combination of Bruce, Brian, two students Stef and Willie plus myself. The students were determined to make it the greatest farting event in the world.

The island was soon buzzing about our event. The media was soon buzzing about our event. Auckland was soon buzzing about our event. Due to the new deck, we had another thirty seats, so we now had one hundred and forty tickets, and they were all pre-sold the day we released them. We were charging thirty dollars per person, with the proceeds going to the Waiheke Community Art Gallery.

Two weeks before the big event, we had another meeting of the farting committee. To get the meeting going, Willie asked if I'd organised the judges. 'Yes. All arranged. We'll have Monsignor Cyril, Archdeacon Johnny and Cardinal Luigi. Cyril and Johnny thought it would be a great laugh when I asked them and Luigi was thrilled at the thought of being a cardinal. But we've got to get them well rehearsed to avoid any stuff-ups.'

'That will be arranged,' Stef advised.

'Now, contestants. There are always stacks of good healthy farting backpackers coming over from the city. We could offer them a free return trip, accommodation, a party that night, then a dirty great feed of baked beans and cabbage for lunch. Student Job Search could be a good source as well. Any student with a few brains who can put on an accent can enter as anyone from anywhere.'

'We'll get onto that, Whacker,' said Stef.

'I think it would be OK if the contestants cheated a bit and used a few props,' I told them.

'What kind of props? A hooter or a fog horn?' asked Brian.

'A couple of years ago I was in a joke shop in San Francisco and came across this remote-controlled farting machine.' With that I brought out a battery-operated remote-controlled farting machine that'd caused a lot of laughs in the ad agency. 'Listen to this.' I pushed the bulb and 'played' the first few bars of 'Baa Baa Black Sheep' out of the small speaker in fart noises. Brian, Bruce, Stef and Willie laughed themselves silly.

'We have six of these coming by DHL from Miami, where my daughter lives. I phoned her a couple of nights ago, and yesterday she phoned back to say she'd tracked them down at the local joke shop.'

'The farting meter isn't ready yet,' advised Bruce. 'Ed, the engineering student who helps Horse in the bar reckons he's nearly there, and Mal's finished the farting post.'

'We're having trouble getting gas masks for people in the front row. Looks like we'll have to use fans,' Stef reported.

'Good thinking! But keep trying the army-surplus stores, real gas masks could be fun, even if we only get a couple. It would look great on television. Something else too . . . because it's The Magna Farta, and out of respect for King John's *Magna Carta*, I think we should commence the event by having somebody fart "God Save the King". Listen to this.'

I then played a minute of the anthem on the farting machine. The committee went into hysterics. 'We can sew the speaker into someone's pants. They can come out, bow, bend over in front of the microphone lowered to the right height and with bum facing the audience, play the anthem to open the event.'

'The patrons will stand up for it, won't they?' inquired Brian.

'Of course. They must show respect for the throne of England. The calibre attending our Magna Farta will be top shelf, with one or two exceptions. Like four of my ex-wives. They missed out on the Miss Fresh Fish extravaganza, but have insisted on coming this time. I tried to get them to enter, but no such luck. It's a pity, Number One's a great farter.'

For the next two weeks Stef and Willie worked their butts off. We had several in-depth meetings and even conducted our own farting competition with the farting machines when they arrived. There were more logistical problems than with the beauty contest and the nearly-nude race, and I was beginning to understand why there weren't too many farting competitions.

I had homework to do. A lot of homework. As the MC, I was the person who would have to describe the blow-by-blow events. The local library didn't have too many books about farting, nor did the island's bookshops. Creativeness was required. I had to do some thinking. Belinda was a good judge of some of the descriptions I came up with — you need a good sounding board when you're trying to name farts. She was great.

'Fellow fartologists,' I announced to the patrons. 'Welcome to our earth-shattering World Championship Farting Competition, The Magna Farta, proudly sponsored by the very café in which you are now sitting, with a wonderful new deck and stairs to the beach.' The crowd showed their appreciation.

'All this week we've been holding elimination bouts to bring you the very finest of the world's farters,' I lied. 'Fabulous farters who will bring credit to their country. Today they are farting for a first prize of one thousand dollars, plus this magnificent Magna Farta Cup.' I held up an old trophy Bruce and Brian had found in a Ponsonby junk shop. Cleaned up and freshly engraved, it looked magnificent.

'Second prize is a massive seven hundred and fifty dollars and third prize is five hundred dollars. The order of farting today is in the programme I hope you have all acquired. I would like to remind patrons you are here at your own risk. If anyone is allergic to strong smells, earth-shattering noises or may have any other problems caused by rumbles from the bowel, I would ask you to move to the rear of the café immediately. I would also like to point out that we have a nurse in attendance to cater for any emergencies.' Nobody moved.

'Judging for today's event is being conducted by three highly respected members of our religious community. First, I would like to introduce Monsignor Cyril from Surfdale.' Cyril stood up and was widely acknowledged.

'Our second judge, also from Surfdale, is Archdeacon Johnny.' He stood up to much clapping. 'Our third judge has flown all the way from Italy to be with us today. Please give a great island welcome to Cardinal Luigi of Rome.' Luigi got a standing ovation and stood there smiling from ear to ear.

'The official farting-meter controller, and the creator of this marvellous machine, is Rabbi Ed of Takapuna. The coordinator of the farting post, and builder, I should add, is Bishop Mal of Orapiu.' These two were duly acknowledged.

There was a pause. I caught Brian's eye, and started to play the drumroll. 'Because today's event is The Magna Farta, closely aligned to King John and his *Magna Carta*, we have chosen as the opening anthem, "God Save the King". Our United Kingdom representative, the very beautiful Sarah, will play this for you. Would you all now please stand.'

Gorgeous, slim Sarah bounced onto the stage to rapturous applause. The patrons stood, Sarah turned her back to the audience, bent over so her bum was right in front of the microphone, and, with the help of one of the farting machine, produced 'God Save the King' from her backside. The patrons went ballistic and screamed for an encore. Sarah, with the most amazing range of vowels in her bowel, had just created musical history. How many times do people scream for an encore of a national anthem? They screamed out for more. What a dynamic opening for The Magna Farta. I was so proud of Sarah and her musical backside.

'Fartologists, it is with great pleasure I announce the first event in this momentous competition . . . the Waiheke

Island High Density Fart. Our first competitor, and representing Waiheke Island, is our very own Bishop Wally of Oneroa.'

Wally came out, in his bishop gear; fairly inebriated I should add, as were a couple of the other competitors. A necessary antidote for stage fright — and to get them to damn well participate! I should also add that we were making pretty good use of props for the competitors. Not just the farting machines, but farting cushions, bulbs and other ingenious devices the students and participants had created. He bent down to the international regulation forty-five-degree position, clutched the farting post and let fly. On purpose we'd planned to make the first one loud to really get the event under way. Willie had given him the right prop to do the job — he just about blew the windows out.

The sight of a fifteen-stone bishop leaning over and delivering probably the loudest fart ever heard on Waiheke Island was too much for the patrons. They were simply hysterical. In fact, one woman was gulping for air and our nurse rushed over to see if she was all right.

Rabbi Ed had the very important job of controlling the farting meter. It looked like one of those vertical poles you see at fairgrounds, where you hit the base with a sledgehammer to see how high you can get the pointer. Controlled by a foot-operated bulb, he had to decide instantly how hard to press it and decide if it was worthy of a ten, an eight, a seven, five or whatever.

Wally's magnificent fart got a ten. And when a ten was reached the alarm went off at the top of the pole. Noisy! Spectacular! It took a while to calm everyone down. Looking at my watch, I could see we'd all be there until midnight if we didn't start moving. We had patrons booked for dinner, so we couldn't have that.

The next contestant was a backpacker from Finland. He tried to do the real McCoy, but was a dismal failure. Seizure of the bowel, I believe it's called in the profession, also known as rectum fright. Not even a beep after much straining and effort. But he was generously awarded a three for effort.

Our third contestant, Trev, was an Australian. A solid construction worker, who lived in Onehunga. He cheated magnificently and let go a forty-seconder. It went on and on and on. The crowd went into raptures. Music to their ears! A well-deserved ten was given.

Asia was represented by a student from Malaysia. Thin and small, but with a big grin, he made a moderate effort that could be heard by those at the back of the café, but not by those across the street. A seven was awarded.

And so it went on. A total of fifteen competitors from around the world, with Wally and Trev the only two to score a ten in the Waiheke Island High Density Fart.

The second event we introduced to our competition was The Sound of Music Fart. The competitors could use their musical imagination here, with a time limit of thirty seconds.

Robin, a colourful individual from Los Angeles, but now living in Piha, played a magnificent rendition of 'Yankee Doodle Dandy'. The rabbi gave him an eight.

Sarah was next. Although she was really a third genera-tion Kiwi flatting in Mt Eden, we'd made her an honorary Pom for the event. So, representing the United Kingdom, she selected, from *My Fair Lady*, 'The Rain in Spain Stays

Mainly on the Plain'. It was brilliant. The patrons just loved it. Henry Higgins would have too. She got a nine.

Dave, a solid Kiwi from Student Job Search, had become a Russian for the event and given the name Vlad. He came out, grabbed the post and treated the patrons to a rendition of the finale of 'The 1812 Overture'. Tchaikovsky would have been so proud of him. He had the farting machine turned up to its highest level and when the cannons let fly, stunning stuff! Vlad got a standing ovation, and the patrons shrieked for an encore. He was awarded a ten. The only person in this segment to achieve that magnificent score, I should add.

Wally let the island down a bit in this segment. He'd chosen Tina Turner's wonderful song, 'Simply the Best'. Unfortunately he played it too slowly and was a little flat. But he still got a seven. I could tell it was the booze. He was very grateful for the farting post to hang on to. Mal gave him some comforting words.

One other outstanding contestant in this category was Paddy, from Ireland. He chose 'Danny Boy'. He lost it at the end though when the machine got stuck on one note and he couldn't change it quickly enough. He was on his way for a ten, but because of that, ended with an eight. Paddy got a wonderful ovation. The rest of the contestants went through their musical contributions, but it was Vlad and Sarah's segment with a ten and a nine.

We had one other serious problem on our hands. Time. It was taking about seven minutes for each contestant — mainly due to the clapping and laughter and the time it took to settle the patrons down. We had thought it would only be a couple of minutes each. It was now after five o'clock and we had to have it wrapped up by six at the absolute latest. At the rate we were going, this wasn't going to happen. There had to be some instant decision-making. I announced that due to time constraints, we'd go straight into the finals, with five finalists selected from the first two segments. This meant we had to abandon The King John's Fart, The Rotorua Fart and The Fart of Love, The Amazing Kamikaze Fart and The Prime Minister's Fart.

The three reverent judges handed me the list of the five finalists. 'Fart fans! The first finalist, representing Australia, is Trev.' He joined me, grinning from ear to ear and the crowd showed their appreciation.

'The second finalist, representing France, is Pierre.' Pierre, the quiet but consistent French Farter (really a panel-beater from Half Moon Bay), who scored two eights, moved forward, wearing his beret. He had extra padding in the rear of his pants to show a considerable, and powerful, rear end. Very creative.

'The third finalist, from the United Kingdom, is Sarah.' She was the crowd favourite and the patrons gave here a standing ovation.

'The fourth finalist, from the United States of America, is Robin!' Robin joined the other finalists, waving an American flag and looking so proud to be representing his country.

'Farting enthusiasts, the final finalist in The Magna Farta is . . . ' I paused, looked around theatrically, and the announced: 'Representing New Zealand, and one of our very own, Waiheke Island's Bishop Wally of Oneroa!'

The crowd loved our Wally, especially after that ear-shattering opening achievement, and did they show their appreciation. They cheered, stamped their feet and clapped. But there was a problem. Wally couldn't get up. Mal rushed over to help him up, but to no avail. He was past it, boozed beyond participation.

'Fart lovers, I regret to announce Wally is all blown out, so we'll proceed with four finalists. The four contestants will playing the national anthem of their respective countries. Time limit of one minute. Please pay respect to each country, by standing during the presentation. To get the ball rolling, let us welcome the United States of America's official entrant, Robin.'

Robin clutched the farting post and thrilled patrons of his rendition of 'The Star Spangled Banner'. It was so stirring, I swear I saw tears in the eyes of some of the patrons as they sat down.

Next, Trev from Australia treated us all to an excellent performance of 'Advance Australia Fair'. It was a pleasure to see the reception our neighbour from across the ditch received.

Pierre farted 'The Marseillaise' to bestow almighty credit on his beloved France. If ever there was an anthem created for farting, this must be it. What a beauty! The laughter was continuous and it took a good five minutes to calm everyone down for the final number.

'Please welcome Sarah, representing the United Kingdom, our final contestant for the night, playing 'God Save the Queen'. She performed magnificently and the standing ovation went on and on. It was after six by now, and I had to get the contest wrapped up. I pleaded for quiet and went across to the judges to get the results. They were unanimous.

'Connoisseurs of the art of farting; in third place, representing the United States of America, Robin.' I paused while Robin came forward, to receive his certificate and cheque.

'In second place, representing France, Pierre the magnificent French Farter!' The crowd gave him a wonderful reception, and I had an effort to get them to stop, so I could announce the winner.

'Fellow fart lovers, it gives me great pleasure to announce the winner of the Whacker McCracker's Café's Magna Farta — all the way from the United Kingdom — Sarah!'

Pandemonium struck the café! The patrons clapped, cheered, screamed and carried on as they do at any final of any world championship. Sarah was a very popular winner. I gave her the cheque and presented her with The Magna Farta Cup. She was so happy and looked so pretty, the media loved her. Because let's face it, Sarah wasn't exactly the contestant they'd have picked to win.

The patrons started moving out fairly quickly, as a lot of them had to catch the next ferry. I made my way over to the bar where Horse had the coldest beer on the island waiting. The health inspector joined me. 'Happy with the way it went?' she asked.

'We really cocked up the time factor. Big mistake. But, all things considering, I think it went off OK. Pity Wally flaked, especially when he made it into the finals.'

Pete Morosey came over. 'Brilliant show, Whacker. How did you jack it up so the pretty babe won?'

'It was the judges' decision. A good one too, I should add.'

'Brilliant. What else is in the pipeline, Whacker?'

'Something to get people here over the winter months. A little miniature-golf course on the empty section below the café. You'll enjoy it, Pete.'

The bar rapidly filled up with participants, organisers and patrons. Sarah, studying law at Auckland University, was just a wee bit embarrassed about the win. Her parents were both rather conservative accountants and she hadn't actually told them why she'd come over to Waiheke.

They would soon find out. Later in the week *Truth* had her on the front page, in the standard forty-five degree position, clutching the post, under the headline *St Cuth's Old Girl blows her way to glory!*

The publicity achieved by The Magna Farta was great for business. We had a television set in the bar and over the following weeks every second patron wanted to see the video. It made everyone laugh, and when you have laughter in your café, you have happy people who relax, enjoy themselves, and spend a little more than they intended. Business was good.

We added the farting post to the décor in the bar and the patrons loved having their photo taken with it. A sign was put up giving instructions on how to assume the official forty-five-degree pose.

A video was edited of the event and again we shoved twenty-five dollars on it. It sold like crazy. One of the ingenious students working for us started making little model farting posts, and we sold these too.

Several other items had been added to the merchandising items we now sold over the bar. Three different T-shirts, four 'funny' certificates, and a book of *Whacker's Thoughts*, which we printed on the island. We looked into food — baked beans was an obvious one. However, there wasn't going to be enough volume to do it profitably. A cookbook, featuring our wonderful cuisine, was also talked about, but nobody seemed very interested in writing it.

30

With winter coming up, I was very aware we would be facing what the island businesspeople called 'The Hundred Days of Hell'. Winter. With that in mind, since acquiring the lease of the section below, I'd been planning a nine-hole miniature-golf course. The idea was for patrons to come over from Auckland, enjoy a game of golf, have a drink or two and a very pleasant meal. I wanted to have it ready for Easter, but it wasn't going to be just any old mini-golf course.

Waiheke is blessed with a number of very creative people, and Gordy Rugg was one of them. I first met Gordy at one of the exhibitions the arty mob held over the holiday period. He specialised in larger sculptures so I phoned him and asked him to call by the café and discuss a business idea I had in mind. A few days later he did.

'Gordy, see that block of land down there?' We were sitting on the nearly completed deck and I pointed to the empty section. 'I've got an idea that could make you famous. On Waiheke.'

'What are you after, Whacker? A couple of sculptures to beautify the site?'

'Something along those lines. I have in mind an adult nine-hole miniature-golf course. Naked life-sized concrete people my customers could fire golf balls into.'

Gordy nearly wet himself. He cottoned on immediately what I had in mind. 'You mean a porn golf course?'

'No, no, no, Gordy. Nothing pornographic. This would

be art. Very beautiful sculptures of the naked body golfers would really appreciate.'

'What you're saying Whacker, is you'd have a sculpture of a girl lying down and you'd fire the golf ball into a hole between her legs — or in her mouth. That kind of thing?'

'Could be her bellybutton, Gordy. Yes, you've got it in one. That's exactly what we should do. But it mustn't be grubby — they need to be very classy sculptures.'

'Bloody brilliant!'

'Are you interested then?'

'Am I what, mate. It's right up my alley. Reckon I could create the most unique adult golf course in the South Pacific.'

The commission was finalised and Gordy agreed to work on the project in top secret. As I had some ideas in mind, he agreed we'd work on the nine concepts together, with Easter Saturday to be the opening day.

I got to know Gordy well over the final weeks of summer, spending hours in his shed as we worked together on what we called Project Hole. I'm no artist but it's amazing what can be done with basic stick drawings. Gordy was a clever artisan and after extensive brainstorming converted the ideas into life drawings and then sculptures. I also made available to him photos of various women I felt would look great immortalised in concrete.

The final nine sculptures were decided on. Hole number one was very simple, the classic woman lying with her legs open, with the golf ball fired between her legs. The second hole to fifth holes were variations on this theme. The sixth hole was of a man, with the ball shooting up and into a hole in his rear. The seventh was a woman, with her head on the ground and the ball fired into her mouth.

Hole number eight was another gent with the ball entering his rather large appendage. The final sculpture, my
favourite, was the vase. A beautiful sculpture of a young
lady lying on her back with her open legs up in the air.
One had to chip the ball into the hole in the appropriate
place. (We called it the vase because one day when I arrived
at his shed, Gordy had cut some flowers and was using
this particular sculpture as a vase.)

Easter weekend was going to be a big one. Not only
were we to have the opening of the golf course, but the
Waiheke Island Jazz Festival was on and the café was hosting bands every day, so there'd be heaps of people over
from Auckland. I wanted as many of them as possible to
see the new venture, because hopefully they'd come back
over the winter with a friend or two, to participate in a bit
of adult golf.

The week before the holiday weekend, Mal, Wally and
myself got the tees finalised on the section below, mowed
the lawn and got everything sorted out for the arrival of
the sculptures. The section was also fully fenced by yet
another friend of Mal's. I went across to the big smoke and
got a stack of second-hand putters and a pile of old golf
balls. We got some scorecards printed up and managed to
find cartons of half-sized pencils at the local stationery
shop that had been there for decades.

As the golf course wasn't a commercial venture, we
weren't breaking any bylaws and didn't need a permit or
the dreaded resource consent. It was for the friends of the
café to play on, at no cost. (Brad, who checked it out, told
me to emphasise this to any official dorks who might come
and try to play silly buggers. He also told us to make sure
the sculptures weren't permanent — that they could be

removed.) Although it was no secret that we were installing a mini-golf course, nobody but Gordy, Brad and myself actually knew what it was to consist of. And, surprisingly, nobody else on Waiheke found out until it opened. I hadn't even told Belinda. I wasn't quite sure how she'd take it and thought she might try and talk me out of it. I decided to give her a wonderful surprise.

At midday on Good Friday, the first truckload of five of the well-wrapped sculptures left Gordy's shed on the back of Ben Broccil's truck. Ben and his brother Phil, who was helping him, were sworn to secrecy. We hired tents to pitch over each of the 'art items' so nobody would see them until opening. Wally and Mal in particular were banned from the scene. With their inability to keep a secret, they were the last people I wanted there!

The four of us spent the afternoon getting them into position, with some very pleasant background music from the jazz bands playing in the café above. Saturday was an early start to get the other four holes finished. Official opening was scheduled for two o'clock, so we were under pressure. The good news was that by noon it all came together beautifully. An hour before the official opening, the sculptures were draped in some red material Cyril had lent me, and the tents taken down.

The actual official opening ceremony had been in planning stages over the previous couple of weeks. Invitations had gone out to the media and some close friends. The fisherfolk were to attend in their costumes, and a pro-am tournament was planned after the opening. Fisherfolk as the pros; media as the ams.

Miriam Webber had very kindly consented to open the

183

golf course. She told me she'd played golf for many years and was a great fan of the game.

By one o'clock I was back to the café getting into my Archbishop of Waiheke gear. It was a happy café, with a wonderful New York-based band playing jazz. The fisherfolk in their religious gear were starting to congregate in the bar and the media, invited friends and Miriam Webber were enjoying a lovely fish lunch. I joined them for a quick bite.

Two o'clock approached and off we all trekked, down the beautiful new staircase to the golf course where Gordy, Ben and Phil were waiting. We'd sent down a nice lunch for them and a couple of bottles of wine. The nine sculptures remained covered. Above us on the café deck, the patrons congregated to watch proceedings. Some of them couldn't get a good view, so they walked down the stairs. People everywhere were waiting in anticipation to see the new venture. The fisherfolk positioned themselves around the covered sculptures. They'd been advised that when given the nod from me the covers were to be removed.

'Religious leaders, Miss Miriam Webber, other honoured guests, ladies and gentlemen. Welcome to the opening of Waiheke Island's newest tourist attraction, our nine-hole miniature-golf course. Over the winter months, I'm sure this course will give the customers of our café untold pleasure.' I paused. 'These simply wonderful sculptures have been handcrafted by a Waiheke Islander, Gordon Rugg, who is here with us today. Gordy, I know these sculptures will bring you fame and fortune.' The crowd showed Gordy their appreciation.

'The official opening will be carried out by an old friend of the café's, Miss Miriam Webber. Following that, we will have a golf tournament with invited guests and members of the media matched with one of our wonderful religious leaders for a round of golf. The winning team will be awarded this magnificent silver cup, which will be played for monthly and be retained in the café.' I held the cup aloft. More clapping and cheering.

'Ladies and Gentlemen, I would now like to ask Miss Miriam Webber to move to the first hole and pour a bottle of champagne over the sculpture. As she is doing this our religious leaders will remove the remaining covers and you'll see for yourself what a magnificent golf course Gordy has created.'

I walked over to the first hole with Miriam, to where a bottle of champagne on ice was waiting. I offered to open it for her, thinking she might be a little past opening champagne bottles. 'No way Whacker! I love opening these things,' she said. With a whoosh, the cork flew out and she poured the champagne over the cover. 'I hereby open Whacker McCracker's Café's golf course!'

I gave the nod. The covers were pulled back. Nine very naked life-sized concrete human beings in various sexual positions were unveiled.

The cheering, ranting and raving started on the café deck and worked its way down to the golf course. It became pandemonium. All around me, everyone was gaping, laughing, cheering, gasping — and utterly flabbergasted.

Except the person beside me. Miriam Webber. She had a look of horror on her face. Belinda was nearby, so she came across and gave her a cuddle and said she'd take her back to the café for a cup of tea.

'I don't know if I'm very proud of you over this one, Whacker,' she said, as she lead Miriam away.

The pandemonium continued.

'Nice one,' commented Mal. 'That'll cause a bit of a stir.'

'Thanks for including a couple of boys,' said Brian. 'I'll be playing hole number eight over and over again.'

By now, practically everyone had come down to take a closer look. It was crowded and there was no way we'd be able to get the pro-am tournament under way for quite some time.

The media were requesting shots of some of our religious leaders playing some of the holes so we handed out some putters and balls to Rabbi Esky Bill, Mother Superior Tina, Cardinal Heke and Bishop Wally.

It doesn't take long for word to spread on Waiheke. I purposely hadn't invited a representative from Her Majesty's Finest to attend the official opening, but within twenty minutes we were gatecrashed by two officers in blue. Constable Lucy and Sergeant Jack.

They came down the stairs from the café on the run, as if they were chasing a gang of multiple rapists. The sergeant stopped and cast his well-trained eyes on sights he possibly hadn't enjoyed for a while. The crowd was quieter now, waiting for his reaction. There wasn't any. He seemed to be stunned.

I decided to break the ice. 'Afternoon, Sergeant Koster. Can't remember seeing your name on the invitation list.'

'McCracker. I don't believe what I'm seeing,' muttered Jack, seething with anger.

'Well Jack, seeing you're here, do you want to challenge The Bishop of Oneroa to a round? Hey Wally,' I called out. 'Come over here, mate. I think our friend wants to give you a game.'

'You're in deep shit this time,' Jack replied slowly. 'You're going inside. This is pornographic.'

'Get real, Jack. God Almighty, in 1644 Michalangelo sculpted David and shoved him on the main street of Florence. All over the world you'll find statues of naked people. All we've done is bring fine art to Waiheke — hundreds of years after Mike did it in Florence.'

'This is different, it's filth. Perversion. Disgusting. Cover them up. Immediately.'

'C'mon, Jack, don't be so bloody stupid. You're making a fool of yourself in front of the world's media.'

'Cover them up immediately.'

'On what grounds, Jack? Give me a legal reason why I should have to cover a naked sculpture? And you'd better make it good, because art lovers around the world — and lovers of the human body, will be very interested to hear it.'

'It's pornography. Straight pornography. Constable Simmonds, cover up these pieces of filth.'

That proved to be impossible, as the covers had been quickly whisked away by Gordy, Ben and Phil. The crowd roared their disapproval and the media was in its element.

'We need covers! Nine tableclothes from your fish and chip shop. My constable needs them now.'

'Tableclothes cost thirty-five dollars each. Tell you what I'll do, I'll let you have nine for three hundred dollars. Cash.'

'I'm taking you to the station, Mr McCracker.'

'Are you arresting me, Sergeant Koster? If so, for what offence?'

'I'm taking you into the station for further questioning.'

'Question me here.'

'You can't take him away, Sergeant,' called a voice from the crowd. 'I'm a lawyer and unless he agrees to go, you can't make him. Besides, on what grounds? This isn't porn. You're making a real dick of yourself, mate.'

The crowd agreed wholeheartedly.

Sergeant Koster was not a happy copper. 'Mr McCracker, will you agree to accompany me to the station for further questioning?'

'Nice of you to ask Sergeant, but the answer is no. And Jack, do you really think I'd be stupid enough to go ahead with this without getting legal advice? It's all quite legal, so I'm sorry mate, you haven't got a leg to stand on.'

'You're a bloody pervert, McCracker! A bloody pervert!'

'Hey, Whacker,' called out the lawyer's voice from the crowd. 'He's slandering you. You could sue him. You've got plenty of witnesses.'

'Thanks mate,' I called back. 'No, deep down he's not a bad cop. I think he just got overexcited at the sight of seven naked concrete women. Or was it the two concrete blokes, Jack?'

Roars of laughter from the crowd.

'I'll get you, McCracker. I'll fuckin' get you,' Sergeant Jack Koster advised me, as he turned away and stormed off up the hill with a very embarrassed Constable Lucy in tow.

The crowds started chanting 'Arsehole, arsehole, arsehole,' as he left. It was music to my ears.

I was concerned about what Belinda had said to me as she departed with Miriam. She hadn't come back so I made my way back to the café to check up on her, but she'd already left to drive Miriam home.

The pro-am was finally starting to get under way, so I made my way back to the golf course. The biggest problem was getting the patrons off the fairways and back up to the café to listen to the jazz. Eventually some of them did, but most stayed, pleading for a game.

Charlie Daily from Radio Pacific was my allocated partner in the draw and we had a very funny round of golf. There were a few teething problems. Some of the holes were harder than we intended and slowed down play because it took too long to play them. The last hole, the vase, was the worst. We had a ramp to help get the ball in but it didn't quite work. A little more island ingenuity was going to be needed to make the island's newest tourist attraction easier.

Cardinal Heke of the Surfdale parish and Jean Witten, a writer with the *New Zealand Woman's Weekly*, were the eventual winners of our first pro-am.

While it was still going on, I phoned Belinda. 'Hi my lovely lady. Where are you?'

'At Miriam's.'

'Why? The party's here. Are you just a wee tiny bit annoyed about something, Belinda?'

'No I am not a wee tiny bit. I am very, very annoyed.'

'What have I done?'

'You used Miriam. You knew damn well she'd freak out at your grubby little golf course. You didn't have to do that to a lovely old lady. You've got heaps of no-hoper friends who could have opened it for you.'

'But Miriam loves golf. That's why I asked her to open it.'

'Bullshit. You really upset her.' She hung up on me. I tried again but only got cellular secretary. I left a message asking her to phone back.

It would seem I had a problem. Excusing myself from

the function, I made my way back to the café, where I quickly changed out of my archbishop's robes. She had the Skoda so I grabbed the keys for the Suzuki. I drove a short distance to the local florist; rushed in, bought a bunch of flowers and proceeded to make my way to Miriam Webber's place.

When I got there, the lime green Skoda was still parked in the driveway. Pausing for a minute or two to consider my plan of action, I decided I'd go to the door, ring the bell, hand over the flowers, apologise in a round-about sort of away, take the drink they would then very kindly offer me and all would be sweet.

Unfortunately, at certain times of my life, for some extraordinary reason, I've discovered that women don't always think the same as I do. This moment happened to be one of them. I walked up the steps, reached the veranda and rang the doorbell. My beloved answered the door. The glare was one of the classic glares only women are capable of. 'Hi gorgeous,' I began. 'Just thought I'd come out and say many thanks to Miriam again for . . . '

'Leave, Whacker. Right now.'

'Belinda, don't be . . . '

'Go. Fast. We don't want you here at this particular moment.'

'But I've bought Miriam some flowers.'

'Take them with you. Goodbye.'

I didn't see Miriam coming along the veranda. With a broom. She let fly, collecting my shoulder. I stumbled and fell over, down eleven steps. I heard the crack as I handed at the bottom and felt a searing pain.

To get to hospital in Auckland from Waiheke Island when you've survived an attempted assassination by a little old lady with a broom, you go by helicopter. By the time the helicopter landed on the paddock next to Miriam's house, I was so well drugged by the local paramedic I could have just about flown there under my own steam.

Within moments of the incident, as I lay in agony at the bottom of the stairs, Belinda, closely followed by Miriam, were no longer the two ladies from hell. They were the kindest of kindest Florence Nightingales. Belinda made me comfortable and held me in her arms. After Miriam had phoned for help, she came back with blankets, pillows — and a million apologies. She placed a gentle hand on the shoulder she'd hit.

I told her the flowers, now scattered all over the place, were for her. I didn't want them wasted. As soon as the paramedics had surveyed the situation, they called in the chopper. The media, still at the café golf course when they heard the news, got there not long before the chopper arrived, so they managed to get some close-ups.

I can't really remember too much more until midday on Sunday when the anaesthetic started to wear off. Belinda was on the chair by my bed when I stirred and started to come back into the world. She was holding my hand.

'Don't say anything, Whacker. You're OK. It's only a broken leg. And I love you.'

I slept on and off for the rest of the day, feeling rather secure.

The hospital kept me imprisoned for five days. The sister in charge of the ward believed I broke the record for the most visitors in that period. Belinda was there most of the visiting hours. Mal, Wally, Bets, Peg, Bruce, Brian, Screwzy Suzy, Cyril and Johnny all came to see me. Miriam Webber too. Along with numerous other friends and acquaintances from the island, plus all my mainland friends and business colleagues. The five exes, yes, even Number Five, couldn't wait to come and see their ex-beloved immobilised. Most of the visitors thought the whole thing a bloody great hoot and there was little sympathy for the poor bastard flat on his back with his leg up in the air.

Heaps of flowers filled the room and there were cards galore, and lots were from café patrons. So when a wreath arrived I wondered who had the warped sense of humour. I should have realised. The card read *Rest in Peace – Jack Koster*. Nice of him to think of me.

The media had a couple of great stories to tell. The opening of the golf course was a pretty good news event, but having the owner of it bowled over by the little old lady who opened it, was a wonderful bonus. 'Whacker Wacked!' headlined the *Sunday News*.

Brian reported that the Easter weekend had been an absolute boomer for the café, except for a shortage of fresh fish for the evening diners. It had all gone during the day. The jazz proved so popular he felt we should make weekend jazz in the café an ongoing event over the winter. As for the golf course, it was a smash hit. The only problem was patrons wanting to be photographed in 'erotic' poses with the concrete sculptures.

'They are keeping their clothes on aren't they, Brian?'
'Most of them.'
'What do you mean most of them?'

'Well, we've had a couple of pissheads getting their gear off and trying to bonk them.'

'Jesus, don't let the bloody law see them doing that!'

'Don't worry, the novelty'll wear off soon. One thing we hadn't realised though is it doesn't run itself. We've had to have someone there all the time to keep an eye on things. That's another cost.'

'Have to work on that one, mate. No further visits from Jack?'

'He came in on Sunday wanting to know if you were still alive, and said it was a pity you hadn't landed on your head.'

'What about the golf course? Did he say anything about it?'

'Only for about a quarter of an hour. Non-stop.'

'Tell you what we'll do when I get back. I'll get Gordy to make a sheep. We can make it a practice hole and the patrons can fire the ball up its bum. Beside it, we'll have a sign dedicating it to Sergeant Jack Koster. What do you reckon?'

'I reckon if you did that he'd make life very, very difficult for us. No, Whacker. Just put it in your great ideas' file.'

'We'll see Bruce. You never know.'

The helicopter doesn't take you back to the island from the hospital. Five days later, Belinda helped me back in a wheelchair to Mr Fuller's ferry. Hugsy, the gangplank-attendant-and-just-about-everything-else on the boat, rushed over to help. 'Great to have you back, Whacker.'

'Thanks, Hugsy. Good to be getting back.'

'Just keep well clear of the old sheilas though, mate.'

'Miriam's all right. She didn't mean to break my leg. Come and have a game of golf sometime. You'll enjoy it.'

'I'll be there for sure. Thanks, Whacker.'

A wheelchair taxi was waiting at the wharf when we arrived at Matiatia and took us to the café for lunch. I'd given strict instructions that there was to be absolutely no fuss when I got back. There wasn't. All of the originals joined me at one of the round tables and we had a very pleasant fish lunch, with some glorious Waiheke red. I was also eternally grateful for the bureaucrat who had made it compulsory for licensed premises to have wheelchair dunnies.

'What's next, Whacker?' asked Mal. 'The golf course is old news now.'

'We've got to make it more playable, me old mate. Some of the holes are just a wee bit too difficult.'

'Bloody right there,' commented Wally. 'That last hole, the vase; no bugger can get into it. Four and eight are the other problem ones.'

'Lucky you shoved in a couple of those concrete blokes, Whacker, ' said Brian. 'We had a group of women's libby types here on Easter Monday and they got quite stroppy about the course. They thought it was all women. However, once I pointed out holes six and eight they calmed down and then thought it was a hoot. They played for ages. Perhaps we could add a couple more male statues — there's room.'

'No, let's keep it like it is for the moment. We'll just work on making it easier. How have the locals reacted? Anyone besides Jack complained?'

'The *Gulf News* came out at lunchtime and it's got three letters condemning it.' Bruce slid a copy of it across to me.

'Three's not bad. Look's like they're the regular moaners. Surprised the paper even published them. Hey, I like the write-up they've given us! Thank God we have some people on the island who want to drag the tourists across from the big smoke. They reckon it'll be a major attraction. I like that.'

Sitting back, with a glass of Waiheke red wine in hand, wonderful friends around me, and a very successful café, I was feeling pretty good. It wasn't to last.

'Hello, what have we here? A chimpanzees' tea party with a white-legged ape in a wheelchair the guest of honour?'

Sergeant Jack Koster had arrived.

'No, the ape's still standing,' I quickly replied.

Everyone laughed. Even Jack. 'Guess I asked for that. How are you feeling Whacker?'

'Much better until you arrived.'

'The island's been a better place with you tied to a hospital bed for the past five days. It's a great pity they couldn't have kept you there.'

'Thanks, Jack. Would you like a wine?'

'I'm on duty.'

'Oh yeah, it's Thursday. Burglars Galore Day on Waiheke. I forgot. Thanks for the wreath. Very nice of you to remember me.'

'I laughed myself silly when I heard the news. You deserved it.'

'I agree Jack, I probably did. I should have asked you to open the course. You can open the next one.'

'What next one?'

'Oh, haven't you heard? This one is already so success-ful I'm going to buy a bit of land down the south end and make an eighteen-hole adults-only sheep golf course. Gordy's working on it already. Trouble is, we're having trouble finding eighteen different positions for the sheep. Perhaps you can help us?'

'Just you try that Whacker McCracker and you'll really have the book thrown at you. Now the reason for my visit — it concerns the piece of filth below this fish and chip shop.'

'You mean our wonderful miniature-golf course that's already proving a great drawcard for the island?'

'I was talking about the nine filthy concrete statues with no clothes on.'

'You mean the golf course.'

'I wouldn't call it that. I'm just here to tell you that you have twenty-four hours to paint some clothes on them.'

'What?'

'You heard me. You have twenty-four hours to paint some clothes on them. By this time tomorrow they are to be clothed.'

'Jack, is this your idea of a joke?'

'Here's the ordinance.'

I was handed an official notice and a copy of the regu-lation that had been broken. I asked the sergeant for an explanation.

'If your legal man had done his homework, he would have discovered that in Oneroa you aren't allowed to run around naked. You might get away with it on Palm Beach, but not here. This is a residential area.'

'But Jack, these concrete statues ain't running around. They're not people. They're solid concrete.'

'Tell that to the judge next week. I'll give you until this time tomorrow and if they're not painted by then, you're going to be charged with displaying obscene objects. A very serious offence. See you this time tomorrow.' With that, Jack smiled and departed.

We all looked at each other, and shook our heads. And saw the funny side.

'What are you going to do?' asked Peg.

'I'm thinking Peg, I'm thinking fast. We may just be able to capitalise on this. Anyone know what the weather's going to be like tomorrow?'

'Looks pretty good,' said Bruce.

'Good. Listen, I've got an idea. It's so hilarious, I reckon we should go along with what he wants us to do, but let's use watercolour paint. The first bit of rain'll wash it all off. If we do this for tomorrow, we'll probably get a bit more publicity. It'll also get Jack off our back and give us a little more time to sort everything out.'

'He's going to look the ultimate dork over this one,' Wally commented.

'Never has a truer word been spoken, Wally.'

Twenty-four hours later, the statues were dressed. Fully painted by Wally, Mal, Bruce and Brian. From their ankles to their necks. Bright colours and simply dreadful designs.

When the media we had quickly contacted arrived, the cameras were quickly flashing. Rude comments galore were made about the colour schemes and choice of designs.

Just after three, Sergeant Koster arrived, accompanied, reluctantly, by Constable Lucy.

'Afternoon Jack. Good to see you, Lucy.'

'Sergeant Koster and Constable Simmonds to you, Mr McCracker.'

'Oh, we're having one of those days are we?'

'This is more like it,' said the hater of naked statues, casting his eye around. 'Much more like it. Quite respectable.'

Laughter erupted from the media. A glare erupted from the brow of Sergeant Koster. The media shot from every angle they could, including a couple of ingenious ones, using the sculptures to the fullest advantage.

'Yes, much more respectable, but still totally disgusting. This will do for starters. Be assured that next time I'll be bringing you an ordinance to close this piece of lowlife down.'

'What's wrong with it, Sergeant?' asked Paul Masters.

'C'mon Paul, you live on the island. Open your eyes and look.'

The rest of the media started asking questions. The sergeant refused to answer and retreated to the café with his constable.

Brad had advised me not to cause too much more trouble, so I didn't get into a raving argument with him, although I knew the media wanted me to. We handed out copies of the ordinance and I advised those present I'd spoken to my lawyer again about it and we were quite within the law. The clothes were painted on as a gesture of peace to Sergeant Koster, who seemed to have a real problem with what we'd done.

One of the young reporters from Radio Hauraki had her bottle of water resting on the third hole and accidentally knocked it over. The paint started to run. Raw concrete started to appear. She was smart and instantly realised what we'd done. 'Hey Whacker,' she called out. 'You've used watercolours! It'll all come off in the first shower!'

The publicity that followed was extensive — and made the police look pretty stupid. Dick Dawson, the police area commander, even phoned Brad later in the week and said the whole thing was ridiculous and as far as the police were concerned, as long as kids under sixteen weren't playing on the course, the matter was closed.

I phoned Jack up to ask if it was true that he was being transferred to Rakino Island.

'McCracker, I'm going to fuckin' get you. I promise you I'll have you cracking rocks before the year is out.'

Numbers One and Three decided to come over for lunch a couple of weeks after the assassination attempt. They wanted to see the 'vile golf course that was the talk of Auckland'. I was grateful they phoned me first, as there was something I wasn't too keen for them to see.

'Mal. Numbers One and Three are coming over for lunch today. Could you do us a favour and cover holes one to five on the golf course, and put a sign up saying they're closed for repair.'

'Why Whacker?'

'No real reason Mal, I'd just feel easier if they were covered.'

'No worries. I'll do it right away.'

There were hoots of laughter when they arrived and saw

me hobbling about on crutches. 'Now, Whacker, can we have our game of golf before lunch?' asked Number Three.

'Got a problem with it today, my old loves of my life. Half of it's closed, there are only four holes open. Why don't you wait until next time and have a game then?'

'We've heard it's the ultimate in vulgarity, and I'm dying to see it,' said Number One. 'Four holes are better than none.'

I stood on the deck and watched them go down to the course. They stood and looked at the five covered holes for a minute or two, then played the remaining four holes. When they came back they naturally pretended to be quite disgusted, but I knew them well enough to know they both had a good sense of humour.

'What's wrong with the first five holes Whacker?'

'Er, water damage, Number One.'

'We couldn't see any water problems,' chimed in Number Three. 'Seemed dry down there, and doesn't sandy soil absorb water?'

'Oh, it's nothing serious. They should be open by the weekend. Let's go inside where it's warm and have a glass of wine.'

'Whacker, you don't need to hide anything from us. We're both broadminded — as you should know. You're acting as if you don't want us to see those first five holes.'

'Don't be so ridiculous.'

'Well take the covers off after lunch so we can play them.'

'I've got a broken leg, Number Three. But next time you come over, I'd love to have a game with you. Always a pleasant experience to beat the ol' exes in anything, especially golf.'

'Still an arsehole. No wonder the old lady bonged you with the broom.'

Much laughter. I allowed it. Anything to get them off the subject of the first five holes.

'Whacker, you should make this café a brasserie. Much classier than a café.'

'Good idea Number One. Excellent idea.'

We discussed the advantages of brasserie over cafés. That took ages. By the end of lunch, my two sophisticated exes had me thinking that perhaps the café should become a brasserie.

Wally took them down to the wharf in the Suzuki. As they left, objecting like hell about their mode of transport, Number Three called out, 'As soon as you're out of the cast, we're going to have a big reunion of the five previous loves of your life Whacker. Yes, even Number Five, now that she's single again. So you'd better have the golf course up and running.'

That sent a shiver down my spine. The five of them together. Playing golf. On a golf course. That had five holes dedicated to them in a rather concrete, intimate, sort of way.

I followed through with the brasserie thing. Perhaps it was classier — and I could creep the prices up a bit! The day after lunching with forty per cent of my ex-wives, I phoned up Sam the signwiter to ask him to look at putting a new sign on the building. He wasn't there. He'd left the island for a fortnight to check out the scene in Australia. I got his stepfather, Bert.

'Been in signwriting all me life, Mr McCracker. Just looking after the shop while young Sam's away.'

'Well Bert, all I want is to change the big sign on the front of the building from Whacker McCracker's Café to Whacker McCracker's Brasserie. Any problems?'

'Piece of piss mate.'

'Any chance before the weekend? Then it will be ready for the Queen Street Willy Woofters.'

'I'll do it for you on Friday, Mr McCracker.'

'Bert, I won't be around. I have to go across to the hospital to get my crook leg checked. If you could do it and have it up by then it'd be much appreciated.'

'Piece of piss, Mr McCracker.'

On the Friday morning, I hobbled my way aboard Mr Fuller's ferry and up to Auckland Hospital. After umpteen hours of waiting, the doc finally spent a couple of minutes with me, said everything looked fine and to come back in another two weeks to have the cast taken off.

I taxied back to Belinda's pad and waited for her to finish inspecting the health of restaurants out west. Together, we caught the six o'clock ferry back to the island in time for Friday night turmoil at the café. Sorry, brasserie.

When we got back to Oneroa, the new sign looked pretty good. Number One was right. Brasserie did look better than Café. Already I could see a difference. Much classier. Belinda started to laugh.

'What's the big joke?'

'Nothing, Whacker, nothing.' She started to laugh again. I put it down to female hormones, because I couldn't get the joke.

Ron the chemist was next. He called out, 'Hey Whacker, got any Elle Macpherson bras on special tonight?'

I wondered if he was entering the first stages of Waiheke looniness, gave him the fingers and hobbled into the café. Cyril and Johnny were on duty and they looked at me, smirking, as I came in. Belinda started laughing again.

'What the fuckin' hell is the joke? Is it because we're a brasserie?'

Suddenly a patron called across 'Got any 38Ds?'

Somebody else called out 'Have you got any fancy knickers?'

I grabbed Belinda by the arm. 'What's going on?'

'Go outside and read your new sign again.'

I did. It read 'Whacker McCracker's Brassiere'. The stupid bugger had misspelt Brasserie. We were a bra shop.

When I got back inside, the whole 'brassiere' exploded with laughter. I was fuming. 'Cyril, didn't you check what Bert was doing? You knew he was from Waiheke. No doubt born on the island which makes him even madder than most. And, I suspect, a chronic pisshead. Surely you could have checked what the idiot was doing.'

'Sorry, we've been flat tack all afternoon. First we knew about it was about an hour ago when a patron asked us if we had any nighties for sale. I went outside, saw what had happened and phoned Bert on his cellphone. He's at the RSA. I told him what the problem was and to come back and fix it. He said that was how he was taught to spell brasserie at school and then he told me it was Friday night, he was on the piss and to get stuffed. I told him you'd hit the roof. He told me to tell you to get stuffed too.'

We stayed a brassiere shop for the entire weekend. Bert wouldn't come and change the sign until Monday. We took a lot of flack. A *lot* of flack. By Monday morning, I was sick and tired of brasseries and brassieres. When Bert finally arrived, I told him to make it café again as quickly as possible.

'Make up your mind Mr McCracker. You had café last Friday. I changed it for you. Now you want to change it back again. Sure you don't want me to call it something else. Restaurant perhaps?'

I envisaged Bert changing that to rest rooms. 'No Bert. Back to café will be fine. Any problems?'

By early afternoon we were a café again. Bert, when he came in for his beer or two, said the cost was six hundred dollars, plus GST. Or, two hundred and fifty for a cashie. I didn't argue with him. I took the very generous discount.

Gordy, the golf-course sculptor, decided to flee the island for winter and spend it in Spain. A very sudden spur-of-the-moment decision. I found this out when I tried to get hold of him to look at making a few changes to the first five sculptures. I was starting to feel a little uneasy about the five exes coming over for the reunion. Perhaps they could be fattened a little and made a little less realistic. But he'd gone, so no changes were made.

I decided I'd like to find a bit of land, build a house, grow a few grapes and live happily ever after. Hopefully, with Belinda at my side. We were getting on really well. But, after five marriages, I was just a wee bit cautious. I passed the word around that I was serious about finding the right piece of land. Wally got me aside, and after ensuring my absolute confidence, said he could help. His Uncle Joe was currently back on the island and he knew where the best property was. He arranged a meeting with Uncle Joe.

'Whacker, there's land and there's land on Waiheke,' said Uncle Joe.

'I'm very aware of that, Uncle Joe.'

'Wally tells me you're OK. Straight as straight and all that.'

'Hope so, Uncle Joe. What have you got?'

'I have your absolute confidence?'

'Of course.'

'Well, to get grapes really growing on this island you need the right piece of land. There are vineyards and there are vineyards. Understand?

I didn't really but I said I did.

'The reason some of these vineyards have grapes growing out their ears while others don't isn't due to anything all them academic guys tell you. Understand?'

I didn't, but nodded.

'There's only three vineyards on this island producing red wine by the truckload. Only three. Do you know why?'

I didn't know why.

'I'll tell you. But in absolute confidence. Understand?'

Uncle Joe was assured of the confidence factor. I have to admit I was intrigued to find out what the hell was so confidential.

'Those three vineyards are all on top of very large Maori burial grounds. Over the centuries many thousands of my ancestors were buried under them. As those bodies have decomposed, adding untold minerals and everything else that umpteen thousand of my dead ancestors would add to the soil. That's what makes those three vineyards' production so high.'

'You're having me on!' I started to laugh.

Uncle Joe was not amused.

'It's not a laughing matter,' he said quietly. 'The owners of the three vineyards, who also have knowledge of this secret, would be horrified to hear you laugh. And so would my ancestors.'

'Uncle Joe, if they were Maori burial grounds, surely they'd be sacred and there'd be no way anybody could grow — or build — anything on them.'

'You're wrong. The fact of the matter is that for most of this century nobody knew about them. For years the land was scrub, then it was sold for farming. And, now, these three are vineyards.'

'Well, why don't you claim them back?'

'Very difficult. We'd have to buy them back and that would be financially impossible.'

'Why are you telling me this, Uncle Joe?'

'Whacker, I do have your complete confidence on this, don't I?'

'Of course, Uncle Joe.'

'Because there's one more.'

'One more what?'

'One more ancient Maori burial ground.'

'Where?'

'It's on five hectares.'

'Is it farmland or what?'

'Good farmland.'

'Why isn't it a vineyard?'

'Because the guy farming it only leases it to graze sheep. He owns the block next door.'

'Who owns it?'

'It's been in a friend's family for generations. He inherited it.'

'And he wants you to sell it. Right?'

'Only to the right person. To a person who would take the secret of what's under the land to his grave.'

'Like your umpteen thousand ancestors eh, Uncle Joe.'

'I'm serious. You're the first person to be offered this land.'

'Why doesn't your friend respect your ancestors and make it an historic site?'

'If his cussies and rellies knew about this, that's exactly what would happen. But he wouldn't get any money, he'd have to give it away. The thing is, he's having a bit of a cash crunch at the moment. Otherwise, he'd do exactly as you said.'

I've met some characters in my life, but Uncle Joe was one of the best, a warmhearted bloke with a wonderful smile. I was sure he was having me on, but he was so sincere, and had spun such a wonderful tale, I had one or two doubts. His sales story was certainly good enough to get me to chug out with him in the lime green Skoda to take a look at the land. I must admit I wasn't expecting much. Perhaps an inland block on a hill facing south with no view. How wrong I was! The land was a couple of miles south of Onetangi, part of it flat, part of it a slight hill, facing north with an unobstructed view of the blue Pacific Ocean.

'This is it. You're on one of most sacred burial grounds on the island. Look at all that plush grass.'

207

The grass didn't look too plush to me. It looked like ordinary grass.

'You'd grow the most wonderful grapes here. Get double the amount per vine than anywhere else.'

What really appealed to me about the place was the peace. And the view. I could see a vineyard café selling our own wine. Perhaps some accommodation. It was a bit like how I felt when I saw *The Glorious Ocean View Café* for the first time.

'How much, Uncle Joe?'

'Whacker, if you bought this, you'd have to swear to me to keep the secret. If that got out, my friend would really be in the shit for selling. And you could be in a spot of bother yourself.'

'Understood. How much, Uncle Joe?'

'Because you're a friend of my niece and nephew, Bets and Walter, I'll make it available at a very, very reasonable price.'

'Cut the bullshit. How much?'

Uncle Joe took out his pen and wrote a figure on the back of an old bus ticket he found in his pocket and handed it to me.

'I'll think about it. Give me a day or two.'

We got back into the Skoda and chugged our way back towards Oneroa, Uncle Joe continuing to list the many benefits of purchasing the island's last available Maori burial ground. 'Just one thing, mate. I've lost my eftpos card. Going to take a couple of days to get a new one. You couldn't lend me fifty bucks until it arrives, could you?'

'Of course, Uncle Joe. Is that enough?'

'Well, if you could make it a hundred I'd really appreciate it. Just for a couple of days.'

I gave Uncle Joe the money and told him I'd get back to him.

When I got back to the café, Mal was propping up the bar talking to Horse. I joined them for a five o'clocker. 'Saw a nice piece of land today guys. It'd be great to have our own vineyard with a little café and bar. Perhaps a few rooms to rent out.'

'Wally's uncle show it to you?' asked Mal.

'Yes, Uncle Joe.'

'I thought I saw him in your car. Did he spin you the one about the ancient Maori burial ground?'

'That's confidential, Mal.'

Mal roared with laughter. 'He's spun that tale for bloody years. Best salesman on the island, that guy.'

'You mean it's all bullshit? That piece of land isn't for sale?'

'No, no the land'll be for sale. But not too many dead ancestors under it mate. Every time Uncle Joe gets out of jail and comes home a couple of the local real-estate agents use him to line up sales.'

'Jesus! I almost believed him.'

'So does everyone. He's the best. Bloody character. How much did he get you to lend him?'

'Hundred bucks.'

'You were lucky. You won't see that again.'

'What about the land? I really liked it.'

'It's real. In a couple of days a real agent will contact you and you'll take it from there.'

'But what about Joe? Will he get a buck out of it? If he hadn't been so insistent, I wouldn't have gone to see it.'

'He'll be looked after by the agent. But it won't last long. Bloody Wally should have told you about him. Still, guess that's family looking after family. He's got his good points though. He came across a heap of Johnny Walker a couple of years ago. Ten bucks a bottle. That was different. A bloody good deal. Everyone on the island bought some.'

Mal was quite right. The next day Fred Daisy from the real-estate office down the hill called in to yarn about the five hectares. I went out with him again and had a good look. Then I phoned Brad to check it out and see if we could put a licensed café, with accommodation, on the site.

He came back to me in a couple of days to say we probably could, but it would be a matter of time and resource consents. We both agreed it would be a logical extension for the café, and the business was so profitable borrowing the money wouldn't be a problem.

I bought the land, and Fred assured me Uncle Joe would be well looked after. Unfortunately he had to leave the island rather quickly, so I didn't have the pleasure of his company again.

Bets and Mal had a baby boy! Mal was with Bets in Auckland for the event, so we waited until they were back to celebrate wetting his head at the café. A dinner was organised for them on the Sunday evening they returned to the island. All of the originals were invited, plus the fisherfolk and some other friends.

Because Sergeant Jack Koster was such an old acquaintance of Mal's, I decided to invite him too. 'The thought of another Mal in this world is not an event I wish to celebrate, McCracker,' he told me, when I phoned him up. 'I'm sure I'll be seeing him a lot more of him later in life, in my professional line of duty, so I'm in no hurry to start seeing him now.'

'Jack, at that police school you somehow managed to bribe or cheat your way through, did they tell you to start judging people when they're just a couple of days old?'

'No. In certain cases, one minute after they were conceived.'

I decided we most certainly didn't need Sergeant Jack at Mal junior's party, and what a happy party it was. When Bets and Mal arrived with the baby, there was love, real love, in the café that night. Bets was smothered in flowers and there were gifts galore. There was no way Bets was going to be parted from the little guy. He was tucked up in the bassinet beside her. Belinda got clucky too — the things babies can do to women.

Wally declared a toast. 'Bets, Mal,' began Uncle Wally. 'Shit-hot effort. Bloody great that he's a bloke.' Moans from the women. Cheers from the men. 'We're all really proud of what you've done and anyway, here's a toast to yous.'

We all toasted the new baby.

Mal then got to his feet and announced he wanted to say a few words. Bets was beaming. 'I just wanna thank all you bunch of bastards for coming and giving us stuff. And thanks Wally for opening up your big ugly trap.' Much laughter all around, then Mal continued. 'I know you're all wondering what we are going to call the little guy. Bets and me would like to name him after a bloke we both really admire who's been bloody good to us. If it's all right with you, mate, we'd like to call our little boy Whacker.'

I don't very often get teary. But as I started to stand, tears poured down my cheeks. 'Bets, Mal, thank you, I'm honoured. Whacker Junior, you're lucky to have two such wonderful parents.' I was so emotional I couldn't say any more. Belinda gave me a cuddle as I sat down, before we got down to some serious head-wetting.

The café's first birthday was coming up. It had been quite a year. We planned to have a wonderful birthday party and use the occasion to announce our own birthday honours, followed by an investiture. Because so many friends would be coming over from Auckland, we felt a Sunday lunch would be easiest. Invitations went out to our business colleagues, friends, media contacts, suppliers and others who'd helped us in some way from day one.

Ten days before the big bash, my five exes walked into the café for golf and lunch. It was a crisp, fine Thursday. I was getting my hair cut in Surfdale when they arrived, but Brian contacted me on my cellphone. 'Your exes are all here, Whacker.'

'How many?'

'Well it looks like four. Plus a daughter.'

'That'll be Number Five. God. Look after them until I get there and keep them away from the golf course.'

'Why? They've already told me they want to play a game. That's why they came across early.'

'Brian, please, please, please try and keep them away from the course.'

'Could be almost impossible. They've already got putters.'

He did manage to stall them for a short while, but by the time I reached the café, it was too late. They were down on the golf course. And had made some startling discoveries. 'You know, Number One, this first hole is the spitting image of you. Was that the way he used to bonk you?'

'Jesus, Number Three, I hadn't really looked at it that closely. You're right. It does look like me.'

'Number Four, that fourth hole is definitely you,' said Number Two.

'God, you're absolutely right.'

'And look at this fifth hole. That is very definitely me,' cried Number Five.

Suddenly there were five shrieking women. 'The arsehole. The absolute arsehole. He's used us as models for this pornographic golf course,' fumed Number One.

Anger and much swearing rained down upon on Waiheke Island's hottest new tourist attraction. And then, the hero of the moment walked down the steps. Yours truly.

Back in Roman days a humble gladiator might have to face up to five starving tigers in the Coliseum. Today I was confronted with something ten times worse. Five snapping, snarling, embittered wives who had reason to believe their sexual attributes were forever immortalised in solid concrete.

'You arsehole,' chorused five ex-wives.

'My darling ladies. It's wonderful to see you again. I gather this is the reunion. Welcome, welcome. Especially you, Number Five.'

'These first five holes are us aren't they?' said Number One. 'How could you be so low?'

'Don't be so stupid, Number One. They're far too ugly. You five are gorgeous.'

'Bullshit,' sniped Number Five. 'That number-five hole was our favourite position? Boy oh boy, this is going to cost you.'

Numbers One, Two, Three and Four then stated something similar. Feeling a little stronger, I told them to get real. 'Even if you were immortalised in concrete, how many people have that claim to fame?'

'Not many decent, ordinary people. Exhibitionists, yes. But decent people. No. Ex-wives in wild sex positions? No way.' Number One had her camera out and proceeded to go click crazy. Her speciality seemed to be to have them each lie down next to their respective sculptures.

Number Two had made a triumphant telephone call. Her lawyer was coming across on the one o'clock ferry, and would represent the five of them. Boy, could she smell money. 'This is going to cost you megabucks,' she yelled at me.

Never had truer words been uttered.

They continued to rant and rave and I continued to deny, deny. It got to me, so I stormed back to the café. How I could have married one of them, let alone the whole bloody five, was totally beyond me.

Eventually they came back up to the café, as Number Five put it, 'to await the professional advice' due to arrive shortly from Auckland. I was made to very feel unwanted and given five turd-stopping glares.

'Everything is on the house today, my lovely ladies. My shout,' I told them, trying to cool down the situation.

'We're not charity cases,' sniffed Number One. 'We're quite capable of paying for ourselves. And will. Please arrange for a professional waiting person to look after us.'

I looked at her and she mouthed that dreadful four-letter word to me. Mal gallantly agreed to tend to their culinary needs.

Woman lawyers are a difficult breed. In three out of five of my matrimonial settlements, poor old Brad had to deal with a woman lawyer. They're tough. And the toughest of them all was Eileen Begg. Number Two's lawyer. I recognised Eileen when she walked into the café.

'Good morning Eileen. Nice of you to come over and visit the café.'

'Mr McCracker. I believe I'm expected.'

'Over in the corner, Eileen. Five gorgeous ladies await the pleasure of your company. And may I apologise in advance for them dragging you all the way here over such a trivial matter.'

'We'll see about that, Mr McCracker.'

Five minutes later there were six women in earnest conversation. A couple of minutes later, they all left the table and proceeded down to the golf course.

I felt I'd better get some legal advice myself, just in case Eileen started to get a bit stroppy. I caught up with Brad, who told me he was trying to enjoy a cold meat pie and a warm Coke at his office desk.

'Eileen Begg is here.'

'Well, give her a nice feed, Whacker. Like you do to everyone else. She is human you know.'

'No, no. She's here on official business.'

'What kind of official business?'

'Well the exes have dragged her across.'

'Your ex-wife. Which one?'

'The whole lot. The five of them. They surprised me with a reunion lunch.'

'You are an extraordinary man, Whacker. Not many guys would be sharing a lunch with their five ex-wives.'

'Well, they're here and there is a tiny, tiny problem.'

'What's the tiny problem, Whacker?'

'The golf course seems to be upsetting them.'

'Your famous filthy golf course has upset quite a few people from what I've heard.'

'They seem to have got upset over the first five holes.'

'Go on.'

'Well, the silly tarts have got it into their heads that the concrete sculptures are actually them.'

'Are they?'

'They're solid concrete. How the hell could they be?'

'Were the five ex-delights of your life used as models?'

'Not directly. I did give Gordy a few photographs of the old dragons to help him. Inspiration, I believe it's called. As you know, they were all quite attractive women when I first met them. Different story now.'

'Whacker, if you've reproduced them so they can be recognised, you could be in a spot of bother. The sculptures are nudes aren't they?'

'Damn right they are.'

'Were the photos of the exes you gave to your sculpture mate nudes?'

'Not going to answer that one. Bit personal.'

'I believe you've already answered it.'

'You should have been a mind-reader.'

'Now, are those five sculptures in sexual positions?'

'In a round-about sort of way.'

'Are they in positions you may have performed with any or all of your ex-wives?'

'Brad, you're getting a bit bloody personal.'

'I think I'm getting the feel of what all this is about. If it is, how the fuck could you have been so stupid?'

'I thought it'd be a bit of a laugh. I was going to change it after Numbers One and Three came over a few weeks back, but Gordy's gone to Spain.'

'Didn't they see them then?'

'No. I had warning they were coming so we covered them up. Today, they just arrived.'

'You could have quite a problem on your hands. My advice at this stage is to admit to nothing. The less you say about it the better. They may see the funny side of it and laugh it off, or hopefully ask you to make a few changes. Let's see what develops. Keep in touch.'

'Thanks Brad. Cheers.'

As I gazed down at the golf course, it looked like a feminist's convention. Six woman stalking around, pointing things out, jabbering away and taking yet more photos. I wasn't inclined to join them.

It was probably another half-hour before they returned. I greeted them with a smile. 'All sorted out now, girls? Not the spitting images at all are they? They're straight from the head of Gordy.'

'Mr McCracker,' said Eileen. 'I have advised my five clients not to discuss this revolting case of sexual exploitation with you.'

'Fair enough, Eileen. I won't discuss it either then. Case closed. Now sit down and enjoy a lovely piece of fish. On the house.'

Surprisingly, the six of them chose to stay for lunch, although they insisted on paying for their food and drinks. The offer of free café transportation to the ferry was declined and a taxi van called. They chose to totally ignore me. I couldn't resist giving them the fingers as they walked out the door.

'Belinda, do you think we should make Miriam Webber a dame?' It was the Friday night before our party and I was at home finalising the birthday honours. They had to be finished that night. Cyril and Johnny wanted to have the names, titles and honours in the morning so they could finish the official certificates.

'Are you sure it's all right to give out titles?'

'Of course it is. Everyone would love to have one. Look how popular the fisherfolk have become. They're only honorary ones. What about Mal? Should I make him an earl? Earl Malcolm Scudd sounds pretty good.'

'He's already a bishop. Isn't that enough?'

'So you think those already blessed with a religious title shouldn't get another one?'

'Over to you. But if you want to show appreciation to a

bishop, you promote him through the ranks of the church. Perhaps you could make him the Archbishop and give yourself a fancy new title, like Duke Whacker.'

'Prefer Lord Whacker. Quite fancy being a Lord. Fair enough. I'm quite keen to make Jack Koster a sir. Then, when I knight the bugger with that old sword we got from the second-hand shop, I could chop his head off at the same time.'

'I can't imagine Jack accepting it. Is he coming?'

'Yep. With his missus. Do you think Screwzy Suzy should be a duchess?'

'What's she done to merit a title like that?'

'Given a lot of pleasure to a lot of blokes on the island, Belinda. Ladies like that should be rewarded in some way. We need more of them.'

'You're disgusting. Is there anyone deserving, besides Miriam, getting one of your loony titles?'

'Brad. He deserves it.'

'And what may I ask is that lawyer who's made umpteen thousand dollars out of you going to be?'

'A count.'

'A what?'

'A count. For a lawyer, it has a nice ring to it. Actually, thinking about it, that would be a bloody good title for Jack. I'll give it to him instead. Count Jack of Waiheke Island.'

'Careful, Whacker.'

'I'll make Brad a KC. A King's Counsel. There are lots of QCs around but no KCs. There's heaps of kings in Africa and Europe he can counsel.'

'I'm sure he'll be most impressed.'

'Hugsy from the ferry is going to become an admiral.

He steers a lot of business our way, telling passengers to come here for lunch. Plus, he's a bloody good bloke. A pisshead, too. We must look after the island's pissheads.'

'Well you'd better balance it up with someone from Alcoholics Anonymous.'

'Good thinking. What could we make Horse? Let's make him a baron. Baron Horse sounds pretty good.'

'And who else are you going to embarrass?'

'Well my old darling, I think you'll just have to wait and see.'

'Have you heard any more from that lawyer?'

'Not a word. I think it's a dead issue. Not a leg to stand on. I don't know if the exes are coming, none of them have replied. I invited them because they've sent quite a bit of business to us over the year. Perhaps I could award them all the Order of the Dragon. Make them Dragons One, Two, Three, Four and Five of Waiheke Island.'

'Don't, it'll only cause more trouble. Still, no news is probably good news. Have you changed the sculptures yet?'

'Can't. Brad phoned me back and said not to. If we did, we could be seen as admitting they were actually the exes.'

'Which of course they are. You're a silly bugger at times, but I love you. C'mon, it's getting late. Let's go to bed.'

Sunday morning, the big day of the birthday party, and it was pelting down. There was no way the fishing boats could get out, but it didn't matter. After a lot of debate I'd managed to convince Brian that we'd serve the original menu.

It was all hands on deck at the café from nine o'clock. Lots of decorating, balloons to be blown up, tables re-arranged and seating allocated, with each table including one of the fisherfolk.

As we still hadn't heard from the five exes, it was assumed they weren't coming. That meant five more of our new local friends, 'on the waiting list', could come. The party was due to start at twelve-thirty and we'd arranged for a couple of buses to pick up eighty-odd guests coming over on the midday ferry.

All of the fisherfolk were asked to arrive by twelve to get changed into their robes. As an incentive to get them there on time, they were told the bar would be open from noon and they could drink from then, provided they were dressed in the religious robes. It was a good incentive. They all arrived early. Several, very early.

It was wonderful to see so many old friends and business colleagues. Naturally a number of them were extremely rude to me, when they saw me dressed in my archbishop's gear. I quietly blessed them. Jim Morran wanted to know how I drove the Skoda with my mitre on. I told him one just opened the sunroof.

Greg, my accountant, gave me some news I didn't particularly want to hear. 'G'day Whacker, looks like quite a party. Nice of you to invite your exes.'

'Don't think they're coming, Greg.'

'Well, they were on the ferry. You won't miss them.'

He was right. They arrived on the second bus. Each of them had gone to considerable trouble to dress in concrete-coloured garments, made in the shape of a sculpture of their own bodies. In respective order, they had signs on them reading: Hole No 1, No 2, No 3, No 4 and No 5.

'Well, if it isn't my holy ex-wives. What a wonderful surprise,' I lied.

'We've only come to highlight to everyone what a simply appalling thing you did to us,' said Number Two.

'Being relegated to a pornographic golf hole is extremely embarrassing. We want others to understand our embarrassment,' raved Number Five.

'Do you feel better now seeing your golf holes jumping into real life?' asked Number One.

'Well, girls, that's a bit of luck, your coming dressed like that. We didn't know you were joining us so there's no seating for you. You can just sit on the floor and pretend you're real sculptures. Might even hand around a few putters and some golf balls for my guests to fire at you! Indoor living golf!' My joke wasn't appreciated.

We had a fairly tight schedule, as the plan was to have some of our city guests back on the three o'clock ferry. We were going to start serving lunch at one, then have speeches and the presentations at two. I went to the stage to get the show underway. The band stopped playing. I welcomed everyone and asked our guests to be seated. 'If anyone can't find their allocated place, we are fortunate enough to have five slabs of real-life concrete present. You may wish to sit on one of these. I assure you they can be most comfortable.'

This earned me one of those infamous glares, while everyone else laughed. (Wonderful Belinda had found them somewhere to sit.) The food, wine and music flowed. The fisherfolk all seemed to be doing a great job hosting their respective tables and I circulated, endeavouring to make everyone feel welcome.

Just before two o'clock, I went to the small dais we'd

built and asked the twelve fisherfolk to join me. It was a very colourful sight. Bishop Wally of Oneroa and Bishop Mal of Orapiu flanked me. I started by welcoming everyone. 'Ladies and gentlemen, there are some people in particular to whom I would like to show our appreciation for helping this café become so successful. It is with enormous pleasure I announce the instigation of the Whacker McCracker's Café Birthday Honours. These will be awarded annually at this time, and as with our religious fisherfolks' titles, these are honorary Waiheke Island-only titles.

'However, those of you honoured with one of our awards may of course use them anywhere in the world. I'm sure they'll help get you instant upgrades on aircraft and hotels for a start. You'll be invited to every top-shelf cocktail party in Remuera. Gentlemen, women will swoon at your feet. Ladies, gentlemen will swoon at your feet. Those who receive titles will be able to wear, at important events at the café and on the island, the appropriate robes we will create for each title. These will, like the fisherfolk robes, belong to us and be kept at the café. I know they will always be worn with pride.'

'It is now with great pleasure that I announce the very first of our birthday honours. To our great friend, the saviour of our streakers' race, I am delighted to announce Miss Miriam Webber has been made a Dame of Waiheke Island. Come hither, Dame Miriam.'

Miriam received a standing ovation. She was a great sport. To save her kneeling, I had my trusty second-hand sword in my hand and gently tapped her on each shoulder. 'I pronounce you Dame Miriam Webber of Waiheke Island. Congratulations.' I handed her a medallion and certificate and gave her a kiss.

'Next, I would like to announce a nautical award. For outstanding services on Mr Fuller's ferry, Hugsy Appleby is hereby appointed Admiral Hugsy of Waiheke Island.' Many cheers as Hugsy came forward and received a medal we'd found in a box of leftovers from the *Stratford off Avon* shop. He was very proud of his rapid elevation and beamed from ear to ear.

'For services rendered to the humanitarian and hospitality fields, our very own Screwzy Suzy is to be known from this day forward as Duchess Screwzy Suzy of Waiheke Island.' Suzy came forward, laughing like she'd never laughed before. I wasn't quite sure what the formality was for officially appointing a Duchess — or any of the other titles for that matter, so I asked her to kneel and then lightly tapped her on each shoulder with the trusty sword. When she arose, she was no longer a member of the great unwashed.

'Ladies and gentlemen,' I continued. 'For another person who has given truly amazing service to the bar, it is with the utmost pleasure that our barman Horse, from this moment on will be known as Baron Horse.'

For contributions to catering, I was very proud to be able to make Bruce a Duke and Brian an Earl. The new Duke of Waiheke Island and Earl of Waiheke Island were ecstatic. Bets and Peg were both made Dames and Johnny and Cyril were knighted. For outstanding legal work I elevated my lawyer, Brad, to the ranks of KC. He made a short, brilliant speech and said he would swear his allegiance to King Boom Boom of the Congo.

Sam Hankle, QC, was given a posthumous WSM (Whacker's Service Medal) for achieving publicity beyond the call of duty. From the local council, Joe Blakely and

Terry Verson also received this award, though not posthumously. These were awarded for professionalism in the area of allocating important permits and consents.

'Friends of the café,' I announced. 'Only one birthday honour is now left for us to award. And, this is indeed to a very close colleague of the café. From this moment Sergeant Jack Koster of the Waiheke Island Police Force will be known as Count Jack Koster.'

The crowd laughed as Jack came forward to be dubbed and decorated with a big badge we'd found at the Ostend flea market. He scowled at me but went along with it, saying quietly as he was dubbed, 'One day I'm going to fuckin' get you.'

With the investitures finished, I asked everybody to stand to join in singing happy birthday to the café. While this was happening, I'd arranged for a big birthday cake to be wheeled in and Karen Blomfield, of Sam Hankle fame, was to jump out topless. It had cost me five-hundred dollars to get her to do it, but I knew it would be a memorable climax.

As we started to sing, two casuals wheeled in this fabulous cake. I felt really excited. This was going to be a truly memorable event. The singing stopped and three cheers were called for by Bishop Mal. Once that had been done, the drummer did a drum roll. All eyes were on the cake. Suddenly, a person crashed through the top of it. Only, it wasn't a topless Karen Blomfield. It was Eileen Begg. Very definitely fully clothed. With a document in her hand.

'Mr Whacker McCracker,' she began, standing in the cake. 'This is a writ for damages for sexual exploitation of your five ex-wives by using them in obscene poses on your filthy golf course. They are seeking three hundred and fifty thousand dollars from you by way of compensation. Each.'

The café was silent. And then the jeering started. Soon it was so loud you could hardly hear a thing. Eileen struggled out of the cake. Nobody helped her. I thought Brad, who rushed over, was going to thump her. She resorted to using language one only learns in the Australian merchant navy and at one particularly exclusive Auckland private girls' school.

Brad kept me away from the exes and Eileen. He told me I wasn't to say anything to them as it could make matters worse. Others, lots of others, did it for me. I caught the eye of the five slabs of concrete. They were smiling a revengful type of smile. I mouthed them that dreadful four-letter word in plural. Five mouths mouthed it back.

By four o'clock, several very stiff Scotches had been poured down my throat. I was still furious that Eileen Begg had wrecked such a wonderful party. The only bit of good news was that Hugsy, sorry, Admiral Hugsy, had done his first official duty, in his new capacity as Admiral of Waiheke Island. The five exes and Eileen, were black-balled from leaving the island by public transport. He'd phoned up his pisshead colleagues, and they agreed to stop them from catching any ferry. He then went down to ensure the ban was professionally carried out. It was a wet dark day so they wouldn't be able to fly home.

The two casuals, both students from Auckland, had done a runner. Obviously they'd been well bribed. Poor Karen was found locked up in a cupboard.

Brad and his wife had to get back to Auckland on the four-thirty ferry for a family occasion. He said he couldn't do much more, but would take the papers, evaluate them in the morning and seek advice from a couple of colleagues. Belinda offered to drive them down in the Skoda. I said I'd go along too. It was pouring. We drove down to get as near to the wharf as we could get and from there, they made a run for the ferry. As we slowly turned around, the back door was suddenly opened and in jumped a soaked ex. Followed by another one. And then, somehow, three more. 'Stop the car, Belinda.' She did. 'Now, out. All of you.'

'Please Whacker,' cried Number Five. 'We're soaked and freezing. We can't get home. And it wasn't our idea.'

'Where is that bitch of a lawyer?'

'There.'

I looked to where she was pointing towards us. For the first time for a couple of hours I smiled. There she stood, soaked to the skin, yelling something in our direction. I wound down the window, gave her the fingers, and told the sixth love of my life to drive off.

Belinda sorted things out as we drove back up the hill. 'Girls,' she said to them. 'You've got to get out of those wet clothes fast. I'll drop Whacker off at the café and then we'll drive down to his bach where you can have a shower and put on some dry clothes. We'll sort things out from there.'

'Sorry Whacker,' said Number One. 'We had no idea about the cake. That was Eileen.'

'What about the three hundred and fifty grand? Each?'

'Stop it,' said Belinda. 'With seven of us squashed up in this car, let's not get into an argument. Here we are at the café. Whacker, I'll come back and join you shortly.'

I walked in, made it to the bar and asked the newly appointed Baron Horse for another Scotch. (We only had a beer and wine licence, but for the boss and good friends there was always Scotch and a bit of other top-shelf stuff hidden away under the counter.)

'Feeling a bit better now?' he asked.

'Horse, you're not going to believe this. Do you know who's going down to my house at the moment, using my hot water and getting into my dry clothes?'

'No idea.'

'My five fuckin' ex-wives.'

'You're bloody kidding me. What about that Eileen bitch?'

'Ha, that's the one bit of good news. She's down at the wharf. Soaked. The word's gone out pretty quickly around the island about what she did. The island's pissheads have arranged for her to be blackballed from every ferry, taxi and bus on the island.'

Hugsy phoned in shortly afterwards with more devastating news. Because the seas were so big, it had been decided to cancel all remaining ferries for the evening. Waiheke was isolated from the world. Horse poured me another very large Scotch when I heard that. I got on the phone to tell Belinda the situation.

'Hallo. The residence of Archbishop McCracker,' answered the voice at the end of the phone.

I recognised the voice. It was Number Four. 'You tarts still there?' I enquired, as nicely as I could, given the circumstances.

'Oh, it's the Archbishop. Yes, your Bishops' court is still occupied by your five glamorous, exciting ex-loves. What is the reason for your call?'

'Put me on to Belinda.'

'Manners, Whacker. Say please.'

'Please.' Belinda came to the phone. 'She's bloody pissed. What are you all doing down there? Getting stuck into my grog?'

'They needed a couple of drinks to thaw out. It's very wet and cold. I just hope someone is helping Eileen.'

'Unlikely. The word's out around the island. Hey listen, we have a hell of a problem. The ferry's stopped running for the night. It's too rough.'

'Oh no.'

'Well, don't worry about it. You and I have got a roof over our head. It's those other five. You'd better tell them they've got a choice of spending the night in either the Matiatia or the Oneroa public toilets.'

'They'll have to stay here.'

'You have to be joking. After what they did today, do you really think I'd have them under the same roof? No way.'

'We'll work something out. I'm coming back up soon.'

'OK. We'll have something to eat here. There's stacks of food left over.'

'See you shortly.'

Horse poured me another Scotch and I was starting to feel a little better. Mal, Wally, Johnny and Cyril joined us and we started to see the funny side. Naturally they thought it was hilarious that it looked as if I'd be sharing my home that night with all my past wives.

The phone went. It was Sergeant Jack Koster.

'Evening, Jack.'

'McCracker. I am at home. I am off duty. But, I thought l you might like to know that the charming woman who jumped out of your cake is, at this very moment, having a hot shower at the police station. Apparently she's near death, but claiming on her deathbed that those mad ex-wives of yours and herself were banned from leaving the island on the ferry. She's blaming you. If I discover you are in any way responsible for this, I give you my assurance I will personally escort you to the High Court.'

'Thanks, Jack. Really appreciate the call. Glad she's found an appropriate place to put her head down for the night. That's the best news I've heard all afternoon. Perhaps making you a Count is going to make you an even nicer person.'

'Sleep well, Whacker. Dream of losing three hundred and fifty grand times five. Quite a bit isn't it?' With that, he hung up.

'What was all that about?' asked Horse.

'That old bitch who jumped out of the cake is up at the cop shop!' We were still laughing when Belinda came in, five exes in tow.

'What's the big joke?' she asked.

'Hey girls. Guess what! Eileen Begg's in jail!'

There were eight of us around the dinner table, in the café, at the end of the day to celebrate its first birthday. Seven women and myself. Five ex-wives, each suing me for three hundred and fifty thousand dollars. A lawyer who had totally fucked up the café's birthday celebrations. And, luckily, a partner I loved. It wasn't the kind of meal I would like to make a habit of repeating.

Sharing an older-styled, two-bedroomed, one-bath-roomed holiday house for a night with the same seven women, was an experience I do not wish to write about. The one memory I do have is lying awake and wondering why I thought it was so funny when I heard these particular ladies had been stopped from catching the ferry. They should have been given an armed escort to make sure they caught it. I had to concede that men, particularly Waiheke Island pissheads, do make the odd mistake.

A taxi picked them up in the morning to catch the eight o'clock ferry. I didn't come out of my bedroom to say goodbye. I stayed in bed, and, for the first time, began to feel that perhaps I could be entering the earliest stage of the proverbial Waiheke Island looniness.

Brad phoned me just before lunch. 'What did you do to Ms Begg last night?'

'Fed her in my café then put her up in my house for the night. With the five exes.'

'Jesus, has she got it in for you. I've just had an earful from her on the phone. Reckons she's going to sue you personally, and completely clean you out.'

'What's her problem?'

'Claims you stopped her from leaving the island yesterday and because of that she nearly expired from hypothermia. What did you do?'

'It wasn't me. It was the pissheads. They banned her from the ferry and all public transport. Funny at the time, but in hindsight, we should have frogmarched the old bitch on to the ferry with the other five troublemakers and just got rid of them.'

'Wish you had done that. She's after blood. Listen

Whacker, I'm concerned over this writ. I've spoken to a couple of my partners and we don't like it at all. I'm not going to get into what you did. That's done and we know all about it. I just want to try and extricate you from it.'

'Well let's do something to Eileen for a start-off, for fucking up my bloody party yesterday. She's a corrupt old bag, bribing those students and shoving Karen into the cupboard.'

'Perhaps we can get Karen to lay an assault charge?'

'Don't think so. Brian told me she admitted, after a few drinks, that Eileen gave her some money. God, so did I — five hundred bucks. All she had to do was sit in a broom cupboard for ten minutes.'

'My advice is we lay off Eileen, unless she starts getting really silly about the ferry business. If she does, we'll look into it then. Meanwhile, we have this writ problem, and also another problem could possibly be looming.'

'What's the other one?'

'Haven't liked to worry you about it because I thought we could sort it out, but it's proving difficult. It's the fishing thing. That lawyer for the Ministry of Fisheries called me last week and again this morning. She reckons the 1884 legislation was made invalid during the First World War, in 1917 apparently. You haven't got any letters sitting over there from her have you? There seem to be a couple I haven't seen.'

'We've had so many, I've been ignoring them. It got so silly I started to give them to Wally and Mal to analyse. Their legal opinions were cheaper than yours. Given me some excellent advice.'

'Well you'd better see if you can dig them up and fax them over. They could be important.'

I searched around and found three letters from the Ministry of Fisheries I'd received the previous fortnight. They didn't make very happy reading. The implication was that the loophole we'd used to obtain our fresh fish was invalid. Every day since we'd started our fresh fish scheme, we'd been breaking the law and could be liable to a substantial penalty. It requested that we stop supplying fish immediately. I faxed the letters to my legal man pronto. An hour later, Brad phoned me back.

'Whacker. Got the letters. Wish I'd seen them a bit earlier. What's the story with the fish situation at the moment?'

'Well, it's fairly quiet at this time of the year. Only five boats went out this morning. We got thirty-two fish today. Come the weekend and we'll see if we can get sixty each day.'

'It might be an idea if you start buying a few whole fish through the legal channels as well. You know, from the local fish shop.'

'Why?'

'Because if you suddenly get a visit from a Ministry of Fisheries wanting to seize your fish, you might be able to arrange it so they seize legitimately bought fish.'

'Good thinking. I'll pop along to the fish shop shortly and get a few snapper. Guess we could use the fish in a pasta or fish pie.'

'Make sure you get a receipt — and take a while buying the fish too so the person behind the counter remembers who's buying them. I'll get back to you as soon as we've clarified this 1917 bit. Cheers.'

When I got up to the fish shop, Charlie Harrison couldn't believe it when I told him I wanted some of the 'six-week-old' snapper he had in the window. 'Bullshit Whacker. Bloody near as fresh as yours. And, a bloody sight more legal. What do you want them for?'

'To shout the cats on the island a late birthday treat, Charlie. You know we wouldn't serve this to humans.' Charlie roared with laughter.

'Might come back and get a few more each day, mate. Trust that's OK.'

'Fine, Whacker. Everything else going OK? Hear those bloody sheilas are after millions from you. You'd think they'd be bloody proud to have themselves featured on that golf course wouldn't you?'

'Women are a strange breed, Charlie. A strange breed. See you tomorrow.'

Back at the café kitchen, I showed Brian the fish and advised him of the new situation. He put them on ice and into a bin that was easy to see, just beside the main bench. Our real freshly caught fish were placed in a cupboard. If we were ever 'inspected', hopefully only the bought fish would be found.

I told him to feed it to the local pussycats just before he left for the night.

Brad phoned me first thing on Wednesday morning with some devastating news. 'Have you been getting some of that legit fish?'

'Yesterday and the day before. The local cats have been very well fed.'

"Good. Get some more today and order heaps for tomorrow.'

'Why?'

'Whacker, through a contact I will not divulge, I've just learned that tomorrow the Ministry of Fisheries is coming

234

across to raid you. They'll seize all your fish. Don't let the fisherfolk go out tomorrow. Quietly tell them to have the day off.'

'Jesus, Brad, is the 1917 thing definite?'

'They reckon it is. We're not so sure. The information is they have enough evidence for a test case against you.'

'Are you coming over?'

'I can't. If I was there, it would be pretty obvious you'd been tipped off. They'll realise that soon enough when they find out the fish aren't locally caught. Don't tell them that when they come though, let them seize legit fish as evidence and then we can make them look like real dorks. Be sure to get a receipt for all the fish — and make sure your mate at the fish shop remembers you bought them. Take a witness with you.'

'What's likely to happen?'

'A couple of flunkies from the ministry will come in, claim you're serving illegal fish, seize the fish and then I guess the legal hassles will commence.'

'So I'm not going to get arrested or anything like that?'

'No way, Whacker. Phone me if there's any problem.'

When I went up to Charlie's to get the day's order of snapper, I told him the fish he had been giving me over the past couple of days had been so delicious, I wanted to order a heap for the next day. So the fisherfolk could have a rest.

'How many do you want, Whacker?'

'Let's make it forty-three snapper, Charlie.'

'Why forty-three?'

'Sounds about right. Any problem?'

'No problem at all, Whacker. I'll phone the order through and you can pick them up at the same time tomorrow.'

I didn't sleep too well that night. I wanted to talk to someone about it, but, because it was so confidential, I didn't and spent one of those 'tossing and turning nights'. The one good thing was that the fisherfolk were all having a nice sleep-in, because I'd told them to take Thursday off.

☕

I took Wally with me the next morning to collect the fish. Charlie had the snapper ready, iced and in a bin. He gave me an invoice, showing forty-three snapper purchased. I asked him, for professional reasons, to keep quiet about the purchase. He agreed. After a bit of a yarn about nothing in general, I said to Wally we'd better be on our way. 'Drive down to Surfdale, Wally. We have a bit of time to kill.'

'What's going on, Boss? Why buy all that fish?'

'The fisherfolk are having the day off today, so we'll use this fish. Don't tell anybody though. Nobody. If we happen to meet any inspectors or anything, don't say where we got it from. OK?'

'Gotcha, Boss.'

We waited a little longer, then I told Wally to drive back to the café. I wanted this diversion so that if these arseholes from the Ministry of Fisheries were spying on us, they would see the fish arriving in the usual fashion. There was a park right outside the café so we parked there and I wandered in. Wally followed me in with the fish. Two official-looking gentlemen followed him in, and one representative of the Waiheke Island Police Force. Sergeant Jack Koster. A smiling Jack Koster. One of the officials stopped Wally, as he was about to carry the fish into the kitchen. 'Stop right there, young man. I represent the Ministry of Fisheries and I'll look after the fish.'

I came on the scene. 'What's going on?'

'These fish are illegal,' said the official.

'Bullshit,' I replied.

'Mr McCracker, it is illegal for you to acquire fish from the seas surrounding Waiheke Island.'

'Those fish are legal, mate.'

'Mr McCracker, we've watched your jeep turn up daily with illegally acquired fish. Today, we are seizing your load of fish and charging you with illegally acquiring fish. Sergeant Koster, would you please take over.'

'Delighted to. Are you Mr Whacker McCracker, proprietor of this infamous fish and chip shop?' beamed Sergeant Jack Koster, loving every minute of it.

'No, Jack. I'm Captain James Cook.'

'I have reason to believe you are Mr Whacker McCracker,' continued Jack, ignoring my sarcasm. 'I have here a warrant for your arrest for the illegal acquisition of these fish from the seas surrounding Waiheke Island.'

'There are forty-three in total, Sergeant,' called out the second official, who had donned plastic gloves and finished counting them.

'Forty-three fish illegally acquired, Mr McCracker,' said Sergeant Jack Koster. 'I must ask you to accompany me to the police station.'

'Jesus, Jack. You can't do that. I'll make a call to my lawyer so you won't be making a fool of yourself.'

'Mr McCracker, you will be entitled to make that call from the station. After you have been photographed and fingerprinted. Now, would you please put your hands behind your back so I can handcuff them.'

Peg raced over. 'Jack, you can't do that,' she said.

'Don't interfere, or you could end up in the same situation. Hands behind your back, Mr McCracker.'

All the staff on duty, a few patrons and some of our neighbours, who by this stage had been attracted to the drama, started jeering and booing. Paul Masters arrived with his camera and started clicking away. Bruce was on the portable phone to Brad, but Jack wouldn't let him hand it to me. Brad instructed Bruce to tell me that I didn't have much choice. He said he would wait by his phone for my call.

'One phone call from jail, Mr McCracker. That is the law.'

Wally came up to me, looking really concerned. 'You OK, Boss?'

'Fine, Wally. Remember, not a word.'

'Gotcha.'

I was bundled into the police car and driven up to the police station. There, I was taken into an office and the handcuffs were removed. Jack then surprised me by saying the police launch would soon be arriving in Matiatia, and, because of the seriousness of the case, I would be taken to Auckland Central police station. I was allowed to phone Brad and tell him what was going on. He told me to enjoy the private launch charter and not to worry. He'd be waiting for me at Central and he'd get things sorted out there.

At an enormous cost to the taxpayer, I was again handcuffed, driven down to the wharf, un-handcuffed, taken across to Auckland on the police launch, handcuffed, then driven from the wharf to Central, where I was again un-handcuffed. Brad was waiting for me.

Bail was set and I was to appear in court in two weeks

time. By five, I was having a Scotch with my legal man at his club. 'They haven't got a leg to stand on. All of those fish today were legitimate. We can prove it and they're going to look pretty bloody stupid. The only thing is, you're probably going to have to knock the fresh-fishing thing on the head. Sadly the 1917 thing does look legit.'

I phoned back to the café and told Brian what the situation was and to tell him to stop all the fisherfolk from going out the next morning. Also, to get hold of Charlie and arrange to buy more Auckland fish from him.

'Just leave it to me. Actually, that Auckland fish isn't too bad. I'm sure the customers won't complain.'

Over the next couple of weeks we prepared for two court appearances. We knew the fishing one was going to be easy. Charlie and Wally were to be key witnesses and the fisherfolk had signed affidavits saying they hadn't gone fishing on the day of the raid.

The other business with the ex-wives was proving a lot more serious. Brad told me that in the barrister's view, in his view and in his partners' view, I was indeed guilty of grossly exploiting my five ex-wives and it would be damn hard to win. The suggestion was that we should consider an out-of-court settlement to each of them. I suggested a dollar each. The general feeling was it wouldn't satisfy the Piranha-snapping, Pauanui-loving ex-loves of my life.

'Whacker, if you plead not guilty, the court costs on a case like this could be horrific. Your five exes are already wealthy women and they can share the costs. It could drag on for a week or two. And, me old mate, due to your fuckin' stupidity, we don't think you will win.'

'How much do you reckon we should give them then?'

'We recommend that you go in at fifty grand. Each.'

'No way.'

'Whacker, they'll get more if it's fought through the court. And just imagine if you end up with a woman judge.'

'Could such a dreadful thing happen?'

'Of course it could.'

'Hadn't thought of that. But Brad, that's a quarter of a million bucks.'

'Oh come on, Whacker. You're a businessman. You'll recoup that in a year. Think of the publicity.'

'Will I have to change the five holes on the golf course?'

'Probably.'

'I'll just make them fatter. I'll leave the negotiations in your capable hands.'

My legal eagle negotiated. And negotiated. And negotiated. The claim came down from three hundred and fifty thousand to three hundred thousand dollars. Each. And, there the old bitch stopped. I got on the phone to Numbers One, Two, Three, Four and Five about it but they refused to discuss it.

'You are a vile man,' said Number Four, pretty well summing up what the others said. 'Speak to Ms Begg about it.'

'But that extortionist has stopped negotiating. Jesus, Number Four, get real. Three hundred grand is ridiculous. You should be bloody proud to be immortalised in concrete. I bet David in Florence was. In fact, you should be paying me.'

'Whacker darling, surely you know by now that ex-wives never pay ex-husbands for anything.'

'You are so right. Next time I come back on earth Number Four, I just hope I'm a woman.'

'Oh, at times you already are.'

'Goodbye Number Four.'

Dreadful Tuesday rolled around. Eileen Begg had come down another twenty-five thousand to two hundred and seventy-five thousand. Each. We had gone up to a massive hundred and seventy-five thousand each. Already, I knew the writing was on the wall for the café. I'd probably have to sell it. Or arrange a good flash flood or fire.

On the court steps, Brad raised it to two hundred grand. Each. One million in total. The old bitch wouldn't concede, so into court we marched. The five exes had all acquired new dresses for the occasion. With the amount of money they knew they were in for, they had good reason.

Our judge was a bloke — Judge Martinbrow. He listened, looked at the photos, called Brad and Eileen over to his bench and asked if they could agree on a settlement once and for all. Brad said two hundred. Each. Eileen said two hundred and fifty. Each.

'I would suggest you meet in the middle. Two hundred and twenty five thousand. Each,' suggested Judge Martinbrow, looking at his watch and giving the feeling everyone was wasting his time.

'With costs, accepted,' said Eileen.

Brad looked at me. I nodded. 'Agreed,' he icily replied.

Five rich manipulators from hell smiled sweetly at me.

I mouthed that not very nice four-letter word to them. They returned it, by the same method.

Brad walked me quickly out and away from the court. I think he thought that if I lingered around, I might have pushed the exes and Ms Begg down the front steps. 'One good thing, Whacker.'

'What on earth could that be Brad?'

'They didn't ask for the sculptures to be changed. You can keep them exactly as they are. Perhaps you could start charging for a game to help pay off this cost.'

'That's over a million bucks those fuckin' exes have extracted from me this time. I'm going to have to sell up to pay that off.'

'Sell your five hectares, take a mortgage out on the Oneroa property and you'll be able to pay. You know you're good at business and you'll soon get it back. Treat it as a challenge. At least we have no worries for Thursday. We know we'll win that one, plus costs.'

Belinda had taken the day off, so we had a quick lunch down at the waterfront, then got the two o'clock ferry back to the island. The café was in full swing when we arrived and the originals were very sympathetic when they heard the full, sad story. I told them the café would probably be able to continue, using the plan Brad had suggested. But we'd have to work that much harder to pay off the enormous extortion. I then got stuck into the booze with Mal and Wally. Belinda understood.

The *Herald* featured the case the next morning at the bottom of the front page: 'Waiheke Café King loses sex-ploitation case'.

Thursday morning, and after breakfast with Brad, we again made our way to the court. Wally and Charlie were waiting to meet us. Brad was full of confidence — after all we had the receipt for purchasing the fish, Wally and Charlie as witnesses and the fisherfolks' affidavits if they were needed.

Judge Maxens was due to hear the case; however, just before things got under way, we were told a different judge would be taking over. Judge Arnold. Brad leant over and told me he was a bastard — commonly known as Judge Arsehole. Not that it would affect us of course. He'd also done Sam Hankle's eulogy, so Brad and myself were a little concerned that he could have a grudge over the café where his friend had snuffed it.

Events got under way with the charge of supplying illegally fresh fish to the café patrons being read out. The judge then asked me how I wished to plead. I confidently called out, 'Not guilty'.

Sergeant Jack Koster was first up and explained how he had seen forty-three fish arrive in the café in our jeep. He had also been with the Ministry of Fisheries officials when they were seized. He was smiling as he said it, looking directly at me.

Brad then got to his feet. 'Your Honour. First, I must apologise on my client's behalf for wasting your time, and the court's. The defence has got their facts very wrong. Allow me to go on.'

'Yes, yes of course you're allowed to go on,' said Judge Arsehole.

'On the said day, these forty-three fish were legally bought at the local fish shop. I have the receipt for them here. I also have present two witnesses. Walter Katira, the driver of the vehicle, who delivered the fish to the café, and Charles Bonney, the owner of local fish shop from where they were legally purchased. '

I looked over at Jack Koster. Our eyes met. I smiled. He smiled back. I was surprised — I expected a glare. Brad showed the invoice to the Judge and called Wally to the witness box. Wally confirmed what Brad had said. Charlie was next and confirmed he had indeed sold us the fish that day.

'Does the prosecution have anything to add?' asked the Judge.

'Yes we have,' said the Ministry's lawyer. 'We have reason to believe inside knowledge was obtained forewarning the visit of the ministry officials to the café. We would like to call a special witness to the stand.'

'Permission granted,' said the Judge.

Brad and I looked at each other in surprise. What was going on? A minute later, I knew how Jesus Christ must have felt when he was betrayed.

It was one of my own fisherfolk. Monsignor Poofter Pete of Kennedy Bay came in the courtroom door and entered the witness box. He began by describing how I'd given the fisherfolk that particular day off, then proceeded to tell all the inside secrets of our fishing system.

Brad tried to interject and get him to shut up, but the judge let him talk.

The Ministry of Fisheries lawyer was next and went on

and on about how we'd been illegally fishing for three hundred and fourteen days, because in 1917, the legislation of 1884 was changed.

Poofter Pete was recalled to the witness box to tell the court more about our operation.

Brad endeavoured to say all of this had nothing to do with the day in question. On the day the charges were made, the fish were purchased legitimately. Judge Arsehole didn't agree. He believed it was very relevant.

We had a break for lunch and Brad was very concerned. 'I don't like the way it's going at all. What's the story with Poofter Pete? Has he got a grudge against you?'

'Not that I can think of. I bet he's being paid.'

'Jesus, if I'd known it was going to go in this direction, I'd have got a QC. I thought it would be an open-and-shut case and I'd be back in the office by now.'

'What happens if we lose?'

'The penalty is horrific. They could go you up to ten grand a day for every day you've been illegally fishing. And you could get shoved in the slammer.'

'Holy shit! What are we going to do?'

'Hope like hell Judge Arsehole has a nice lunch.'

The judge did not have a very nice lunch.

Brad did his best, but I have to admit the lawyer for the ministry really knew her facts and threw the book at me, with the help of Poofter Pete. It was terrible.

Judge Arnold took about ten minutes to sum up before saying there was not a doubt in his mind that I was guilty.

Sentence would be given in two weeks' time. Further bail was granted.

I sat there mortified for a moment, then staggered out in a blur. Brad steered Charlie, Wally and myself into the nearest bar. I just wanted to get out of the godforsaken city and back to the island. Shortly afterwards Charlie, Wally and myself caught the ferry home. Sergeant Koster was also on board, but I managed to stop Wally from throwing him overboard. It was nice to have such a loyal employee.

The *Herald* the following morning had me on the bottom of the front page for the second time that week — 'Waiheke Café King guilty in fresh fish case'.

Waiting to be sentenced is a horrible experience. Never had I felt so close to Belinda. She was just marvellous. The island community also rallied around and tried to give me support. Business was still great, helped by all the new publicity.

The pissheads made sure Poofter Pete paid the ultimate price. He was totally banned from the island. A total blackball, meaning he couldn't get home. There was a very strong feeling he was paid handsomely for his betrayal, as he'd been having serious financial problems.

I put the five hectares on the market, spoke to the bank about mortgaging myself to the hilt on the Oneroa properties and worked out I'd probably would be able to square off with the five ex-wives. However, the concern was what the fine could be from Judge Arsehole. Brad was hoping, because it was a test case, it would be mild. Perhaps five thousand dollars, ten thousand at the outside. He laughed when I asked about going inside.

'No way Whacker, not for a first offence.'

'Are you sure?'

'Judge Arsehole would be pretty bloody low if he did that, mate.'

Belinda came with me to the court for the sentencing. So did all the originals and other friends I'd made on the island. Finally, the moment arrived and I was asked to stand in the dock.

'Mr Whacker McCracker, the court has found you guilty of catching and supplying fish on Waiheke Island in an illegal manner. On three hundred and fourteen days, to be exact. On the day of an official inspection, by using inside information, you supplied legally acquired fish and endeavoured to make a mockery of the Ministry of Fisheries, the police force and this court. I am aware you have had a significant award given against you in another court case recently, and I am taking this into account when sentencing you. But, at the same time a deterrent must be given to stop others from trying to do the same. For every day you have been breaking the law, I hereby fine you two thousand dollars. Plus, I sentence you to one year's imprisonment.'

I nearly collapsed. Shortly afterwards, a strong arm was at my side and a gentleman in a blue jacket escorted me out a side door, down some stairs and into a cell.

I felt so humiliated, I didn't want anyone to see me in a jail cell, other than my lawyer. 'Jesus, Brad. I thought it was going to be a small fine. What happened?'

'Hell, Whacker, I'm devastated. I can only assume they felt they had to throw the whole bloody book at you as a deterrent.'

'But, jail. A year's jail.'

'You'll be out in a few months. And it won't be a high-security one.'

'Thanks. Plus a six hundred and twenty-eight grand fine. With the one million, one hundred and twenty-five thousand I have to pay the exes, I'll have to sell everything.'

'Things will work out. Always does with you. Three out of your five divorces were seven-figure settlements and you always managed to pay them.'

'I've had a lot of fun over the past year, but I never expected this. The thing is, if I hadn't done it I wouldn't have met the best bloody woman in my whole life. No bullshit, non-spoilt, hardworking, honest, loveable Belinda. I guess this is going to be the test. Will she stand by me?'

'Of course she will. She was very upset. Are you sure you don't want her to come in for a minute?'

'No. I don't want her to see me in jail.'

'I'll keep an eye on her. You'll work it out.'

'What happens now?'

'Well, you'll probably go to Mt Eden for a day or two then you'll be send down country to a low-security farm, where it should be a bit of a cruise.'

'Can you please get hold of Greg and see if he can

come and see me while I'm still in Auckland so I can get a handle on the financial situation.'

A prison officer came and advised me a van was ready to drive me back to Mt Eden. I shared it with five others. I don't think any of them would ever have been members of the Auckland Club.

I am not going to go into detail about the four days I spent in Mt Eden. All I will say is that they weren't the happiest four days of my life. Simon, my cellmate, a professional burglar doing time for the fourth time, and with the word Waikato tattooed on his dick, smelt vile.

Greg did come to see me and we worked out that by selling everything on the island and using all the money I had left from the sale of the ad agency, I'd be able to pay the exes and the fine. But I would have practically nothing left.

I wrote an open letter to all my wonderful staff and the fisherfolk thanking them for what they'd helped me achieve. I wrote another open letter to the *Gulf News* thanking the people of Waiheke Island for all the wonderful support they'd given me. It had all been a lot of fun and if they would have me, when I got out of this mess I would love to come back and grow old and loony on the island. I meant it too.

Finally, I wrote one more letter. To Belinda. I thanked her from the bottom of my heart for the amazing support she'd given me over the recent weeks, and for being such a fantastic friend, lover and companion over the past year. I told her again that I didn't want her to ever see me in jail and I really did mean that. I hoped she would go over to the café as much as possible until it was sold, to help keep morale high. My bach was there to be used and as spring was arriving, it was a lovely place to stay. Provided I was a good boy, it looked as if I would be released early in the New Year. Right in the middle of summer. Finally, on the day I got out, would she marry me?

The day after I mailed these letters, I got sent down to 'the farm' in a mini-bus with four other fairly decent types. It took about five hours, including a loo, cup of tea and a lukewarm pie stop at Hamilton Central.

My roommate was a guy called Nev, who'd pinched a cople of hundred grand over three years from the Whangarei City Council. A nice enough bloke, whose only vice seemed to be the horses.

I phoned Belinda the second night I was there.

'Got your letter, Whacker.'

'Oh, that's good.' I waited for her to say something else. My stomach went all funny.

'Everything all right down there?'

'As good as one can expect. But I still don't want you to come here and see me. Not while I'm inside.' I wanted her to say something else.

'I can't wait four or five months.'

'You'll just have to, my darling.'

'I'll try. I'm going over to the island for the weekend. Mal said the café was flat out today. Apparently somebody knocked Number Three's head off down at the golf course and they're trying to put it back on.'

'The whole bloody five of them should have had their heads knocked off if you ask me. And I'm not talking about the sculptures.'

'I know how you feel. Oh, one other thing Whacker . . .'

My stomach was nearly going crazy. 'What's that?'

'Yes.'

'Yes?'

'Yes! I'd love to be Mrs Whacker McCracker the sixth. As long as you promise I'll definitely be the last one.'

I promised and felt like jumping over the moon! We said our farewells and I hopped, skipped and jumped back to the room. 'Guess what Nev! The love of my life has just agreed to marry me the day I get out.'

'Shit, you poor bastard,' replied Nev. 'You'll have to see if you can get an extension when it's time for you to leave.'

It struck me then that my roommate was not the romantic type.

The farm was quite a good lurk really. As long as you behaved yourself, weren't smart to the screws and played the game, it was bearable. I wanted outside work and was allocated to the vegetable garden. A couple of characters were with me — both repeat DIC offenders. Their whole day seemed to be devoted to working out how to get a drink that night. Booze was easily available. Friends and relations hid it in the corner of a paddock and the inmates wandered over and got it when it was dark.

I'd decided to use the experience to get healthy and welcomed the opportunity not to drink or eat big meals, not that there was anything wrong with the food. It fact, it was surprisingly good. Working outside, using the gym and not having too many daily dramas does wonders for one's health. I started to feel pretty good.

Greg and Brad were the only people I agreed could visit. This was for business reasons. Things were happening fast back on the island. The five hectares had sold the second day it was on the market. A born-again Christian millionaire, Dave Arney, bought the café. He agreed to call it by its old name, *The Glorious Ocean View Café* and said he'd retain any of the staff who wished to stay.

There were several things not included in the sale. I wanted the farting post, as a memory of a great event. I wanted my signage — and the right to open another café using my name. I wanted all merchandising we had in stock. And I wanted all the robes. He definitely didn't want to continue the adult golf course, so I also kept the nine sculptures.

My family, friends and the exes respected my wish for no visitors while I was inside. However, I was very surprised when, about two weeks before Christmas I was informed that a member of the Auckland police force had called in to see me. Expecting someone from Auckland Central, I went along to the visitors' room.

'G'day, Whacker. How are you getting on cracking those rocks?' asked Sergeant Jack Koster, thrusting out a hand to greet me.

'Bloody hell. The big Count himself. How are you, Jack?'

'A little worse for seeing you, but otherwise OK.'

'So, what brings you to this part of the world, Jack? Was it the thought of seeing me behind bars? Sorry I haven't got a pick-axe at the moment — or a ball and chain on my foot.'

'I'm driving back from seeing my mum in New Plymouth and I just thought I'd call in and see how the old Whacker is.'

'Attending your parents' wedding were you, Jack?'

'Watch it, mate. How are things going anyway? You look good.'

'I'm surviving. Looking forward to getting back to the island though. Will you be still there, or is it true they're promoting you to head the Hen and Chicken Islands police force?'

'Watch it! Look, Whacker. I just want to say something. I'm sorry. I'm really sorry. I had no idea they'd shove you inside. I thought you'd get a bloody good warning, a small fine and that would be that. I was bloody upset.'

'Thanks Jack. So was I.'

'Tell you something else, Whacker. The island misses you. I don't think people realised how much business and publicity you brought to Waiheke. We were talking about it at Rotary the other day and it was agreed that your year on the island was the most colourful it's ever had. You will be coming back?'

'Depends who's heading the police force, Jack. Had a right prick there this year.'

'Watch it, McCracker.'

'How's Dave Arney going with the café?'

253

'Seems OK. He's a bible-basher, so he's toned a few things down. The range of seafood is pretty good, though the prices are starting to rise. I went in the other day and old fatty and skinny were busy waiting the tables.'

'I assume you're talking about Walter and Malcolm?'

'Yeah, those two no-hopers. Although, the interesting thing is, since that goat incident the buggers haven't been in any real trouble.'

'They're good blokes, Jack. They just needed a chance.'

'And you gave it to them, Whacker. Thanks for doing that. You improved the lives of a number of others too — and gave us a chance to laugh a bit. I'll never forget that ugly bloody dyke winning your beauty contest!'

'You were meant to judge that, Jack.'

'Promise you something, Whacker. I'll be a judge for the first big competition you organise when you get back.'

'No, those days are over. I'll go for the quiet life with lovely Belinda at my side.'

'Nice girl that one, Whacker. Hear you're getting married too. Obviously she has a slight brain problem, but, well, congratulations.'

'Thanks, Jack.'

'Is there anything I can do to help you get yourself re-established? I know it's only a few weeks away, and I do mean it. The funny thing is, well, since you haven't been around, I've realised you're not a bad kind of arsehole.'

'That's probably the nicest thing you've ever said about anyone, Jack. Thanks. Are you still a marriage celebrant? I seem to remember that was one of your claims to fame.'

'Sure am. Do about two a month.'

'Well, when I get back, I don't want to carry any grudges

against anyone. To prove it, how about officiating at my wedding on the day I get out of here?'

'Be bloody honoured. I usually charge a thousand bucks, but for you I'll do it for nine hundred.'

'Fifty bucks to your favourite charity.'

'Done. What are you going to do when you get back?'

'Initially, just relax with Belinda. She's quitting her job with the health department on Christmas Eve. February and March are wonderful months. The weather is great; the sea is warm. Guess I'll look around for a bit of consulting work after that.'

'Might be a job up at the station. What are you like with a mop and broom?'

'I don't particularly want to clean up after pigs, Jack.'

'If you were on the outside I'd have you arrested for saying that.'

'And, as the great crime-buster of Waiheke Island, I'm sure it would be front-page news.'

'Watch it, McCracker.'

'Jack, I'd really appreciate it if you could keep an eye on Belinda when she moves into my bach. She'll be there most of the time by herself. Except over the New Year period, when her mum and dad are going to stay a few days with her.'

'Of course I will, Whacker. Guess I'd better be on my way. If I can be of any other help, just give me a call. Happy Christmas and all that. Bye.'

As he started to walk away, I couldn't resist calling out, 'Watch out for those little old ladies over the holidays. Remember what Miriam did to me.'

He turned around and replied, laughing, 'I'll never ever forget it! She got you a beauty!'

It sounded nice to hear the real Sergeant Jack Koster.

Ten days before Christmas, Greg advised me all my financial obligations had been met. The exes were all paid off.
Her Majesty was paid off. Plus, I even had a little bit left
over. I received a stack of Christmas cards. And five very
nice letters from the five exes thanking me for their unexpected, but most welcome, Christmas cheques. Number
Five was the first one who told me she'd already wisely
invested most of it in a Mercedes convertible. Just to really
piss me off, she enclosed a photo of her sitting in it.

Christmas Day. It wasn't bad, all things considered.
Christmas lunch was chicken and some wine somehow
turned up in the coffee mugs on the table. A couple of
videos concluded what was to be hopefully my first and
last celebration of J.C.'s birthday inside.

January seemed to drag. For the first few months the
farm had been a bit of a novelty and I was fairly busy during the day doing the vegetable gardening. But now there
wasn't much to do in that department. Most days I managed to speak to Belinda and that helped keep me sane.
She always wanted to jump in the car and come down to
see me, but understood why I didn't want her to see me
'inside'. Through her, I was kept up to date with all the
island gossip, so it was great knowing who was doing
whom, what and when. We discussed future plans, and
agreed the first month or two of being together again was
going to be a magic period of our lives. We hoped it would
last forever.

My release date was the second Saturday in February. I

could either be picked up any time after seven in the morning, or catch the seven-thirty bus, at the front gate, to Auckland. It would get there at eleven-thirty. I chose to do that, as I could then connect with the twelve o'clock ferry.

With two weeks to go, I phoned Belinda yet again. 'My darling, just another fourteen sleeps and I'll be with you!'

'I hope I can wait that long, Whacker. It's been ages since I've seen you.'

'I'm looking forward to our quiet afternoon wedding with the family, the originals and a few friends. Jack will officiate. Down on Oneroa beach, in front of our place.'

'It's going to be a fabulous day. Everything is pretty well organised at this end. What ferry are you going to get?'

'Well between you and me, I'll be on the twelve o'clock boat. But if anyone else wants to know, tell them I'll be on the one o'clock one. I don't want a fuss.'

Release day came. I was very fit, tanned and, surprisingly, mentally pretty good. The bus trip back to Auckland seemed to take an age, although we made very good time. Two of us from the farm sat together. Baz Burton had found the great joy of all the pleasures an American Express card can buy. Unfortunately, when it came time to pay for the joys, American Express discovered with great displeasure that Mr Burton wasn't really the right recipient for one of their cards.

At eleven-fifteen we arrived at the Hobson Street bus depot. With time up my sleeve, and because Baz's brother wasn't there to meet him, we grabbed a coffee and muffin. Very nice it was too. We got chatting the breeze a bit and

the next thing I knew it was eleven-forty. The last thing I
wanted to do was miss the ferry. Quickly farewelling Baz,
I grabbed my bag and raced off down Albert Street, turned
right and crossed the road to the ferry terminal.

The ferry had a big blue ribbon on it. And so did the rail-
ings on the wharf. There was a jazz band playing. Then I
saw the banner stretched over the entrance to the gang-
plank. *Fullers welcomes home Whacker McCracker!* Standing
under it to greet me, in the most amazing admiral's costume with a million medals, was Admiral Hugsy. 'Good to
have you back, Whacker. This trip's on us. Welcome home.'

All around me Fullers staff appeared, all wearing a blue
ribbon, and welcoming me back to the island. Admiral
Hugsy then escorted me onto the ferry. The passengers and
bystanders cheered and clapped. I couldn't see them too
well — I had a billion tears in my eyes.

The captain welcomed me aboard and said how much
I'd been missed. He then called for three cheers. A bottle
of bubbles was opened, and the crew all toasted me. I
began to feel like the ultimate returning emperor! The media
was on board in force too, and it was good to see some
familiar faces. Pete Morosey and Paul Masters both told
me how dull the island had been since I'd been away. The
band played continuously and someone kept filling up
my glass. I didn't want to arrive boozed, as after all, it was
my wedding day, so I took it slowly.

I was at the rear of the ferry for most of the trip, so I

couldn't really get a good look at the island. When the ferry slowed down to enter Matiatia Bay, the band headed up to the top deck. The admiral asked me to follow. I did, and walked towards the bow to get my first real glimpse of the island. The wharf was packed! There were blue ribbons on the trees, on the cars, on the wharf. Everywhere, heaps of people were waiting. A big sign was stretched along the wharf, *Waiheke Island welcomes Whacker McCracker home!*, and the school band was playing.

I was given the honour of being the first to disembark. Waiting to greet me, flanked by Bishop Wally and Bishop Mal, in their religious robes, was Sergeant Jack Koster in his police uniform. Over it was a sash reading *Count Jack of Waiheke Island*. I walked over to him and shook his hand. Then he put his hands up and pleaded for silence. It took another minute or two for this to happen as everyone was cheering and clapping like crazy. With a microphone in his hand, he started to make a short speech.

'Whacker McCracker; in my official role of Count Jack I have been chosen by the population of Waiheke Island to officially welcome you back. You put Waiheke on the map. Not just domestically either, but internationally as well. You brought us fun and vitality, and as a result we've been blessed with a staggering boost in visitors, which has substantially benefited everyone. We are thrilled you have chosen to come back to live here and wish you all the very best.' He paused, and the crowd cheered loudly. Then, he raised his hand and continued. 'Whacker, the people of Waiheke Island have got together and in appreciation of what you have done, it is with the utmost pleasure that I announce you have been awarded The Freedom of Waiheke Island.' With that, he pinned a large medal to my chest.

'What does it mean, Jack?' I quietly asked.

'Same as your titles, mate. Sweet fuck all. Might get you on an upgrade on the ferry if you're lucky. Now you'd better say a few words.'

I thanked everyone for the wonderful welcome I'd received and said how great it was to be back home. I kept casting my eyes around, because I was a little surprised that Belinda wasn't there. Soon I was escorted to the lime green Skoda, which was covered in blue ribbons and climbed into the passenger's seat. With Mal driving and Wally in the back seat, we slowly drove off the wharf, following Sergeant Jack Koster in the police car.

'Where's Belinda?' was the first thing I asked Mal.

'She's waiting for you, Whacker. She's waiting for you.'

Slowly we drove up the hill and then down the main street of Oneroa. There was a big blue banner across it reading *Welcome home Whacker!* and everywhere there were people with blue ribbons waving and cheering. And blue confetti!

The Glorious Ocean View Café was decked out in blue, with a sign welcoming me back. Dave, the new owner, the staff and the patrons all waved. I looked hard to see if any of the originals were there, but I didn't see any. We followed Jack slowly to the lower end of Oneroa, with people still lining the street waving blue ribbons.

'Do you know where you're going, Mal? We should be going down to the beach to my place. Belinda's there.'

'There's been a slight change in plans, Whacker. You'll be seeing her in a minute. Mate, Belinda asked me to give you this card about now. I think I know what it's about, so you'd better read it quick.'

I opened it up. The card read: *My darling Whacker. Just*

another minute or two and we'll be together. I can't wait to see
you and am so looking forward to being the last Mrs McCracker.
Your many island friends and myself have thought and thought
about what to get you for a wedding present. In a few moments,
you'll see it. The originals, the fisherfolk and many others have
helped make it possible. Love, Belinda'

'What's all this about, Wally?'

'You're about to see, Whacker.'

Jack slowed down in front of a one-storied building
and stopped. On the front of it was a sign reading,
Whacker McCracker's Café. Lined up under it, in full religious costume, were eleven fisherfolk. The jazzband from
the boat had gone on ahead of us and was playing.

'Here's the front-door keys to your new café. Belinda
told me to give them to you now. It's yours, mate.' Mal
handed me a key, on a fish keyring.

'I don't believe it, I don't believe it,' I mumbled, too
overcome with emotion to say much more.

A red carpet stretched into the café. Duke Bruce and
Earl Brian, both in magnificent costumes, swept forward
to open the door. They bowed. Duchess Screwzy Suzy,
dressed magnificently in yellow, curtsied, and said, 'Welcome home to your new café, Whacker.' She kissed me on
the cheek.

I started to bawl. Tears just kept pouring from my eyes.
I couldn't stop. Behind the duchess, all in their appropriate costumes, I saw Dame Bets, Dame Peg, Baron Horse,
Sir Johnny and Sir Cyril. Brad was there with his big KC
badge and so was Dame Miriam Webber, dressed up as
only an elegant eighty-year-old, plus dame could dress.
Other friends from the island were waiting. I spotted a
group of relations — Belinda's mum, sister, brother, their

partners and kids, plus my sister and her family. But, still no Belinda.

The jazzband from the ferry started to play 'Here comes the bride, fair fat and wide!' Everyone turned towards the door, and then, on the arms of her father, out came Belinda, in the most wonderful bridal gown I'd ever seen. And, very, very pregnant.

'Friends,' called out Sergeant Jack Koster. 'We are all here for a most wonderful occasion, the wedding of Whacker and Belinda. Let's go through the café to the back lawn, where the actual service will take place. The reception afterwards will be back in the café.'

I guess I broke rank then. I bolted over to Belinda and took her in my arms, kissed her, and said, 'The two of you look beautiful.'

'It's three actually, Whacker. Twins. OK?'

'Just fantastic! But why didn't you tell me?'

'I thought you might have run a mile.'

'I stopped running eighteen months ago when I met you.'

'That's good.'

'The café looks fabulous. Who did it? Who paid for it?'

'I'll tell you all about it later. You'll do it all over again won't you?'

'With your help, of course! Thanks a million darling. Hey, if you're free, what say we pop inside and get married.'

'What a fabulous idea!'

We walked into the café. Belinda's dad was on one side of her, and me on the other. Glancing around, I recognised mementoes from the old café, including the farting post. Right in the middle, was the vase, with a beautiful floral arrangement in it. Sorry, in her. The café was beautifully decorated for the wedding. We walked through it and out to the back lawn.

Chairs had been set out and the actual marriage was to take place under a lovely tree. The fisherfolk and the two bishops gathered behind Belinda, her dad and myself. The guests took their seats and then Jack, still in his police sergeant's uniform and the Count sash, got into position to proceed with the wedding.

'Ladies and gentlemen, just before we get underway with this marriage between the island's worst scoundrel and Auckland's most beautiful woman, I have been advised we have caught three gatecrashers. As a police officer, I've used my authority to allow them to also attend this ceremony. So, please let them in.'

Out the café door came my three kids. Jilly from Miami, Zak from Sydney and Paul from London. It was pretty emotional, that one. Especially in front of all the guests. I started to introduce them to Belinda, but was quickly told they were old friends. I asked them to stand by my side.

Jack called for order again, and proceeded with a very informal wedding service. Twelve minutes later, I had a new, and very final, wife. The band came to life. A duke, an earl, a baron and two knights popped the bubbles and started to hand drinks around. We were greeted, hugged and kissed by all our wonderful relations and friends.

After half an hour of mingling, Brad, who was to MC the reception, requested everyone to proceed into the café to be seated. The chairs from outside had been moved in around the tables and once everyone was seated, I noticed two tables were still empty.

Brad got the ball rolling. 'Welcome to all of you, and again my most heartiest congratulations to the beautiful bride and the illustrious groom! Before we proceed further, we do have several other guests joining us for the reception. Whacker, your adorable new wife has invited several more interesting people from your time on Waiheke Island to share this special today. She knows you don't like carrying a grudge and I certainly commend her for inviting some of these . . . friends. First, a very early acquaintance of the original café. From the third day, Sam Hankle's close friend, Karen Blomfield.' Karen came in looking very glamorous in a micro-mini. She paraded around the room with a handbag over her shoulder to wolf-whistles from the guys and disapproving looks from some of the women.

'Next, the first man and the first woman home in the nearly-nude race from Palm Beach to the café, Darcy and Jo.' A spunky couple came running into the café, clad only in G-strings, did a couple of laps around the tables, then sat down. Very much appreciated by the guests too, I should add!

'On this beautiful summer's day, it is very appropriate that we should have our next guest with us today. All the way from Auckland; previously from Te Kuiti, Miss Fresh Fish, Stiffy!' Stiffy, a little chubbier than a year ago, waddled into the café, dressed in her bikini. A remarkable sight. She walked around the café to lots of cheering and quite a bit of jeering, gave the fingers in the direction of the jeerers, which got her more, then sat down grinning. I admired her for that.

'I assure you the next guests were indeed invited by Whacker's lovely new wife. Number One, Number Two,

Number Three, Number Four and Number Five.' The five exes came in, dressed in their sculpture costumes. They all came and gave Belinda a kiss first and then one for me — for old time's sake. Three out of the five managed to whisper that awful four-letter word to me while they did it. I was quite pleased with myself. I managed to whisper it to the whole five of them. They paraded around and took their seats.

'To really prove that Whacker and Belinda don't want to carry any grudges, Monsignor Poofter Pete of Kennedy Point, Ms Eileen Begg and Judge Arnold, were also invited. However, I've just been advised they've been refused entry on any form of transport to get them to the island today. Some of you may have witnessed a confrontation down at downtown ferry terminal. As a lawyer, I am always amazed at the power of the Waiheke Island pissheads.' Brad paused, as there was considerable cheering at that announcement.

'Just as bloody well, mate,' called someone from the back of the café. 'They might have forgiven them, but we haven't.'

Brad went on. 'Finally, all the way from the United Kingdom for this special occasion, the winner of the Magna Farta, the young lady with the most amazing vowels in her bowel, Sarah.'

Sarah came bouncing in, jumped up on a table, put her finger to her lips for quietness, leant over, and graciously farted the first eight bars to 'Here comes the bride'. Wow! Ecstatic clapping from all quarters of the café! She then went and joined the others at the table.

A very simple, but delicious three-course meal was then served. In the tradition of the old café, a fisherfolk was on each table, and other titled people were also allocated to different tables. Brad said a few words at the end of the meal, then called on Mal to propose a toast to the bride and groom. Mal was, by this stage, just a wee bit affected by the evils of alcohol. 'Ladies and blokes, please stand up. All the very best to me mate Whacker, and his up-the-duff missus, Belinda. Here's a toast to yous.' Everyone toasted us.

It was then my turn to get up. I kept it very brief, saying the right things, thanking the right people and said how wonderful it was that my new wife and I were celebrating this occasion with so many wonderful friends and relations. I didn't want to make it controversial in any way, so avoided any comments about Eileen, Poofter Pete and the judge.

The band started up again, a few tables were cleared back, and Belinda and I were requested to start the dancing. We did our five minutes' worth, then circulated. It was wonderful catching up with everyone again and the afternoon flew by. The band played; the booze flowed and friendships were cemented even further.

Around six o'clock, with a lot of guests getting to a very merry stage, three invited guests, who'd been blackballed from travelling to the island, arrived. Ms Eileen Begg, Poofter Pete and Judge Arnold walked through the door. The party came to an abrupt halt.

Admiral Hugsy was the first to act. 'How did you get here? You're banned.'

'Helicopter, dork-face,' snarled Eileen Begg. 'We were invited. It's taken us all afternoon to get here. And, be

266

assured, we'll be taking action against the individuals who tried to stop us from coming.'

'You piss off out of here, Poofter Pete,' called out Wally.

'You do the fuckin' same, Judge Arsehole,' gallantly yelled Mal.

I made my way over and managed to defuse the situation. I lead them over to meet Belinda and Brian arranged drinks and led them to a corner table to get them something to eat.

An hour or so later, Belinda's mum came over and told me that Belinda was tired and I should consider taking Belinda home soon. I agreed.

Everyone poured outside to farewell us. Jack, who'd had a few himself, arranged for Constable Lucy to drive us back to Oneroa Beach in a police car. Belinda had one final act to do. The throwing of her bouquet. She threw it. Bets caught it.

'You'll have to throw it again, darling. Bets is already married.'

'Actually, Whacker,' Bets called out to me, 'we're not. We've never got around to it.'

'But we will now,' called out Mal. 'Next wedding is ours!'

I laughed. Then, with heaps of waving, Lucy drove us away from the new café to our little beachfront bach in Oneroa.

Not too long after we left, as I was later to find out, it was Sister Teresa of Matiatia who started the trouble, by whacking Poofter Pete. Eileen stood up to see who had done it, and was called an 'Interfering Old Whore' by

Canon Bert of Ostend. She took a swing and knocked him down.

Sergeant Jack Koster, seeing what was happening, ran over and pulled out his phone to summon aid. Karen Blomfield grabbed the phone off him and threw it into a fish tank. He went over and grabbed her, and she grabbed him back. They both lost their balance and the next thing, the two of them were on the floor, with Karen's micro-mini slipping up to her ears.

Judge Arsehole copped it next. Number Three started abusing him. Someone gave him a little push and his glasses flew off. As he reached for them, he accidentally hit Number Three. Well, two of the other exes saw that happen. Judge Arsehole didn't have a chance.

Stiffy came rushing over and decided to hit Number Five for no reason at all, except perhaps because of her youth and beauty. Wally saw it happen and went over to defend her. Fat chance. Stiffy socked him one. Then another. Wally hit the floor. Bets came to her brother's aid and slammed a chair on Stiffy's head. It got worse. Brian told me later it was just like what happens in the cowboy movies. Except this was real. He was the one who phoned the police station for reinforcements.

The police arrived not long afterwards and quickly brought the evening to a conclusion. An ambulance was also called, but fortunately nobody was hurt badly enough to need it for medical reasons and it was commandeered into a paddy wagon instead. In total, thirteen were taken away to the local police station.

It was half-past ten at night. I was in bed with the lady I loved. It was also my wedding night. My sixth.

The phone rang. I was going to let it ring, but eventually I answered it.

'Mr McCracker. This is Sergeant Koster of the Waiheke Island Police Force,' slurred Jack.

'Jesus Jack, it's my wedding night. What on earth do you want?'

'I'm phoning to let you know that as of this moment, we are holding in the cells of this police station, three of your ex-wives, two bishops, a canon, a judge, a reverent sister, a hooker, a rabbi, a fuckin' ugly beauty queen, a cardinal and a plump woman lawyer. I have reason to believe they belong, or indirectly belong, to you Mr McCracker.'

'Is that all, Jack?'

'This island has been a peaceful haven for the past few months while you've been away cracking rocks. Within a few hours of your return, chaos has returned.'

'About time you did some work, Jack. That's what we pay our taxes for, so you just look after your guests nicely. If you're going to extend them hospitality overnight, be sure to give them lots of nice fresh coffee and hot buttered muffins in the morning. Goodnight, Jack.' I hung up and left the receiver off the hook.

'What was all that about?' Belinda asked drowsily.

'Nothing, Number Six. Nothing at all. Just Jack Koster getting a little bit excited about some of his overnight guests. God it's good to be back on this loony island again.'